The Essential

HORACE

ODES, EPODES, SATIRES, AND EPISTLES

Translated by Burton Raffel
With a Foreword and an Afterword by
W.R. Johnson

NORTH POINT PRESS
San Francisco 1983

For Elizabeth

Table of Contents

Foreword by W. R. Johnson

I

Each man, it has been said, has his own Horace, and this cliché, like many clichés, has some of its roots in fact. But we need also to remember that each generation and each century tends to have its own Horace as well. For the past few centuries Horace has been, for most readers of Western literature, a rather flattering mirror. See, said the mirror, we are civilized; we are educated; we are tolerant and capable of loving life and being loved by it; we have many humble but necessary virtues: above all, we are sane. Those to whom the mirror kept saying such things neither deceived themselves nor were they deceived by the mirror. Horace was saying, is saying, and, one hopes, will keep saying these things till the end of time: we need to hear them, and Horace says them unusually well. But Horace also says a number of other things unusually well: these things Samuel Johnson and his contemporaries were studiously deaf to; Matthew Arnold, though he heard them,[1] preferred not to hear them.

In making his selection of poems from the Horatian corpus, it would seem that Burton Raffel decided to emphasize the things that the eighteenth and nineteenth centuries could not or would not listen to from Horace. In Mr. Raffel's translations we find, of course, the suavity, the self-control, the unfailing good temper, and the sanity that fascinated our ancestors; but Mr. Raffel has seen to it that other aspects of Horace's work, which were previously minimized or ignored, receive their due: anxiety coexists with suavity, rage with self-control, good temper sometimes fails, and so do benevolence, faith, and sanity. Horace is not always staid. Even toward the end of his life he can lose his temper magnificently. At one moment he can be contemplating human life with detachment, even with tranquillity; at the next, wrapped in a heavy gray despair, he can be meditating on the uncertainties and terrors of the human condition; at the next moment, he can break into wry, rich laughter at the fallacies of human greatness and the facts of human vanity.

This version of the poet may or may not be more accurate than earlier versions of the poet, but, take him or leave him, this Horace is ours. The civilized gentleman that the eighteenth century adored and the wistful preacher-cum-schoolmaster that often charmed (and occasionally bored) nineteenth-century schoolboys are not much on display in this volume. Instead, we are here faced with a moody, mercurial, witty, tough, cheerful, vigorous, melancholy, sensual, intellectual, courageous, malicious, stubborn, gentle, and complicated human being who is always interested in and sometimes horrified by what is going on in

[1]See his essay "The Modern Element in Literature," *passim.*

the world around him. Far less elevating than the civilized gentleman and far less comforting than the wistful preacher, this vital, rather petulant human being is not much interested in elevating or in comforting us. Rather, he is interested in looking out at the world and in reporting to us what he sees with all the imagination, artistry, and honesty that he can command. We shall be wanting to examine the imagination, artistry, and honesty in some detail, but in order to do that we have first to look briefly at the world Horace lived in, at Rome in the last half of the last century before the birth of Christ. We need first to see the turmoil and the confusion that Horace experienced and that he forged into a dynamic unity and a hard, robust clarity.

2

       Horace was born in 65 B.C. and died in 8 B.C. These dates mean, among other things, that he was sixteen years old when Caesar and Pompey finally decided to fight it out to the death even if that meant destroying what was left of the Roman Republic. (That is what it meant.) He was twenty-one years old when Caesar was killed by a mixed gathering of naïve idealists, cynical crooks, and shrewd but desperate idealists. He was twenty-three years old and a graduate student in Athens when he enlisted in the army of Brutus, who was a desperate idealist, and when he witnessed (as he thought then and was to think again much later) the cause of freedom go down the drain. In short, Horace's adolescence and early manhood were spent in viewing the final destruction of the Roman Republic. But the Roman Republic had been in the process of being destroyed for over a hundred years before Octavian and Antony each tossed down the last straw, so civil wars and the death of freedom were not news to the young man who limped home from his defeat at Philippi, grateful for amnesty and for blessed anonymity in the lower ranks of the civil service. The young idealist did what fundamentally sensible young idealists do when realities can no longer be eluded—he marked time. Horace licked his wounds leisurely, became an angry young cynic, plunged into Life, and worked hard at becoming a first-rate versifier.

       From his twenty-fifth to his thirty-fifth year Horace softened his anger and cynicism, learned more about the arts of reflection, and while pursuing, it would seem, the sweet life with commendable insatiability, took time out from this pursuit to learn his craft as no other Latin poet—not even Ovid—would ever quite learn it and to find and to shape the brilliant satiric stratagems that are uniquely his. He spent his decade very wisely. There was no use in worrying about Antony and Octavian or even about Cleopatra. Someone or other would win eventually, for a while: that was what the previous hundred years of Roman history had taught even the most casual observer. So: ignore the morning headlines, have some fun, learn to scan and to scrutinize.

But when Horace turned thirty-six and Antony and Cleopatra were safely interred together in the splendid mausoleum in Alexandria, it began to appear that there was something new under the sun after all. The novelty's name was Octavian and would soon be Augustus. He had seemed to be just another pretty aristocratic gangster, but it seemed now that he was a statesman of genius who had managed, against all hope, to save something from the wreck. Rome would never, of course, be quite the same Rome again, but that was all right, because the old Rome had been a pretty rotten place, and the new broom seemed to have a knack for sweeping clean. Everything had seemed, as always, to be on the brink. Suddenly luck (or what our ancestors called gods) snatched us from chaos and set us, safe and trembling, in the wide sunlight. Perhaps. From his thirty-sixth until his forty-second year Horace palters brilliantly between the music of the Wasteland and the music of the Golden Age Returned. Throughout the first three books of Horace's *Odes* there is an elaborate and moving counterpoint between decadence and despair on the one hand and praise and rejuvenation on the other. The angry young cynic has learned from himself and from the events of the world outside him to say, as he eases himself into middle age: Look, we have come through, maybe.

From his forty-third year until his death (he was fifty-seven), the music of the Wasteland is subtly intensified, and its ironies become more complex and more opaque. The poet no longer says: Look, we have come through, maybe; he says: Look, I have come through, after a fashion. Augustus was indeed a states-man of genius, and he had indeed saved very much from the wreck. But his brave new world is shot through with strange unrealities; this noisy blustering city is not the Rome of our ancestors, has not been restored. Augustus is not a rather obviously permanent consul, he is a king. The nightmare that we warded off through the centuries has come again and will endure: Augustus is a king, we are not free.

Horace spends less and less time in the city, more and more time at his house in the country. He is not alone. Friends come to visit. There are amusing, sometimes rather naughty parties. Horace reads Homer and philosophy. Augustus flatters him, asks him to become a sort of private secretary, asks him to write a few courtly poems. Horace cannot see himself as a secretary, but he sends off a few poems: one of them, a hymn to Apollo and Diana for a religious festival, is not funny; the others are pretty funny. After a while, Horace dies, and Augustus lingers on for twenty-two years.

Horace died thinking that he had spent most of his life watching the death of freedom and the disintegration of a culture and a civilization that he and many of his generation loved as much as their fathers had loved it. Horace was right in thinking this, but he missed the point. One cannot blame him for missing the point, because he was a satirist and a poet, and it is not the task of satirists and poets to get the point. The point was that, after one hundred years of violent incurable sickness, freedom had died, and neither luck nor the gods nor Augustus could bring it back to life. And the fabric of society was shredded, and the old philosophies were no help, and, very soon, Syrians, Jews, Egyptians, Greeks, Christians, Gauls, and Germans would be striding through the streets where Horace had strolled. That was a world he would not have understood, would not much have cared for. But it was not, in many ways, a bad world (as Gibbon knew and as Tacitus could not know), and Augustus had made it possible.

Horace was not a man between two worlds. He was a poet at the edge of a chasm beyond which he could not see. What he saw was the ruin of the world he loved and the death of freedom. His vision was the more bitter because, for a while, he had almost learned to hope against hope that his culture would not collapse and his freedom would not die. But when that hope had vanished, though he could not hope again, he would not give up. The desolation of outward freedom ultimately forced him to search out the inner freedom of the heart that each man has if he wills to find it. Political crisis and cultural crisis had provoked from Horace an astonishing number of complex successful songs in which hope warred against despair and celebration of the human spirit warred against dark intuitions of abiding failure and futility. In the last decade of his poetic activity (roughly, 20–10 B.C.) Horace turned from his ruined dreams of man's salvation in his city and in his culture to the fact of man's salvation in himself, in the courage of his individuality and true independence. Mr. Raffel hits it off neatly:

> Life is lived, truly lived, when we are
> What others think we are. . . .

(Epistles I, 16)

"Become what *you* are!" Prompted by his disenchantment with what Augustus had succeeded in doing (and by his misunderstanding of the necessity that Augustus was grappling with), Horace learned to obey this stern injunction, discovered a freedom that the whims of history could not take away, and became himself. In becoming himself and in recognizing the secret springs of his independence, he did not so much achieve tranquillity and calm (though he achieved them in some measure) as he chanced upon (that is the way he viewed the matter) a courage and an honesty that enabled him to encounter his intimations of disaster without self-pity and without idle rage and idle fear. As his world collapsed about him—indeed, *because* his world collapsed about him—he became, as

Montaigne saw, a vital humanist, that is to say, an adequate human being. Thank you, Augustus, for making us face facts.

3

      At the opening of this essay I expressed some disapproval of earlier versions of Horace. But even if I know that there are many quintessential Horaces and am therefore leery of offering yet another quintessential Horace, I cannot resist the temptation. So I offer a Horace that I think we can live with and that Mr. Raffel's translations marvelously illustrate. The quintessential qualities of Horace are (not ranked in order of importance, necessarily): versatility; nearly infinite variety; stamina; adaptability (hostile readers have spoken of "frivolity" and "inconsistency" in this regard); pleasure in the drudgeries of craftsmanship (this quality accounts for the endless gossip about the impeccable discipline and the classical severity and other like misemphasis); and, above all, a perverse, almost childish propensity for wild, silly laughter at what most of us would regard as "the wrong time." Horace grows up, changes, closes with the tragedies of the center's not holding and the fall of civilization, but from the beginning of his poethood until its end, the man is sly and wicked, always notices that there is usually a strange discrepancy between the way things are supposed to be and the way things are. The man is a satirist born, and he does not bother to stop being a satirist even when he is writing lyric poems (the *Odes*) and philosophical meditations (the *Epistles* and the *Ars Poetica*).

      The core of Horatian poetry, then, is satiric, or, if you will, it is steadily ironic (in the mode of Socrates and of Diogenes—but it is not cynical, in any bad sense of that much misused and much maligned word). Horace's basic instinct is to contradict any proposition that happens to be proffered to him. Pindar is great? Yes, but. The Golden Age has returned? Yes, but. There is nothing to fear from death? Oh? Yes, but. The temperament is essentially irascible (why should we not be irascible in the face of untruth or half-truth?), but the irascibility is not self-serving and is finally governable: the boxing gloves are Socratic and the rules of the game are, as Professor C. O. Brink has splendidly shown,[2] strictly dialectical. Horace enjoys fighting against words, ideas, received opinions, and feelings; not so much because he hopes to win (rather early he began to sense that nobody wins, here below), but because, as Socrates had shown, once and for all, fighting is a way of coming to know, perhaps the best way of coming to know.

      This satiric bias is obviously an advantage when one is writing satire (Horace's first genre), and it is by no means a disadvantage when one is writing phil-

---

[2]See his essay "Poetic Patterns in the 'Ars Poetica' and the 'Odes,' " in *Horace on Poetry: The Ars Poetica* (Cambridge University Press, 1971).

osophical meditation (his last genre). But is it not a handicap when one is writing lyric poems (essentially, his middle genre)? "Typical readers" of the eighteenth and nineteenth centuries (to use another tiresome abstraction and one that has recently been popular) might well have thought so. How can a satirist have sufficient refinement of sensibility, sufficient honesty, sufficient sincerity for the high endeavor of recording one's sensations when they are stirred by the profound mysteries of Nature and Truth? Well, quite frankly, Horace was not interested in the stirring of his emotions or in the refinement and delicacy of his feelings, at least not when he was writing poems. He did not feel, as many lyricists—Virgil among them—seem to feel, that he was at the mercy of life. He sensed that he was best equipped to criticize life, or, to put it more Socratically, to criticize the ways in which human beings (he and others) thought and felt about what they did and suffered. His strategy in writing lyric poems is not usually different from his strategy in writing satires and philosophical meditations; it is aggressive rather than defensive, critical rather than "creative." This does not mean that Horace has no feelings or emotions or imagination (as has sometimes been asserted by some of his warmest admirers, who seem to be themselves deficient in the qualities that they find lacking in him); it means that feelings, emotions, and imagination are subjected to the same scrutiny that he lavishes on thoughts and ideas and ideals. Or, to put it another way, Horace frequently uses lyrical poetry to challenge the postulates of lyrical poetry. He is not interested in celebrating the beauty of reality or the profundities of the human heart or the mysteries of bliss and pain or what we feel when we stand, "strangers and afraid," in the presence of Death and Sex and Seasons. Rather, he is interested in trying to figure out (and to help us figure out) why and how we feel as we do (which is a way of gaining some distance from our feelings, that is to say, a way of letting the heart and the mind do their joint job properly: again, the beast in view is freedom). Or, finally, to put it another way, Horace distrusts lyric poetry (he is in good company: Donne, Herbert, Burns, Baudelaire, Heine, Dickinson, Kipling, come randomly to mind), and so he invents numerous voices (or *personae*, if you prefer the fashionable word) whose beings and temperaments are at odds with the conventional notions and utterances that they make use of. Once that has happened, the dialectic may begin to function properly, and we have some chance of really thinking about what we feel and of really feeling about what we think. "I have come," said Diogenes, "to deface the coinage." Because the old living truths, unless we fight to win them for ourselves, become dead illusions. One cannot inherit truths. Hence the satiric lyric, the struggle of yes-no, yes-no, the wild oxymorons, the coincidence of contraries, *rerum concordia discors*.

Master of satire, of lyric, and of philosophical meditation. His range is immense, but his volume is, considering the range of styles and subjects and genres, rather slim. To whom should we compare him? Why bother? is an obvious and just answer. But one wants to, because, without some attempt at comparison, the greatness of his achievement tends to go unnoticed. Ovid succeeded in writing the greatest poem in the Latin language (as Chaucer, Shakespeare, and Milton knew)—the *Metamorphoses*. Propertius wrote the most original and artistic poetry in Latin (Pound spotted this faster than you can say "but didn't know Latin, really"). Lucretius wrote the most intelligent and most ingenious poem in Latin. Virgil wrote the most imaginative, the most passionate, the most haunting, and the most spiritual poem in ancient literature. Where does that leave Horace? Is he not, after all, the genial, plump don with a flair for sherry and an infinite capacity for platitudes, and common sense, and taking pains?

No, I compare him with Homer, Dante, Shakespeare, and Goethe. My criteria are: breadth of vision and sympathies; maddening facility with language and versification; sheer guts; irony that has outgrown egotism; capacity for change; willingness to confront the tragedies of history without casting oneself (or anybody) in a permanent tragic role; not looking backward too much and not pretending to be able to look forward very far; courage to be free; finally, a deep charity for what sustains what is, for other beings, for oneself.

I have put Horace in very rare company, and I have done this because he belongs where I have put him. Having done this, I now see that Horace is maybe more like Austen than he is like Homer or Dante or Shakespeare or Goethe. How to get out of this huge embarrassment? I guess by including Austen, where she belongs. And the moral of this is (as Horace might say): Make your own list.

Translator's Introduction

In his commentary on the *Third Book of Horace's Odes*, Gordon Williams points out that "not only did Horace regard the *Odes* as a highly personal poetic form but also Romans always read aloud. This means that a poet could count on a far greater sensitivity to tonal changes in readers who were accustomed, as a natural part of the basic process of reading, to discern tones of voice in written words." The advantage is doubly Horace's: English poetry is today read with the eye, not with the ear, but Latin poetry continues to be sounded, even if only silently. To translate Horace's complex, delicate, ear-oriented lines into English is difficult enough; but then to have one's translations eye-read, coldly, without any of the rhythm, warmth, and color that speech could provide, is disastrous.

These translations do not attempt to match Horace's music, or his meter, or his immensely deft manipulation of syntax. These are locked forever into the Latin that created them. The sounds of Latin are not the sounds of English; the meters of Latin (quantitative) are not the meters of English (accentual); and neither the syntax of daily Latin nor the much more complex syntax of poetic Latin is anything like the syntax of English. The linguistic realities, in short, are severely limiting. Translation thus becomes more than usually difficult. It does not, I think, become impossible. Latin is a very great language, but so too is English. The resources and the possibilities are different, but they are not less; one can find, or invent, or approximate devices that carry over a great deal more than just the bare lexical significance of Horace's Latin.

The *Odes* are the hardest of these poems to re-create in another linguistic environment, and I will direct these brief remarks exclusively to them. "Damna tamen celeres reparant caelestina lunae," writes Horace in *Odes*, IV, 7, and I translate "Whatever the skies lose, quick-running / Months repair." This is lexically close; it seems, I suspect, very flat poetically, read off the page. Sounded, however, with major stresses on "lose" and "repair," and a slight drop in pitch on "repair," and a caesura after "lose," and a prolongation of "skies," with "skies lose" sounded as a spondee—really *read*, in short—the English at least measures up to the Latin, at least "matches" it, to some degree, in quality. Not *fully* matches it, not *fully* re-creates it, but *to some degree*—which is mostly what a translation can do. To fully translate Horace, one would need to translate him into Latin!

In the first, much smaller and less representative edition of this book, I wrote the following: Structurally, too, these translations make no attempt to be one-to-one equivalents. They do attempt to create *English* structures that to some degree do things like what Horace does in Latin. In the great "exegi mo-

mentum" ode, for example (*Odes*, III, 30), I have constructed a free-stressed tetrameter line, something rather like classic blank verse, but not blank verse; the
final line is, however, a trimeter. All this, *in English*, does some kind of justice to
the literally unmatchable qualities of the Latin. In *Odes*, II, 20, a very different
poem, I have tried to match Horace's quatrain structure, but have devised, here,
a basic trimeter line, with the final line being in tetrameter. In *Odes*, III, 12 and
13, I have partially mirrored the quatrain structure, though the "quatrains" in
my translation are anywhere from four to seven lines in length. In the moving
"Reglus Ode," however (III, 5), I have felt obliged by the poem's power and dignity to translate in honest four-line quatrains.

In this much enlarged edition, for which I have now translated roughly
four out of five of Horace's poems, in all the four genres he employed, my approach has been slightly different. The new translations match Horace's formal
structures, stanza for stanza, and largely line by line. They are in general less im-
pressionistic about Latin names, though there is bound to be some unhappiness,
still. No classicist likes *anything* to be different, even when moving from Latin to
the very different language I work in. But except where the going becomes truly
desperate—as for example in *Satires*, II, 5, lines 62–69, where no one seems now
to understand what Horace is talking about—I have tried to reproduce Roman
stories and references as clearly and accurately as a new language and a new culture permit. This edition, large enough to approach completeness, required
somewhat higher levels of representative fidelity. All the same, I have not altered
the original translations: the slightly different tack taken in the new versions,
though it perhaps makes them more useful to both teachers and students, does
not involve any major shift in poetic procedures.

Nor have my poetic procedures changed in other ways. I have not rhymed,
in the usual sense of end-rhyme, but I have frequently used internal and part-
rhyme to tie together a poem's structure—as well as alliteration, word play of
the sort English allows, and indeed all the craftsmanlike techniques I know to
weave tonal structure and formal structure and literal meaning into a poetic
whole.

> Persicos odi, puer, apparatus,
> displicent nexae philyra coronae;
> mitte sectari, rosa quo locorum
>   sera moretur
>
> simplici myrto nihil adlabores
> sedulus, cura: neque te ministrum
> dedecet myrtus neque me sub arta
>   vite bibentem

Persian elegance, my lad, I hate, and take no pleasure in garlands woven on linden bast. A truce to searching out the haunts where lingers late the rose! Strive not to add aught else to the plain myrtle! The myrtle befits both thee, the servant, and me, the master, as I drink beneath the thick-leaved vine.

This is *Odes*, I, 38, first as Horace wrote it, then as C. E. Bennett translated it in the Loeb Classical Library *Odes and Epodes* volume. ("I have made an effort to avoid the atmosphere of easy acrimony which sometimes haunts footnotes. Since we have inevitably to stand upon the shoulders of previous scholars, it ill becomes us to step on their toes getting there," Henry Steele Commager, *The Odes of Horace: A Critical Study.*) To turn this delicate, delicious lyricism into English poetry is of course an act of hubris—who but a fool or a poet would attempt it?—but despite the immensity of the problems, there are things that can be done. Joseph P. Clancy has a plain, clear version, one that seems to me to catch the sense well—but not much of the poetry:

> I'm bothered, boy, by Persian elegance,
> expensive garlands are not to my taste:
> stop searching through hidden spots where late
>   roses linger.
>
> I want no fuss, nothing added to plain
> myrtle garlands: myrtle suits us both,
> you as you serve, me as I drink, beneath
>   the close-leaved vine.
>
>   *(The Odes and Epodes of Horace)*

Still, this is a poetic version, and it captures more of the essence of Horace than a prose version like Bennett's can hope (or was intended) to do. It reproduces the visual form, too, and is on the whole smoothly cadenced. Edward Sullivan's much older version takes a very different tack:

> No Persian pomp, my boy, for me!
> No chaplets from the linden tree!
> And for late roses, let them be
>   Unculled, unheeded.
>
> Naught with the homely myrtle twine
> To wreathe your brows, my boy, and mine.
> When drinking 'neath the pleached vine
>   Naught else is needed.

I rather like this; though it is not my own vision of Horace, it has energy and a kind of grace that is at the same time some reflection of the Latin. I think the same can be said of my own version, finally:

> My little slave, forget
> About Persian puffing and blowing,
> And elegant flowers pasted on bark.
> Boy, boy, stop rooting around
> In the woods, hunting winter roses for my hair.
>
> A bit of green myrtle will do,
> Is good for you, my little slave,
> And good for me, your master,
> Drinking here in the shade of these thick green vines.

The question, you see, is not which translation is more "faithful." Faithfulness is a complicated and very human concept, not in the slightest legalistic; surely a person who commits adultery in his mind is unfaithful, though differently unfaithful from another person who commits adultery in bed. No translation, again by definition, is ever definitive or final. I can only claim that, although my version is not Horace, it is an English poem—and sounded aloud, with some sense for its rhythms and its grace notes, it can bring the Latinless reader of the 1980s as close as I can get him to the *Persicos odi* of 35 B.C. I think *Persicos odi* is the better poem of the two; I do not mean mine as a substitute for the original, which *is* definitive, final, and very beautiful. But I do like my version, both as a poem and as a reflection of that definitive original, and I like it better than other English reflections. If I did not, I would not have bothered to make it. Anyone, then, who reads this translation and exclaims, in horror, "Why, this isn't *Persicos odi!*" has my sympathy as a Latinist, and my firm disapproval as a reader of translations. These translations should be read in English, if they are to be read at all.

Post Scriptum on the *Ars Poetica*

Since this much enlarged edition now includes my version of the *Ars Poetica*, and since that is arguably Horace's single most important poem, some supplementary remarks need to be made. I have not handled the *Ars Poetica* in the same way that I have approached either the versions originally made for this book, a decade ago, or the versions newly added. Indeed, I could not treat the *Ars Poetica* as I have treated any translation I have ever done. It is a poem so densely encrusted with centuries of interpretation, centuries of commentary and translation, that in some senses it has, for a great many people, ceased to be a poem at all. And as a document in intellectual and esthetic history, the *Ars Poetica* does in fact make a kind of sense— as any great artistic work can make sense, deprived of the primary artistic thrust that once gave it being, and that for many many people kept it alive long after its author, and his intellectual concerns, crumbled into dust.

Bluntly, my version of the *Ars Poetica* is the freest translation I have ever done, so free that at moments it almost approximates a genre I have no desire to practice, namely what Robert Lowell (and John Dryden before him) called "imitation." But the poet who practices "imitation" is primarily interested in making use of his original for his own purposes; the translator, and I come down squarely on this latter side of the fence, is above all interested in making the original available to readers unable to fathom its language. The difference in perspective is all important—and so too are the consequences. The imitator is apt to be ruthless, and to transform everything he touches into something approximating his own original work. The translator—and again, though I admire much of what the imitator does, I simply cannot imitate *him*—the translator will always, in the final analysis, put himself second and his original first. Translation is as much transmission as it is creation. And while the creator is responsible largely to himself, the transmitter has a host of other responsibilities: to his original, to his original's time and esthetic, to his original's techniques, and to his original's language.

Why then, feeling as I do about these two genres, translation and imitation, have I permitted myself to operate so close to the border between them? Again, because I do not think I had any choice. I have tried to jostle both the poem and its new readers out of their prior ways of thinking and feeling about the *Ars Poetica*. And this is basically because I regard the *Ars Poetica* as a *poem*, not as a historical document. That is, I feel in these lines the living presence of a passionate, committed, wry, and sometimes very funny writer who was reacting—and reacting strongly—to what he saw as the decaying, corrupting forces in his society. An example will make this clearer:

> postquam coepit agros extendere victor et urbis
> latior amplecti murus vinoque diurno
> placari Genius festis impune diebus,
> accessit numerisque modisque licentia maior;
> indoctus quid enim saperet liberque laborum
> rusticus urbano confusus, turpis honesto?
> sic priscae motumque et luxuriem addidit arti
> tibicen traxitque vagus per pulpita vestem;
> sic etiam fidibus voces crevere severis,

et tulit eloquium insolitum facundia praeceps,
utiliumque sagax rerum et divina futuri
sortilegis non discrepuit sententia Delphis.

(Ars Poetica, 208–19)

I have seen commentary which described this passage as gently satirical, in places; it has been said that Horace was here describing the evolution of dramatic performances, in his own day, and intermixing some occasional wry commentary. I think this desperately wrong, a virtually total betrayal of what an angry, excited poet was trying to say. My translation reads, accordingly:

Rome
First staggered the world, then swelled to fill it up:
Spilling wine in their Own Great Name,
Romans now feast like wild pigs, swilling loud.
And how could clods and bankers be quietly mixed,
Crooks and Senators?
So musicians gave up being quiet, grave,
Turning into strolling players,
                              sneered,
                              leered,
Pulled their sacred gowns like balloons across the stage;
The sober lyre was strung like a banjo;
Actors learned a bright melodramatic bray;
And our once-wise chorus began to read tea leaves
Like other gypsies.

A much more literal rendering will show, I think, that the rather savage tone of this is not my invention:

When its conquests were over, the Roman people began to extend their territories, and a broader wall to encompass their cities, and began to propitiate their Genius, on festival days, with wine in the daytime, without restraint: greater license was added both to poetic numbers and to musical tones. For what taste could the illiterate clown, free from his labors, share with the citizen (*urbanus*), the baseborn with the respectable? Thus the musician added both movement and wantonness to his ancient art, and strolling about trailed his robe along the stage: thus also new notes were added to the grave lyre, and bold, abrupt eloquence produced an unusual theatrical diction: and then the sentiments of the chorus, wise in teach-

ing useful things, became prophetic of the future and did not differ
from the mystic oracles of Delphi.

A list of key words, for tonal puposes, in Horace's Latin, might look like this:
impune ("without restraint"), *licentia* ("license"), *rusticus* ("clown"), *turpis*
("baseborn"), *confusus* ("intermingled"), *luxuriem* ("wantonness"), *praeceps*
("bold, abrupt"), *insolitum* ("unusual," in a pejorative sense), *sortilegis* ("mystic," in a pejorative sense). This is a man on the attack, not a placid historian with
an occasional soft complaint. This is an angry man, and I have translated him
into angry verse.

I have not, of course, translated him into Latin verse. Horace's poem already exists in Latin and has been read in that language for centuries. I have translated him into English verse, and the verse of my own country and my own time.
I am keenly aware of the hard fact that Horace died in 8 B.C. and never heard a
word of English, never knew a line of Chaucer, Shakespeare, Donne, Milton,
Pope, Wordsworth, Keats, Browning, Hopkins, Pound, Yeats, T. S. Eliot, Wal-
lace Stevens—the list is endless. Horace surely never heard of the banjo, and he
is unlikely to have had much experience of gypsies, but we, in this time and in this
place, have all heard the banjo (though not the lyre), and we all know a great deal
more about tea-leaf-reading gypsies than we do about the oracle at Delphi. The
problem really comes down to this: what is the point of making a translation,
and for whom does one make it? What is a translation supposed to be and to do?

It is not supposed to be the original. Nor, as I view translation, is it a linguistic art, a matter of expositing the different phonemic and syntactical structures of one language for the native speakers of another language. If you want to
learn Latin, study Latin, and ask syntactical questions of your teacher: he will be
disappointed if you do not, and delighted when you do. But do not come to the
translation of a *poem* and expect linguistic enlightenment. I know, myself, what
sortilegis means, and I can show its development in later languages (French *sor-
tilège*, English *sorcery*, etc.); this is interesting, and useful, and for the translation
of a poem quite irrelevant.

The translation of a poem must turn its back, firmly and forever, on the
original. No translator who keeps the precise shape and style of his original foremost in his mind can, as I understand translation, produce a viable poem in the
language into which he is translating—and if he is not producing a viable poem,
why is be bothering to translate? Would anyone have bothered to read Horace,
all these years, if *he* had written clumsy, confused Latin, devoid of music, hard to
penetrate, flat of tone? Why should anyone read a translation of Horace, written
flatly, clumsily, dully? Is that sort of translation really *Horace*? Translation requires that vitality be matched by vitality, wit by wit, music by music—but not

necessarily, nor even usually possibly, the same vitality, or wit, or music. Read any Latin page aloud, and then read any English page: you are clearly in different sound worlds. Consider, next, that Horace has been dead almost two thousand years, and that man's life on this earth has changed vastly, even if we and the men of Horace's time are all *Homo sapiens*. Clothes, governments, houses, wars, food—it is all different. And poets are not more abstract than the average man in the street—perhaps rather less abstract, if one presses the point. Should a translator assume that these changes are insignificant? Did Horace himself ignore the effects of social change? Hardly !

The translator must turn his back on the original, then, in order to be ultimately loyal to it. He must be free, similarly, in order to be faithful. If he respects and loves his original—and, again, if he does not, I see no point in his translating it—he must liberate it from the boundaries of time, the boundaries of physical change of all sorts, the boundaries of cultural change. He is not to create *de novo*, or *ex nihilo*: he must first master the original, know it as nearly as possible as its original creator knew it, linguistically and culturally, inside and out. He must feel its tone to his fingertips. If he is not certain of a passage, he must return to it, over and over, until he becomes certain, until all fuzziness disappears. A translator cannot work under a blindfold: he must see his way before he can walk it.

I have been superficially free with the Latin text, also, because as a poet and translator of some experience I think I have seen things in that text which previous translators have not seen. It does not seem to me to be a dull set of maxims—it does not seem dull at all—but a spirited and well-organized exposition of powerful and long-matured ideas and feelings. I have seen these things, I suspect, in part because I myself tend to feel the same way about art in my society, its practitioners and its corrupters. "You don't have to *annihilate* it," people have protested, when I tore into a bad poem. But I do have to annihilate it: it is as much an abomination to me as the golden calf was to Moses. I am not speaking casually—and neither was Horace. Bad/corrupt art and bad/corrupt artists spelled moral issues for him, and he reacted like the *urbanus*, the citizen he was.

Some discussion of particular freedoms may be helpful. It is obvious, just as it was inevitable, that my English text is considerably longer than the Latin it translates. Latin is vastly more condensed—but I have also tried to exploit the differing musics of differing line lengths, for the musical requirements of the poem that I have tried to make my translation into. I have used spatial arrangements, too, which do not exist in Latin poetry, spreading the translation about on the page, at times, in order to bring out more effectively what seemed to me the thrust of Horace's poem. All of this has made my translation very considerably longer than Horace's orginal. There has been no ulterior motive (I am not paid by the line!): like all my changes, divergences, and innovations, this particular physical layout has been designed to make the translation work as poetry. Andrés Segovia makes even tuning his guitar part of his musical performance; Picasso never ignores the particular texture of the materials on which he paints. The translator too must use all the resources he has.

Additions—or, again, what seem like additions—to the Latin text need some special comment. The poem begins, for example, with a long passage attacking an inept painter who "joins a horse's neck to a human head, and spreads a variety of feathers over the limbs of all sorts of different animals, collected from all over. . . ." After a sober start—"A painter who puts a horse's mane / On a Man's neck"—I have turned this into the following:

> . . . who pulls feathers
> From canaries
> > and doves
> > > and parrots
> > > > and owls
> And grows them on a sheep's back. . . .

Varias inducere plumas undique collatis membris, says the Latin—and where then are all the canaries, the doves, the parrots, the owls, and that poor befeathered sheep? Well, Horace is plainly talking about "a variety of feathers," and he does talk about spreading them "over the limbs of all sorts of different animals, collected from all over." This takes you within hailing distance of my version; it clearly does not entirely account for it. There are several additional steps behind my version, however. First, Latin is a more abstract language than is English, and Horace is a more abstract poet than, in my own poetry, I am (or than any contemporary American poet is or could possibly be). I have had, throughout this translation, to aim at particularity where, to the taste and sensibilities of *this* time and *this* place, Horace was too abstract. Not abstractly too abstract, but too abstract to hold the interest and catch the minds and hearts of contemporary readers. Again, contemporary readers of English are not the audience of Horace's Latin original, but they are all the audience this translation can hope to have. If their interest is defeated, if the poem *qua* poem cannot get through to them, it is useless and I have labored in vain. But there is more, still, to my additions: ours is a time inured to shock, a time in which the decorum and the modest gravity, which Horace felt being dissipated, are virtually unknown. I recall a photograph, showing a New York City street and the burning corpse of a man, self-immolated, smoking in the foreground. In the background, some few turning to watch, most ignoring the scene, is the inevitable flowing mass of urban indifferents, neither shocked nor making any attempt to help. To say that this would have offended Horace is to say something meaningless: it would not have been comprehended by him, it could only have been understood by him as some kind of mass madness. We are a noisier, more raucous civilization than anything Horace could have dreamed of. Our poetry is noisier and more raucous. Our translations of poetry have to be noisier and more raucous, too. One does not translate (though one may hope to write) for all time. One translates for a particular time, a patricular place, knowing that in x number of years some other translator will need to do the job over again.

There are a few anachronisms in the poem, a very few, and I hestitated before introducing them, but finally felt obliged to. I had hoped, when I began the translation, to avoid anything that Horace would not have recognized as instantly familiar—but I realized, as I worked, that the translation of any poem this old lives, simultaneously, on a number of levels. The reader knows that this translation is a translation; he knows that the original was written in Latin, roughly two millennia ago, but he knows that the translation was written yesterday morning. He reads, accordingly, conscious of both time sequences, his own (and mine) and Horace's. They are necessarily different; in a translation they necessarily coexist—and I simply acknowledge that fact. It would be an empty pretense to ignore it—and so I have tried to turn this recognition, too, into a resource on which my version could draw.

Two very particular freedoms, and I have done:

. . . and any book
Written as that canvas was slopped, empty brained,
Like a sick man's nocturnal
Editions. . . .

This is, bluntly, what Leacock called an execrable pun. I have been told so by friendly critics, but I have not removed it. The objections were not strong enough, and I happen to be rarely fond of it. I have made many other changes, as I usually do when readers make comments and suggestions. No translation is ever perfect, at any stage in its existence, and I do not pretend that "nocturnal editions" is strictly defensible. I just like it. I hope Horace would have. (Catullus certainly would have!)

At the very end of the translation are these two parenthetical lines:

. . . (Do I hear one now?
Run for your life!)

There is no Latin original for these lines. I would maintain, however, that they are not mere additions, but part of the interpreting process which any good translation must also be. This poem as here translated needed those two final lines, and it was my job to supply them. Call them, perhaps, extended gloss, or interwoven footnotes, and they may seem less libertine in character.

Chronology

HORACE'S LIFE	ROME	OTHER WRITERS
Born, 65 B.C.	Cicero's consulate, 63 B.C.	Lucretius, Catullus, died 55–54 B.C.
Military duty at Philippi, on wrong side, 42 B.C.	Caesar in Gaul, 58–50 B.C.	Virgil's *Eclogues*, 37 B.C.
Friendship with Virgil and with Maecenas, 38 B.C.	Civil War, Caesar/Pompey, 49 B.C.	Propertius, fl. 33–16 B.C. Virgil's *Georgics*, 29 B.C.
Satires I, 35 B.C.	Caesar dictator, 45 B.C.	Livy begins *History of Rome*, 29 B.C.
Satires II, 31 B.C.	Cleopatra in Rome; Caesar's death, 44 B.C.	Virgil's death, posthumous publication of *Aeneid*, 19 B.C.
Epodes, 30 B.C.	Brutus, Cassius defeated at Philippi, 42 B.C.	
Odes I–III, 32–22 B.C.		Ovid's *Amores*, 16 B.C.
Epistles I, 20 B.C.	Battle of Actium, 31 B.C.	
Carmen Saeculare performed, 17 B.C.	Death of Antony, Cleopatra, 30 B.C.	
Odes IV, Epistles II, 13 B.C.	Octavian renamed Augustus, 27 B.C.	
Death, 8 B.C.	Maecenas's death, 8 B.C.	

ODES

I, 1

Maecenas, born of kings, O
Protector and patron and pride
Of my life, men live and breathe
For whom Olympic dust on their chariot
Wheels is the purest delight, men
Who feel like gods, rulers
Of the world, if their smoking
Wheels turn a bare inch from the post,
If they take a prize, any prize.
This man swells if a Roman mob
Fights to bless him with triple
Honors; that man glows inside
If his barn doors hide everything
Swept from the threshing-floors of Libya.
A peasant whose pleasure is chopping
His fathers' ground with a hoe
Won't take to the sea, trembling,
Won't plow the Aegean in Cyprian boats,
No, not for all the gold in Asian
Greece. Merchants and traders, afraid
Of vicious storms from the west,
Talk of peaceful fields in the towns
They were born in—then need to eat
And patch the holes in their fleets
And sail to sea. And some men drink
Expensive wine, if they can, and sleep
In the daytime, if they can, snoring under
A pine tree, or stretched on their backs
Where sacred rivers quietly
Bubble from the earth. Oh some men
Long for tents and battle formations,
And bugles and trumpets, and all the bloody
Fighting that the mothers of men
Hate. Hunters forget their wives, running
In the snow, chasing a deer while their hounds
Bay, prodding spears at a wild
Boar smashing out of fine-spun nets.
But I, Maecenas, I want only
Ivy wreaths, the prizes poets earn:

I pray to the gods for cool groves
And dancing nymphs, and satyrs,
And I stay away from vulgar mobs, I pray to
Euterpé, mistress of flutes, to
Polyhymnia, who tuned Sappho's lyre.
And yet, if you call me a lyric poet, my friend,
My forehead will clang against the stars.

I, 3 *to Virgil*

Ship: let the goddess who rules
On Cyprus, let Helen's starflung brothers,
Let the father of winds himself (and no one else)
Guide you—

Ship, which keeps our Virgil
But owes him to us, bring him
Safe to Greece, oh keep that half of myself
Alive!

It took oak and triple brass
Wound across the breast to first sail
On that angry sea, unafraid of African
Gales,

And blizzards from the North,
And dismal rainstorms, and swirling currents,
And all the ocean gods who lift and drop waves
As they please.

And who could fear death, watching with dry eyes
Water monsters swim, noting
The sea as it swelled, seeing rockhard
Cliffs?

Oh, the gods labored in vain, dividing
Land from land: our secular ships
Leap from one to the other, forbidden
But swift.

And men are bold enough, brave enough
To tackle anything, forbidden or allowed,
As Prometheus once was brave enough to steal fire
From Heaven.

Terror fell from Heaven, then,
Wasting sickness and flickering fevers,
And death, who had once been slow, and heavy,
Came faster.

Yet Daedalus flew the empty air
Though no man was given wings,
And by sheer muscle and will Hercules burst
Into Hell.

Is there anything we think too high?
Fools: go on, try for Heaven itself,
And Jove will greet us with his angry
Lightning.

I, 4

Winter weathers away, goes dull as Spring
Blows in, warm; dried-out boats
Creak to the water; sheep run from the barn,
Farmers leave their kitchen fires,
And the white, frosted meadows go brown
And green. Venus is whirling under the moon,
With all her worshipers—and Graces and Nymphs
Cross the earth on gentle feet—and burning
Vulcan comes to the Cyclops' forges.

It is time, it is time: take flowers from the new
Earth and hang them in your hair, hang myrtle
Across your forehead, and bring Faunus what he wants,
A lamb, a kid, and under arching trees
Offer him blood.

Death raps his bony knuckles, bleached,
Indifferent, on any man's door, a palace or a hut.
Life runs short: even your money, Sestus,
Even all your money, won't buy him off.
You'll drop in his darkness, and stay forever
In shadows and mists, down in Pluto's gray hall.
No spinning the dice for toastmaster, then.
No staring, heartsick, at lovely Lycidas,
Loved by all the boys, now,
Loved by all the girls, soon.

I, 5

O Pyrra, who
Is holding you
Now, roses above you, under you—who,
All perfumed, loves your yellow hair

Braided on your back? O fool,
He'll be cursing you, soon,
As new gods come, he'll be staring, soon,
As loving seas go black

And innocent joy, all gold
And bright, all hoping,
Warm, and wrong,
Gets blown, and drowns. How long

They suffer, till finally they know! But me,
I've hung my dripping clothes
In the temple, a sacred offering
To the god of the sea.

I, 8

Lydia, tell me: for all the gods' sake
Tell me: why ruin Sybaris
With love? why does he hate the parade ground,
Who used to shrug at dust and the hot sun?

Where is his armor, why does he never ride
With the other soldiers, neatly checking French stallions
With those lovely wolf-tooth bits?
What keeps him out of the yellow Tiber?

He avoids the wrestler's oil more fearfully
Than viper's blood—oh why? And once he could throw
Discus and javelin half out of sight, and wear
His weapon-bruises with pride. Not now.

Why is he hiding, as Achilleus too hid,
When Troy was about to fall
And he thought that dressed as men are supposed to dress
He'd be quicker dead, and at Trojan hands?

I, 9

See Soratté, limestone mountain
Standing white in thick snow,
Forests bent to the ground,
Rivers turned to ice,

And melt the cold, Thalarchus,
With logs piled high
And seasoned Sabine wine:
Pour it, pour it!

The rest is for gods to decide—
And when they silence the screaming
Wind and sea, no cypress shakes,
No ancient ash tree quivers.

Stop wondering after tomorrow: take
Day by day the days you're granted,
Take love while you're young and you can,
Laugh, dance,

Before time takes your chances
Away. Stroll where baths, where theaters
Bring Romans to walk, to talk, where whispers
Flit through the darkness as lovers meet,

And girls laugh from hidden corners,
Happy as favors
Are snatched in the darkness, laugh
And pretend to say no.

I, 10

Mercury, Atlantis' eloquent grandson,
You who civilized savage man with language,
Whose wisdom created the sandy wrestling-ground
And gave men that gift,

I sing of you, messenger of mighty Jove
And of all the gods, father of the lyre,
Skillful deceiver, cheerful undetected thief
Whenever you choose to steal.

Apollo tried to frighten you, once,
Wanting his slyly stolen cattle,
But he had to laugh when young Mercury
Stole his arrows too.

And Priam carried gold out of Troy,
And was never seen from any Greek camp fire
By any proud warrior,
Because you led him past.

You bring the good into Heaven,
And you lead them there, that airy crowd,
With a golden wand beloved
By gods above and by gods below.

I, 11

Leucon, no one's allowed to know his fate,
Not you, not me: don't ask, don't hunt for answers
In tea leaves or palms. Be patient with whatever comes.
This could be our last winter, it could be many
More, pounding the Tuscan Sea on these rocks:
Do what you must, be wise, cut your vines
And forget about hope. Time goes running, even
As we talk. Take the present, the future's no one's affair.

I, 13

Lydia, when you praise his
Rose-colored neck, his
Waxlike arms, oh Lord,
My liver swells with bile.

My mind and my face change shape
And color, and tears trickle
Quietly down my cheeks, all witnessing
The slow fires burning me up.

I'm tortured when wine whips him on
And you quarrel and he beats
Those gleaming shoulders, when passion
Makes him bite your soft lips, and mark them.

Well, if you'll listen to me
You'll never expect him to be faithful
—Him? So cruel to lips
Where Venus distills her own nectar!

Happy, and happy again, and three times happy,
And more, are those unbreakably bound
Each to the other, their love immune to whining
And quarrels, even to the very last day.

I, 14

O ship of state, new waves push you
Out to sea. Why stand there? Hurry,
Hurry to port! Can't you see
Your oars are gone,

And an African wind has bent your mast,
And your yardarms groan,
And without cables your hull
Can hardly hold together in this raging

Storm? Your sails are shredded,
There are no more gods to call on.
Built of noble timber
From wondrous forests

You treasure your parents and your used-up
Name, but frightened sailors are afraid
Of bright-painted wood. Watch out!
The wind will be toying with you.

Once I worried over you, and was miserable,
But now I love you and wish you well:
Oh be careful of the flowing waves
That heave around and around the shining Cyclades!

I, 16

O girl, lovelier than your lovely mother,
Do what you will with my ill-tempered poems,
Burn them, if you like,
Or drown them in Adriatic water.

Not even the god hidden in the Pythian shrine
Whipping into his priestesses' souls,
Not even Bacchus, not even the Corybantes
Banging their cymbals,

Can grind at the heart like grim anger,
Which no Doric sword can hold back,
Nor the ship-wrecking sea, nor fierce fire,
Nor even Jove himself, crashing down in thunder.

They say Prometheus had to mix
Our clay with a piece of every animal
On earth, and stuck in our hearts
The lion's insane fury.

Anger ruined Thyestes,
Anger has always brought down
Lofty cities, ground them to dust,
And left their walls for the plows

Of insolent armies.
Oh, be calm: anger used to drive me,
Once, when I too was young,
Anger whipped me into

Excited poems. If I could, now,
I'd turn my bitterness sweet,
I'd be your friend, if you could forgive
My harsh words and restore me to peace of mind.

I, 17

And often Faunus changes Lycaonian
Mountains to Lucrine lakes, swiftly
Saving my goats from burning
Heat and rain-bearing winds.

Soft she-goats and their stinking mates
Graze in peaceful thickets, cropping
Thyme and hidden arbutus,
And kids are never afraid of snakes

Nor wolves beloved of Mars—never,
O Tyndaris, once the deep valleys
And smooth rocks echo and echo
Again to Pan's sweet pipe.

The gods protect me, my prayers
And my poems please them. Come,
And fruits of the fields will flow to you
From Fortune's great horn.

Come, and in this hidden valley
Escape the fiery dog-star, and sing
Of Penelope and Circe, sing
Of them struggling for that same hero,

Come, and drink bland Lesbian wine
Here in the shade, Bacchus
And Mars at peace one with the other,
And you at peace with that rude Cyrus,

Who watches you so jealously,
You so helpless, he so importunate:
Here your garland is safe from his hands,
Here he'll never tear at your innocent robe.

I, 18

O Varus, never plant trees instead of holy vines,
Never, here in Tibur's mild soil and in front of its founder's
Walls; Heaven makes everything hard for teetotallers,
Only wine drives off gnawing care.
Who groans about money or war, with wine in his gullet?
Who can ignore you, then, Our Father Bacchus, or you,
Lovely Venus? But moderation, moderation:
Remember the Centaurs, mauling the Lapithae over
Wine, and remember the Thracians and how Bacchus
Levels them, when they're so flown with passion that right
And wrong disappear. Bacchus, it won't be me,
O gracious one, who'll disturb you, or flare into daylight
Your leaf-hidden mystic signs—no wild cymbals, no blaring
Horns, no orgies of blind conceit, with empty heads lifted
Into high places, and with a foolish faith
That betrays its own secrets, clearer even than glass!

I, 19

Cruel Venus, and Bacchus
Too, and my own careless
Lust, compel me once again
To live with what I'd thought was ended.

Glycera's beauty burns me,
It glows more brilliant than Parian marble;
Her face burns me, dangerous to stare at,
And I love her sly laugh.

Flying here from Cyprus, Venus
Falls on me with all her power,
Silences my pen, stops it from singing
Of Scythians, or Parthians, or anything

But her. Slaves! Make my altar here,
Green and lovely with frankincense and leaves,
And a bowl of last year's wine, unmixed:
A sacrifice will make her more gentle.

I, 20

O beloved Maecenas, come
Drink with me, cheap Sabine wine, yes,
But sealed in Greek jars by these two hands
And on that day, dear friend,

When the amphitheater
Rang with such applause, all for you,
That the echoes from Mount Vatican and from your own
Home stream joined in.

You can drink rare Caecuban, you can drink
Grapes crushed by a Calenian press, but
There's no Falernian in these cups of mine,
Nothing flavored by the Formian hills.

I, 21

Sing Diana's praises, O virgins!
Sing the beardless Apollo, O boys!
And sing Latona, great Jove's
Delight.

O girls, sing of her who loves
Swift streams and green groves
High on cold Algidus, or in the black woods
Of Erymanthus or forever-green Cragus!

O boys, sing of Tempé, and Delos too,
Where Apollo was born,
Where his brother's lyre was hung
From his shoulders, and his quiver.

Your prayer will move him, he will
Drive off war and its tears, he will keep us
From famine, he will hold back the plague
From Rome, and from Caesar, and give it to Parthians and to Britons.

I, 22

Fuscus, an honest man,
A man without guilt,
Needs no Moorish spears,
No poisoned arrows,

Wherever he may be—
The boiling Bay of Tripoli
The cold Caucasus, or along
Some ancient Asian river.

I was walking in the woods, far from
My Sabine farm, unarmed,
Happy, singing of my lovely
Lila, and saw a wolf,

And he ran, a monstrous wolf,
Fiercer than Africa's lions,
Huger than the beasts stalking
In Daunus' oak forests.

Drop me in a barren desert
Where the sun beats down, but no leaves
Quiver, or a world of mists
And rain and cold black skies—

Set me where nothing grows and nothing moves
And no one lives and I will love my Lila,
Love her sweet smiles, love
The sweet, silly things she says.

I, 23

Chloe, you run from me
Like a fawn fleeing to its frightened
Mother, leaping through mountain woods,
In terror of every branch and every breeze.

Its heart shakes, and its knees,
If spring rustles across
The leaves, if small green lizards
Peep out of bushes.

But I'm no savage tiger, no lion
Hungry to tear you apart.
Stop this running after mother, now that
You're old enough to take a mate.

I, 24

How be ashamed, how limit grief
For one like him? O Melpomené, teach me
How to mourn, you to whom your father
Gave the lyre and that liquid voice!

And Quintilius will never wake, never
Again? Where will Honor and perfect
Faith, sister of Justice, and where will
Plain Truth find his equal?

How many mourn him! And none
More than you, Virgil—praying,
Oh how uselessly, for the gods to give
Him back: not once they have him!

And if your lyre was nobler than that
Of Thracian Orpheus, to whom the trees listened,
Would life flow through that vague ghost
Driven by Mercury's grim wand

—Would he listen to our prayers?—
Down into the crowded shadows?
It's hard, yes, but what we cannot change
We can learn to live with.

I, 25

The boys don't come knocking
At your windows, now, not often
They don't, and they let you sleep as much
As you like, and that free-swinging door

Of yours hangs on its hinges and hugs
Its posts. Less and less they sing to you,
"O Lydia, how can you sleep the long night
Away, with me dying out here?"

Left in some lonely alley, a hag
Deserted, weeping for lovers'
Disdain, oh your turn will come,
While the Thracian wind howls and the moon

Changes, and burning love and lust
Eat at your cankered liver,
Just the way they eat at
Mares in heat,

And you'll moan because all the laughing
Boys chase after nice green ivy and nice dark myrtle
And leave withered leaves
For Eurus, Winter's mate.

I, 26

And I, beloved by the Muses,
I will send sadness and fear
On the wild winds, out to the Cretan sea,
Without worrying what northern king

Of what frozen country threatens us, or what worries the king
Of Armenia. O sweet Muse,
Who loves pure fountains, weave me
Bright flowers, weave me a garland

For my Lamia! Nothing I can give him
Is anything without You: You and your sisters
Should sing him immortal
With new songs and the sound of the Lesbian lyre.

I, 27

Fighting with wine cups is fit
For Thracians—but no one else. Abolish
The savage custom! Protect Bacchus, who loves
Modesty, from such gross squabbling.

How little Parthian daggers share
With wine cups and quiet lamps! My friends,
Keep your sordid voices down,
Lie with your elbows calm against the couch!

Am I to drink this bold Falernian
With you? Then let the girl's brother
Tell us what wound, what arrow,
Makes him happy to be hit.

No? It doesn't interest you? I'll drink on no other
Condition. Whoever enslaves you to Venus,
Friend, she makes you burn honorably,
As you always burn.

If you've secrets to tell, whisper them
Here in my faithful ear.—Oh Lord, you're unlucky!
What a Charybdis! Lord,
You're worthy of a better love.

What witch, what Thessalian enchantress,
What god, can save you?
Trapped in this triple Chimaera
Even Pegasus could hardly hope to free you.

I, 29

Ixus, you're lusting after Arabian treasures,
Now, and preparing a nasty campaign
Against Syrian kings we haven't yet conquered—
And are you measuring chains for those tough

Persians? After you've killed her lover,
Will you take some savage girl for your slave?
And what perfumed page, out of royal halls,
Will stand and serve your wine,

Though his father taught him to aim
Oriental arrows? But who could deny
That rivers can run up mountains
And the Tiber turn itself backwards

When you, once a scholar and known for better
Reasons, once a collector of famous books,
Are anxious to exchange the Socratic school
For Hispanic swords and armor?

I, 30

O Venus, queen of Cnidos, queen
Of Paphos, leave your beloved Cyprus
And come to Glycera's shrine, where she calls you
With clouds of incense.

Come with your glowing son, and all the
Graces, and the Nymphs, all with their robes
Loose and ready, come with Youth, which is only lovely
In your presence, and come, goddess, with Mercury.

I, 31

Dedicating Apollo's temple, what does the poet
Pray for? What does he ask, pouring new wine
From his bowl? Not for the rich harvests
Of fertile Sardinia,

Not for the dense flocks of hot
Calabria, not for gold or for Indian
Ivory, nor those fields where the silent Liris
Flows. Let those

Blessed by Fortune prune their vines
With Calenian hooks, let rich merchants
Sip out of golden cups,
Savor wine bought for Syrian wares—

Merchants favored by the gods, permitted
To cross the Atlantic three times a year,
Or four, and return. No, it's olives for me,
And onions, and mallow.

Apollo: all I ask is what I own already,
And the peace to enjoy it, sound in body
And mind, and a promise of honor
In old age, and to go on singing to the end.

I, 32

A song, a song is requested. Lying lazy in the shade,
If I've ever sung anything
Worthy to live this year, and next, and more,
O come, my lyre, sing a Roman song,

You who were first tuned by brave hands
On far-off Lesbos, by a fierce poet
Who could sing even in battle, or moored
On some damp beach,

Pour out praise of Bacchus, and the Muses,
And of Venus and the boy clinging to her robe,
And of Lycus with his jet-black eyes
And beautiful brown hair.

O lyre, sworn to Apollo and welcome
When Jove feasts, O sweet
Healer, my solace, help me
When I call!

I, 33

Albius, why such bitter tears
For cruel Glycera, such endless mournful
Laments, simply because she was faithless
And someone younger has taken your place!

Blunt-headed Lycoris loves Cyrus
Madly, but Cyrus chases after cold
Chloe, and she-goats will mate
With Apulian wolves sooner than Chloe

Will give herself to a lower-class lover.
Which is how Venus prefers it, smiling cruelly
As ill-matched minds and bodies thrash
Helpless in her brazen grip.

Even I, though a worthier woman wooed me,
Once entangled myself
With slave-born Myrtle, sultrier than Adriatic
Waves winding around Calabria's gulfs.

I, 34

I worshiped the gods neither fully
Nor well, nor often; I wandered
Lost in foolish wisdom; and now
I need to sail backward, retracing

A way I'd abandoned. Oh, Jupiter can split
The clouds with His lightning, but this time
His iron horses and wind-swift chariot
Flashed through a cloudless sky,

And the dumb earth and the winding rivers
Shook, and deep Hell, and Tanarus' underworld
Cave, and even Atlas, posted at the end
Of the world. God can exalt

The lowest, pull the highest down
To darkness; Fortune on her shrill wings
Snatches a crown from this man, cackles
With delight as she drops it on that man's head.

I, 35 *to Fortune*

O goddess, divinity of delightful Antium,
Ready to raise mere mortals
To the heights, or turn proud triumph
To disaster,

The humble peasant prays to you,
Anxious, afraid, and whoever ploughs
The Carpathian sea in an Asian ship
Prays to you, empress of all oceans,

And fierce Dacians, and wandering Scythians,
And cities, and all lands, and warlike Rome,
And the mothers of barbarian kings,
And purple-clad tyrants

Afraid your careless heel might grind
Their power away, might whip up the people
And stir up mobs—"To arms! To arms!"—
And bring down kingdoms.

Necessity stalks forever in front of you,
Grim, her bronze hand holding
Huge spikes, sharp wedges, molten
Lead, and heavy-jawed clamps.

But Hope walks with you also,
And sometimes Good Faith, wearing white,
Never deserting you even when, angry,
You run in the streets, abandon the powerful.

But the fickle mob will scatter, and the lying
Whore, and even faithless friends will hide
When the wine is all drunk, when
Trouble is too heavy to bear.

Oh watch over our Caesar, soon
To march to the ends of the earth, against
The Britons, and our young armies bringing fear of Rome
To the East, to the shores of the Red Sea!

I shrink in shame for our scars,
And our guilt, brother against brother! Brutal
Generation, have we shrunk
From anything? Left anything undone? Has anything

Restrained our youth, any fear of the gods? What altars
Have they spared? O goddess, reforge
Our blunted swords on new anvils,
Turn them against Arabs and Huns!

I, 36

The gods have brought our Numida
Safe from farthest Spain: sing,
Pour out bullock's blood, burn
Incense in the holy names,

O Numida's many friends, wrapped
In his arms, now. And Lamia
Happiest of all, who sat in the same classroom,
Learned from the same teacher,

Put on man's clothing at the same time.
Hold back nothing on a
Day like this, out with the
Wine jars, and dance, dance

Like mad Salians, let Bassus drink
As much as lovely Damalis who holds wine
Like a Thracian! Let there be roses
At the feast, let there be lilies,

And let everyone wish Damalis were
Theirs, instead of that new lover, he whom
She will not leave for a moment, wound around him
Tighter than ivy clinging to an oak.

I, 37

Drink! O friends, stamp wild
Bare feet on the ground, overflow
Temples with eating
And drinking: it is time!

But to break out the best old wine, before—O
Blasphemy, blasphemy, while that mad queen,
Cleopatra, and her driveling, sick-brained
Camp followers scurried and cried

And tried to pull down the Capitol,
Stupid and weak, but dangerous,
Hoping to stay drunk
On good luck. But her madness ebbed

As one by one her ships sank,
Burned, and her frenzy became fear,
Real fear, as she turned
And fled from Italy, with Caesar

Augustus running behind her, flying
Like a hawk after doves,
Or a hunter tracking hares
In the snow, lifting chains

For her monstrous neck. And she, a woman
No woman, decided on a nobler
Death, not afraid of his sword,
Not sailing for hidden shores.

She could watch her palace in flames,
Calm, she could lift
Angry asps, hold them at her heart,
Drinking black poison through her veins

And lying more fierce, dead, than ever alive—
Too proud for chains and parades, a
Queen with no throne
But a stiff-necked, noble woman.

I, 38

My little slave, forget
About Persian puffing and blowing,
And elegant flowers pasted on bark.
Boy, boy, stop rooting around
In the woods, hunting winter roses for my hair.

A bit of green myrtle will do,
Is good for you, my little slave,
And good for me, your master,
Drinking here in the shade of these thick green vines.

II, 3

Remember, Dellius: keep yourself in
Balance when it's hard, keep yourself in
Balance when all of it comes your way,
All of us destined to die

Whether we live forever sad
Or always lying in some grassy spot,
Celebrating life away
With a jug of choice Falernian.

Why do tall pines and silver poplars
Love to fuse their branches and offer us
Inviting shade? Why does the swift
Stream push its way downward?

Let them bring wines, and perfumes,
And the brief loveliness of the blossoming
Rose, while Fate and Time permit it,
While you're still young.

Those fields, that mansion, everything you've bought: you'll leave it,
Dellius, even that shining villa where yellow Tiber
Washes past, and all your piled-up
Wealth will belong to others.

Descendant of ancient Inachus, and rich,
Or poor and living poorly
Under Heaven, it makes no difference,
All of us belong to pitiless death.

We're all forced down that same road,
Our luck shaken out of the same urn,
Sooner or later we step into Charon's boat
And are ferried into eternal exile.

II, 4

Loving a slave-girl's no
Disgrace, Xanthis. There was Briséis, once,
A slave whose snow-white skin
Tamed even arrogant Achilleus,

And Tecmessa's beauty moved
Mighty Ajax, Telamon's son,
And Agamemnon in the middle of his triumph
Burned for a captive girl,

Once barbarian Troy had fallen
To the Greeks, and Hector's fall
Made it all seem almost
Easy.

Who knows? Your blonde Phyllis
Might have been born to wealth: her parents might
Do you honor, they might be king and queen
Somewhere. You've seen her yourself, weeping for her household

Gods and their cruelty. Surely, loved by you
She's hardly one of the nameless mob—and how
Could anyone so loyal, so untouched by greed,
Come from a vulgar mother!

Believe me, old as I am,
Utterly free of lust when I praise
Her arms, her face, her lovely limbs:
No one, now, could be jealous of *me*!

II, 5

No, she can't carry the weight
Of marriage, not yet, she's not ready
To be bedded, she couldn't bear a full-grown
Bull rushing into pleasure.

Her mind, this unripe calf, still runs
To grassy fields, to cooling herself
In flowing streams, longing
For games played under moist

Willows. Stop, don't pant
For the unripe grape! Autumn will soon enough
Darken green clusters with
Riper purple.

She'll follow you, soon, for Time
Plunges on, and will give her
The years it takes from you, she'll hunt
A husband, she'll hunt boldly,

Loved as Phloe will never be, nor
Chloris, her white shoulders shining
Like a cloudless moon on the midnight sea,
Better loved than Gyges, a boy

So beautiful that, set in a crowd
Of girls, he'd puzzle the wisest stranger,
His hair so flowing, his face
Gorgeously ambiguous.

II, 7

O friend, who fought at my side
And in danger
When Brutus led us to war
And rebellion exiled our names,
Tell me: who brought you
Back to Rome, to your country's
Gods and Italy's skies,

O Pompey, best of friends?
Oh how many times
We've blessed a dragging day
With wine, drunk together,
Syrian perfume
Shining in my hair!

We ran together, at Philippi,
Ran for our lives,
Shields in the dust, courage
Dying, and men dead
In the bloody ground
All around us.

But the wingèd god lifted me
Free, in my fear, swept me
Through dark clouds
And away—while the waves of war
Caught you again, pulled you
Back into foam-whipped water.

Now give Jove what is
Jove's, His banquet, His feast,
And come lie
Here, under my laurel
Leaves, weary of war, and break
Cask after cask, drink
Wine pledged to your name.

Pour forgetfulness
To the brim, fill these shining

Flasks! Let perfume roll out of
Broad-lipped jars—
Who'll weave our garlands,
Quick! who'll bend
Parsley and myrtle,

Who'll sit as master
Of wine and laughter?
I'll roar like a wild
Bull, myself, a Thracian
Bull: pleasure is double
Pleasure when a friend who was lost
Comes home, is won, is a friend
Again.

II, 8

Barina, I'd trust you if
Ever a broken oath had brought you
Punishment, one tooth gone black, a single nail
Spotted, anything to make you decently

Uglier. But no, you swear to everything
And everyone adores you,
You emerge shiningly lovely, all eyes
Follow you.

And it's useful, of course, to swear (and lie)
On your mother's buried ashes, and the silent
Stars, and even all the stars, and the
Deathless gods—

Venus smiles at you, laughs (she does!),
Innocent Nymphs smile, and fierce
Cupid, forever sharpening his hot
Arrows on a bloody whetstone.

And more: all our boys are ripening
Just for you, a whole new generation of your
Slaves—not that your original lovers
Desert you, much as they'd like to.

Mothers shake for their sons, seeing you,
Penny-pinching old men quiver,
And new-minted brides have nightmares
Of you enchanting, enchaining their men.

II, 10

Licinus, life makes better sense
Lived neither pushing farther and farther
To sea, nor always hugging the dangerous
Shore, shaking at the thought of storms.

Cherish a golden mean and stay
Exempt from a filthy hovel
And exempt from the envy
A mansion excites.

It's tall pines that the wind
Shakes, and high towers fall
Harder, and lightning strikes at
Mountain peaks.

A well-ordered mind hopes, when
Nothing goes well, and fears
When it does. Jove makes winters
Return; he also blows them

Away. If you're miserable now, wait
For tomorrow. Wanting to waken the Muse
Apollo plays his lyre, and tries not to
Bend his bow.

Show yourself brave in misfortune,
Prove yourself strong: and when the wind
Is too good to believe, pull in
Your sails.

II, 13

Tree, whoever planted you
Planted on an evil day
And watered you with blasphemous hands,
Planning our village's disgrace
And the destruction of its posterity.

He must have strangled his own
Father—yes, and in deep darkness
Spattered his floor with a sleeping guest's
Blood. Yes. He must have bought
And sold Medea's poisons—

Whatever any criminal does, anywhere,
He must have done it, that infamous
Wretch who put you here on my land,
Put you where you would fall
On your owner's innocent head.

No one knows enough
To run from danger, hour by hour.
Phoenician sailors shake at
The Bosporus Strait, but at nothing
Striking from different directions, unseen.

Roman soldiers worry about Persian
Arrows and quick retreats; Persian
Soldiers worry about Roman
Chains and Roman jails; but death,
Which no one plans for, has swept away generations
And will sweep away more.

How close I came to dark Proserpiné's
Realm, and the throne of Aeácus, Zeus'
Son, Peleus' father, and the fields death
Saves for all good men; I could almost hear
Sappho's Aeolian lyre, hear her

Singing songs of Lesbos girls,
Almost hear you, Alkaios, and your darker

Songs of sailors at sea, of the pain
Of exile, of the misery of war—
And oh, the golden strings!

They listen to you both, the wondering,
Grateful spirits of the dead, listen
In silence; but the pack of ghosts
Pushes, shoulder to shoulder, to hear
How tyrants fell and wars
Were won and lost.

Such songs that the hundred-headed
Monster droops his black ears—
And snakes, twisting in Furies'
Hair, unwind and rest!

Oh, even Prometheus rests, and even
Tantalus, tormented into eternity, forgets
His pain, hearing your sweet songs,
And ravenous Orion rests, he too,
Leaves the frightened foxes, lets
The lions run unharmed.

II, 14

Oh year by year, Póstumay,
Póstumay, time slips by,
And holiness can't stop us drying,
Or hold off death.

Pluto will swallow a hundred bulls
A day, and do what he does
Anyway: three-bodied Geryon can't fly
Away, or giant Tityos

Escape him, down in that sad darkness
Where we all go, everyone
On earth, poor farmers,
And kings on their thrones.

Dodge the bloody war god,
Escape the frantic sea,
Guard your kidneys
From desert winds,

You'll still go there where the black river
Groans, and see Danaeus' bloody
Daughters, and Sisyphus forever
Rolling his stone uphill.

Good-bye to earth, and home, and love
And wife; none of your precious trees will grow green
Where you go—except the cypress,
That sucks on corpses.

He who takes what you took, and deserves it
More, will drain that hidden wine,
Will spill the juice of more glorious vines
Than an emperor tastes.

II, 15

Soon, these royal palaces will be empty
Acres for the plough, fishponds wider than
The Lucrine Lake will be everywhere, and the flat-leaved
Plane tree will push out

Regal elms, and violets and myrtles and hosts of
Fragrant flowers will scatter their perfume
Where once the fertile olive grew
In rich groves,

And thick-branched laurels will keep out
The sun. Romulus never meant it
So, nor long-haired Cato, nor any of
Our simple fathers.

They owned almost nothing, but Rome
Was rich beyond measure: no citizen boasted
A porch paced out in ten-foot lengths,
Open to the cool northern winds,

No citizen would dare offend the gods, would
Refuse to build them wonderful shrines, of rare
Marble, and every city was made a delight
At everyone's expense.

II, 16

O Grosphus, caught on the open Aegean
Sailors pray for peace, while clouds
Hang dark across the moon, and stars go out,
And storms begin to blow;

Warlike Thrace begs for peace,
And Persians carrying rich quivers beg for peace—
But peace, my friend, no gold no diamonds no empires
Can ever buy.

No heap of treasure, no kinglike power,
Can cure misery deep in the soul,
All the fear and worry flitting
High around paneled ceilings.

Happiness sits in a battered
Salt dish, on a thin-spread table,
Lies in sleep too quiet for greed,
Too soft for fear.

Why work so hard to earn so much,
When we live so little? Why run to some different sun,
Seeking fortune? Whoever ran from his country
And escaped from himself?

Worry crawls like rust even on brass-bound
Boats, the fastest horses never
Outrun it, the swiftest deer, even
The East Wind pushing storms in front of him.

Let your soul taste what it has,
Never twist and turn for an unknown future;
Cure bitterness with an easy smile:
Nothing and no one is ever perfectly happy.

Death cut down Achilleus, young; and Tithonus
Of Troy, granted long life, lived to shrivel like a shadow;
And whatever you wanted, friend, and never got,
Might now come to me—who knows?

Your stables may be filled with African
Horses, your fields with Sicilian
Sheep, double-dyed purple wool
May grace your shoulders, and I,

Given this tiny farm by a kind fate,
Blessing me with closed palms, still breathe
Some echoes of Greek song, still live
Blessed with contempt for malicious mobs.

II, 17

Why weary me with your heavy sighs,
Maecenas? The gods won't take me
Before they take you, and I've no interest in going,
O glory and foundation of all my existence.

Part of my life would die, if you
Were snatched away, and I would refuse
To linger, part dead already, and the living
Part no longer lovely to me. Ah, the day

You die, I die! This is an oath, and a true one:
We two will go, oh we will go,
Whenever you lead the way, arm in arm
On that final journey.

Neither Chimaera's flaming breath
Nor hundred-handed Gyges, reborn,
Could tear me from you: this is mighty
Justice's word, and that of the Fates.

Let Libra be my dominant star, or
Evil Scorpio, violent half of my birth hour,
Or Capricorn, ruler of western
Oceans—whatever our horoscopes,

Maecenas, we and our stars
Will agree. Jove's great pulsing
Light kept you, once, from Saturn's
Treacherous grip, saved you

From Fate's swift wings, when the people's
Massed voice rang out, and rang, and rang again
For you; and a falling tree
Would have crushed me, once, but Faunus,

Protector of poets, put out his right hand
And brushed it away. Then remember! Sacrifice in both
Our names, put up a grateful shrine.
And I, I will offer a humble lamb.

II, 18

No ivory gleams in my house,
No golden ceiling,
No marble beams
Held up by pillars quarried

In farthest Africa; I am no startled
Heir of a dead king's
Palace, no noble ladies parade
For me in Laconian purple.

But I am honest, blessed
With a vein of talent, and poor as I am
Rich men court me: there's nothing more
I can pray to the gods for, nor do I beg

More of my powerful friends,
I'm more than happy with just
This Sabine farm. Day follows day,
The new moon rises, and wanes—

Yet you, perched at the grave's edge,
Sign contracts for quantities of marble
And, ignoring death, throw up a palace
And work at pushing the shore further

Into that thundering Baian sea, as if
The shore were not already more than sufficient.
Why insist on shifting property markers,
Nibbling your neighbors' lands, even

Leaping across to lands
You rented out yourself? Man and wife
You toss them out, household gods
In their hands, ragged brats at their side.

Yet Pluto's dark hall, deep in the earth,
Is surely your next home—hell
Is certain for greedy
Landlords. Why struggle for more? The ground

Opens for us all, for poor and rich
And princes alike, and Pluto's ferryman
Is immune to gold, brings no one
Back. Prometheus stays there. And proud

Tantalus, and all his race, stay in
That prison; call him or not, that ferryman
Comes, and when the poor man's labors
Are done he's ferried to freedom.

II, 19

I saw Bacchus himself—oh believe me, men in
Later times!—singing hymns high on the crags,
And nymphs learning his songs, and I saw
Goat-footed satyrs with pointed ears.

Lord! My heart beats with new fear,
Remembering, and my heart rejoices, full of
The god. Lord! O Bacchus, spare me,
Wielder of that terrible staff!

I must sing your endless festivals,
And the fountain of wine, and rivers flowing with milk,
And sing, oh once again, how honey
Fell out of hollow trees;

I must sing your happy mate, high
In the heavens, now, and Pentheus King of Thebes,
His palace destroyed, himself destroyed, for defying
You, and Lycurgus, blinded, killed.

Rivers bend when you call, and the savage
Sea, and on lonely mountains you bless your Thracian
Women, wet with wine, you tie their hair
In harmless knots of vipers.

When slobbering Giants climbed
Toward Olympus, fought the steep slopes of the sky
To attack your father Jove, you became a lion, tooth
And claw, and hurled them down.

They say you're happier dancing, and laughing,
And playing, you're unhappy with a sword
In your hand, but you've had a hand
In war as in peace.

Glorious with your golden horn, even Cerberus
Stared and could not harm you, but gently
Wagged his tail, and when you left licked
Your feet with his triple tongue.

II, 20

Poet of double nature, I shall soar
The liquid air on no common, feeble
Wings, nor linger here on earth, but fly
Beyond envy, beyond all the cities

Of earth. The son of poor parents, yes,
Maecenas, and one you call your friend, but
I will never die, never be
Imprisoned by the waters of the Styx.

Now—now—wrinkled skin comes winding around
My ankles, and the rest of me mutates, becomes
A swan, snowy white, soft feathers
Sprout on my shoulders, my hands.

And now, singing in the clouds, I will go to
Murmuring Bosporus, I will visit Africa,
Swifter than Daedalean Icarus I will come
To Hyperborean fields.

Men of Colchis will know me, men of Dacia,
Pretending not to be afraid of our armies, and
The distant Geloni too, and the learned Spaniard, and he who
Drinks from the Rhone.

No dirges, no womanish weeping
At this mock funeral! Be silent,
Forget this talk of death, and above all
Waste no time on a tomb.

III, 2

Let young men learn how suffering
Ennobles, let them be patient soldiers, severely
Tested, and then be horsemen feared for their
Lances, pursuing fierce Parthians

To their lairs, in troubled times living their lives
In the open air. Let the wives of warring
Kings, and their grown daughters, watch them
From city walls, and sigh, and say:

"Dear Lord! Keep our royal son
And brother safe from this raging lion,
Keep our awkward prince from this bloody
Hero, who cuts through the center of our army!"

How good, how noble to die for your country.
Death chases those who run from him,
And catches them, and never spares a coward
Or a womanish boy.

Virtue has no concern with reputation,
Shines for its own sake, neither takes up
Arms nor lays them down
Because the mob tells it to.

Virtue opens Heaven for many who deserve
To live, guides itself by its own light, unknown
Except to the virtuous, soars above this cloudy
Earth on wings the vulgar are forever denied.

And honest silence has its own rewards:
He who betrays the sacred rites of Ceres
Is forbidden to share a roof with me,
Or sail in the same fragile boat;

Ignore angry Jove, and he's likely to
Mix up innocent and guilty, but lame-footed
Vengeance manages to find whoever she seeks,
No matter how fast they run, or how hard, or how soon.

III, 4

Calliopé, come down from Heaven
And let your flute blow long lovely
Melodies, or sing out in that clear voice, or
Sing to Apollo's lyre.

Do you hear her? Am I deceiving myself?
I feel that I hear her, I feel myself wandering
In sacred groves, where quiet streams
Trickle and soft breezes blow.

As a child, sleepy with too much playing,
There on Apulian Vultur (oh mountain stretching
Far from my home) I lay, all covered in fresh green leaves,
Dropped down by fairy-tale forest

Doves—a story to startle everyone
Living on lofty Acherontia, or deep in the
Bantine woods, or along the fertile
Valley of Forentum:

Where were the vipers? Where were the wolves?
How could I sleep safe, unafraid, sheltered
With sacred laurel, and with heaped-up myrtle?
With the gods' help I could, and I did.

Oh, and I am yours, Muses, yours still
When I climb these tall Sabine hills, when I visit
Cold Pranesté, or descend to Tibur, or across to
Cloudless Baiae, as fancy takes me.

Our armies ran at Philippi, and that cursed
Tree tried to kill me, and Sicilian waves
Off the strait of Palinurus: I survive,
Friend of your fountains, your dancing, your song.

With you beside me I'll smile
As I sail the raging Bosporus,
I'll brave burning
Syrian sands,

I'll visit murderous Britons,
And the Concani who drink the blood of horses,
And the Geloni with their bristling arrows,
And I'll cross Scythian rivers, and be always

Safe. For it's you who refresh Caesar
Himself, resting a moment in Pieran grottoes,
His tired troops quartered
In town. It's you

Who make him mild, help him delight in
Doing good. And all men know how mighty
Jove, who rules this lifeless earth, and its
Cities, and the stormy ocean, and those dark

Kingdoms under the ground, controlling
Mortal and immortal with even hand,
How he crushed Titans and Giants
With his sweeping thunder.

An insolent mob, arrogant, fierce,
Struggling against Heaven:
They struck terror, for a moment, even in
Jove's great heart.

But even Typhus and huge Mimas,
Rhaetus and Enkeladus, who hurled trees
He uprooted himself, even immense
Porphyron,

What could they accomplish against
Minerva's ringing shield? And there was
Vulcan, more than ready, and there was Juno,
And Apollo who never lowers his bow,

Apollo god of Delos and Patara, who
Dips his flowing hair in Castalian
Dew, who hunts in the forests of
Lycia, who rules at Delphos.

Force without wisdom falls of its own
Weight. Even the gods require sense of themselves,
And work better for its guidance. They hate
Evil no matter how strong.

See, hundred-handed Gyas
Proves it, and Orion, who hunted pure
Diana and fell to that virgin's
Arrow!

Earth mourns, falling eternally on her
Own monsters, burned into Hell
By Jove's lightning; flaming Aetna
Stands unconsumed forever;

The vulture who eats out
Tityus' liver eats on, and on;
And amorous Pirithous lies wrapped
In three times a hundred chains.

III, 5

Hearing his thunder, we believe
Jove in Heaven; and Augustus will be
A god here on earth when Britain
And Persia complete the Empire.

Are any Romans, captured in Persia,
Disgraced by barbarian wives, growing gray
—Oh our ruined Senate, our corrupted Rome!—
As soldiers of their enemies, Apulians,

Oscans, serving Persian kings while Rome
Still stands, forgetting the eternal Vesta, Roman
Names, Roman togas, the sacred
Shields, and Jove himself?

Regulus, captured by Carthage, saw
Too far in the future, refused freedom
For his friends and himself, knew
What ransom would mean for Rome;

Sent as a messenger, sworn to return,
He asked a vote for death instead of bribery.
"I've seen," he said in the Senate,
"Roman flags hung in Carthage's shrines,

"Swords taken from unresisting soldiers,
I've seen freemen, Roman freemen, tied
Like slaves, and the gates of Carthage carelessly
Open, fields being plowed and sown and tilled.

"Romans bought back with gold will fight
Better for their vacation! No! Shame will be doubled
By a waste of money. Dye your wool
And never see its true color again.

"Nor does courage come back;
Once gone it's gone forever.
When deer fight like lions,
Freed from traps, then fools

"Who surrender to their enemies, trusting
  An enemy's good faith, will be brave
  Too, and soldiers tied with Carthage's rope
  Will crush Carthage's armies,

"Though death frightened them witless, once!
  They know nothing of life, they take peace
  For war. Shame! O mighty Carthage,
  Grown mightier by Rome's disgrace!"

  Knowing himself a slave by war, Regulus
  Turned from wife and sons, refused
  Their touch, stood staring grimly
  Down at the ground, until

  A hesitating Senate accepted
  Advice new to it, then left
  His weeping friends, hurried back
  To Carthage, an exile departed in glory.

  Oh he knew what barbarian tortures
  Were waiting, and knowing, knowing, he still
  Pushed friends and relatives
  Aside, people trying to stop his going,

  Leaving the Senate like some lawyer
  Who had argued his client's case
  And now was off to Venafrum for a rest,
  Gone down to Tarentum to lie in the sun.

III, 7

Astera, why weep for faithful Gyges,
When Spring's first gentle winds
Will blow him home to you,
Rich with Bithian wares?

Winter drove him east to Epirus,
When the goat-stars raged, and there
He lies, sleepless, through the frozen
Nights, and he weeps for you.

And yet his love-struck hostess
Has her servants feeding him thousands
Of lies, telling him how she sighs
For him, and only him, and how her love burns

Exactly like yours. They tell him how trusting
Protus was betrayed by a
Scheming woman, and stern
Bellerophon died;

They tell him how Peleus came close to
Hell, for avoiding Hippolyta—
And all they tell him are tales
Pointed toward sin.

But in vain: your lover listens, as deaf as the
Cliffs of Icaros, his heart as whole
As ever. But you, *you* be careful of Enipus
Your neighbor, already too well liked:

Granted, he rides as fast and as well
As anyone, on Mars' hard grass;
Granted, he swims the Tiber
Swifter than everyone:

Just keep your doors and windows closed, at night,
Never watch when he wanders the streets,
His plaintive flute playing, and no matter how often
He calls you, never hear him.

III, 8

Maecenas, learned in tongues, tell me
Why an ancient bachelor busies himself
With the Kalends of March, fusses with flowers
And incense and rows of burning coals

Laid out on the grass?
I promised Bacchus a banquet
And a white goat, when he kept
That falling tree from killing me,

And here on this day, each time the year spins
Around, I'll pull a well-pitched cork
From a wine-jar sealed in
Tully's time.

Drink a hundred cups, Maecenas,
To celebrate your friend's escape!
Let the lamps all burn till dawn,
Let all anger and bustle be banished!

Forget your official concerns:
The Dacians are well defeated,
The Parthians are fighting each other
In a lovely civil war,

Our old enemies, the Spanish Cantabrians,
Are finally in chains, and even the
Scythians, their bows unstrung,
Are contemplating peace.

Be private, this once, forget responsibility,
Let the people worry for themselves!
Take with a smile what the hour brings,
The devil with all seriousness!

III, 9

Horace:
"When you still loved me
    And no one you loved better could kiss
    Your snowy neck, I lived
    Happier than a Persian king."

Lydia:
"When you loved me best
    And even Chloe meant nothing,
    Then famous as I am I lived
    More glorious than the Mother of all Rome."

Horace:
"Thracian Chloe rules me, now,
    With her sweet voice and skillful lyre;
    I would die for her, unafraid,
    If the Fates would let her live."

Lydia:
"Calas of Thuria consumes me, now,
    And I him; I'd die for him twice over
    If the Fates would let the beautiful
    Boy live."

Horace:
"What if dead love rekindled, and golden
    Chloe were put aside, and though long-parted
    We were joined once more, the door reopened
    For poor neglected Lydia?"

Lydia:
"He may be handsome as a god, and you
    Less stable than a cork, stormier than the windblown
    Ocean, but I'd gladly return, it's you
    I'd love to live and die with."

III, 10

Lyca, living in frozen Russia, drinking from the
River Don, married to a fur-clad savage, still
You'd never throw me to the North winds
As I lie here at your indifferent door.

Can't you hear it howling, that cold blast, creaking
Your gate, moaning in your trees,
While Jove in his cloudy majesty
Glazes the fallen snow?

Be careful: disdain runs back like a
Rope on a pulley; remember Venus, who loves
Lovers. You're no Penelopé, born to a
Tuscan father, immune to all men.

No presents impress you, no prayers move you,
Not even your lovers' purple pallor,
Not even your husband's passion for his Pierian
Mistress—oh, though nothing can bend you,

No gentler than the rigid oak, no softer
Of heart than a Moorish snake—spare us!
How long can I last, here on this cold portal,
With Heaven's rain pouring down?

III, 11

O Mercury, who taught Amphion to sing
Rocks in motion, and you,
My lyre, tuned sweetly on seven
Strings, once neither lovely

Nor welcome, now heard at the tables
Of the rich and the temples of the gods,
Sing to Lydia, bend her stubborn
Ears, who leaps like a filly

Three years old, runs
In the fields, plays in the meadows, and
Runs most from men, still unripe,
Still unwilling to be mated.

Mercury: you can stop rivers, pull tigers
And trees behind you;
You charmed Cerberus, grim
Gatekeeper of Hell,

Though a hundred serpents
Twist on his head, and his breath
Is pure poison, and blood dribbles
From his three-tongued mouth.

Oh, even Ixion and Tityus
Smiled, and let the wine-jar stand
Idle, while you flattered
Danaus' daughters.

Listen, Lydia, hear how those girls
Were guilty, and were punished,
Hear how Fate can
Punish wrong even down in

Hell. Evil! Who could have done
Worse? Perverted women,
Able to stab their wedded
Husbands to the heart!

But one, only one, was worthy of
Hymen's torch, gloriously false
To her treacherous father, noble for all
Time to come.

"Wake, wake!" she whispered to her young
Husband, "or you'll fall into endless
Sleep, and at hands you've never feared.
Escape my cruel father, my evil

"Sisters, greedy lionesses leaping
On steers, and now, now killing them!
My heart is too soft, I could not kill you,
I could not chain you here.

"My father can lock me away
For pitying my helpless husband:
He can sail me to the darkest
Corner of the world!

"Run, go where your feet and the wind
Take you, hurry, while Night and Venus
Smile on you! And carve my mournful
Fate on my tomb."

III, 12

When love hurts, girl, and needs love,
How miserable not to love, not to forget love, and need,
In sweet, sweet wine, only to tremble
At some uncle's lashing tongue!

Aphrodité sends her son, O Néobulé, to steal
Your basket of wool; you see Hebrus, come from Sicily, and
His beauty drops your hands from your loom,
Everything you've learned drops away

As soon as he wets his oil-rubbed shoulders
In our River Tiber. He rides his horse
Better than Bellerophon, who rode on Pegasus,
No one runs races faster, or wrestles stronger,

Or stalks terrified deer, weaving madly in the grass,
With surer aim, or stands, quick and straight,
As Hebrus stands while a boar charges, wild,
Exploding out of thick bushes.

III, 13

Bandusia, Fountain, clearer than glass,
Worthy of wine spilled in Your honor, of flowers
Poured in Your name, tomorrow I will bring you a kid,
Horns sprouting on his forehead, swelling

With life: in vain.
He came from an amorous flock,
But tomorrow Your cool water
Will be red with his blood.

You, Fountain, untouched by the dog-star's heat,
Cool to straggling cattle,
Cool to weary oxen
Free from the plow:

Fountain, You too are famous, now,
As I sing the oak tree jutting above You,
Rooted in the hollow rocks
You leap from, noisy, bright.

III, 14

Romans! They said that Caesar like Hercules before him
Hunted a fame
That only death could bring, but Spain
Returns him to us, triumphant.

Now let his wife, rejoicing in that matchless
Man, sacrifice to the evenhanded gods:
Behold her, and Caesar's sister,
And mothers of Roman virgins, and of Roman

Sons spared by Mars, their foreheads wreathed in
Supplication. O virgins, O young men
Unmarried, guard your tongues,
Be careful!

We will celebrate, truly celebrate,
This day. I fear no violence,
No civic cares, nor even death
Itself, while Caesar rules the world.

Bring me perfume, slave, and garlands,
And wine that remembers the Marsic
War—if the Spartans left any
Unbroken.

And tell my sweet-singing Naera
To hurry, to tie up her hair, fragrant with myrrh:
If the doorman is rude, ignore him,
Leave!

Well, I'm milder, now, than the hot-tempered
Fellow I was in Plancus' time:
Grey hair does wonders, calms a quarrelsome head,
Soothes a brawling mind.

III, 15

O wife of poor Ibycus, enough!
Give up those sluttish habits, finally,
No more bewitching!
Death approaches, leave

The girls to themselves, let
The stars shine unclouded.
What's right for Phloe is wrong
For you: leave

Seduction for your daughter,
Shaking to Bacchus' drum:
Love for Nothus makes her leap
Like a wanton she-goat—

But soft Lucerian wool fits you,now,
Not cymbals and zithers, not the damask
Rose, and oh, old woman, not
Wine-jars drained to the dregs!

III, 16

A bronze tower, and oak doors, and
Fierce watchdogs could have kept
Princess Danae safe, locked away
From midnight lovers,

But Jove and Venus laughed at her
Anxious father, king of the
Argives: they knew how it would go
Once the god turned golden!

Gold blows down walls better than
Thunder, loves to walk through
Jailers; it was gold
That ruined the Greek prophet,

Destroyed his family; cities
Burst open for the Macedonian hero, and
Kings toppled, at the touch of gold;
Even hardened sailors melt in its hands.

But gold brings both greed and
Trouble on its back. O Maecenas, glory
Of Rome, I've been right to fear
Fame, to hide in the shadows.

The more you keep from yourself, the more
The gods give you. Having nothing
I hunt others who own as much,
I abandon riches and rich,

And yet I'm as wealthy,
Old friend, as if my barns
Were packed with everything ploughed
On all the acres in Apulia.

My clear, pure water, my acre or
Two of timber, the tiny cornfield
I know I can harvest, make me happier than the
Lord of fertile Africa.

I've no Calabrian honeybees, no wine
Mellowing in Lamian jars,
No French sheep growing fat
In my fields,

Yet no one could call me poor;
If I asked for more, you'd give it,
Maecenas. My money goes farther
Because I use it less:

Why try to own the world?
Those who desire too much, miss
More; the gods' true blessing
Is exactly enough, not a grain over.

III, 17

O noble Aelius, descended from ancient
Lamus, father of all Lamiae
And of your father, and
Recorded in our oldest

Annals as founder of your race,
He who first ruled the Formian
Walls, and the river Liris
Where it laps at Marica—oh,

A mighty ruler! But tomorrow a storm
Will blow from the east, and unless
The raven, prophet of rain, deceives me,
The forest will be filled with leaves

And the shore with seaweed. Get your dry wood
While you can! Tomorrow let your
Slaves rest, cherish yourself
With wine, and with a suckling pig!

III, 18

Faunus, nymph-fucker,
Cross my fences quietly
And leave luck
Here in my sun-filled fields:

I'll smoke incense in your name,
Kill you a soft-eared kid—
O friend of Venus, famous wolf-hater,
I'll pour you wine and wine and wine.

Sheep and goats dance
December, in your name;
Peasants and oxen lie in the grass
And drink and laugh,

O Faunus, lambs prance
And ignore the wolf,
And plowmen stamp, stamp, stamp
On that damned hard ground!

III, 20

Pyrrus, Pyrrus, an African
Lion fights for her cubs:
Do you know what danger you're in?
You'll run like a frightened rapist
As soon as she charges your band
Of beardless boys, hunting
Her beautiful Neárchos. She'll fight you,
All teeth and claws, and god only
Knows who'll get him. You flex
Your bow, yes, she files
Her ghastly fangs—but calm
Neárchos, waiting to decide
The winner, covers the palm-wreath
With one bare foot, and stands
Letting the soft breeze cool
His shoulders (covered with perfumed
Hair), stands like Niréus,
Next to Achilleus most beautiful
Of Greeks, or Ganymede, swept
From Ida to Olympus by hot-eyed Zeus.

III, 22

Diana, Virgin, keeper
Of mountains, of trees,
O three-shaped goddess
To whom women in labor call,
Three times over,
And who comes, making
Birth-death go,

Diana, I dedicate
This pine tree, brushing along
My roof, to you, and year-end
After year-end I will smile
As I splash it, in your great name,
With the blood of a boar
Too young for a perfect sideward
Slash of his tusks.

III, 23

O rustic Phyllis, lift your prayerful
Hands to Heaven when the moon is
Born new, burn incense to your household
Gods, offer them fruit and a fat pig,

And no vicious wind out of Africa
Will rip at your vines, no mildew rot
Your corn, no lambs sicken and die in autumn
When the trees grow ripe.

Fate's victim, grazing now on snowy
Algidus, cropping among the oaks and holm-trees,
Fattening in Alban fields, will dye
The priest's axe with its blood.

No need to slaughter
Wholesale: crown those tiny
Images with garlands of rosemary, with
Myrtle, and they will reward you.

Pure hands lifted at an altar
Better satisfy the gods with sanctified
Grain and crackling salt
Than with any costly sacrifice.

III, 24

Richer than treasure-full India
Or unknown Arabia, your palaces
Crowding everywhere, pushing
At all the oceans,

If Destiny drives her iron nails in
Your roof, your soul will quiver
With fear, and your life
Will lie in Death's hands.

Better to live like rambling Scythians,
Pulling their houses behind them, or
Those tough Thracians roaming
Uncountable acres

And plucking fruit and harvesting
Corn as they please, staying
Anywhere a year at a time, and moving
On as another moves in.

Stepchildren are children, there, with a
True mother's love, and husbands
Rule wives, and wives seek
No glib lovers.

Children inherit virtue and
Chastity, steady, sure, ashamed
Of sin, aware that crime
Is punished with death.

Oh who will block these
Bloody wars among ourselves?
Carve "Father of Rome" on his statues,
Whoever dares to stop

Lust run wild and leave us
Something to leave our children! Oh we
Despise virtue in the living, worship it
In the dead: horrible, horrible!

What good is complaining, if crime
Goes unpunished?
What good are laws
Without morality? All empty.

If the merchant can go
Where he wills, glowing Africa
Or the frozen North,
Without restraint—

If sailors crisscross stormy
Oceans, if poverty is the greatest
Sin and we do anything, suffer
Anything to avoid it, and avoid virtue

As hard and unpleasant—then let us drop gold,
That seed of all evil, and diamonds and all
Precious stones, in the nearest
Ocean, or ship them instead to

The Capitol, where the crowd
Will applaud them, and us. Repent?
Can we repent? Lust and depravity
Must be wiped from our hearts,

Our enfeebled minds taught
The stiff, unwelcome truth. No youth
New to horses can ride,
Is afraid to hunt, now,

Knows Greek games better, and
Forbidden dice, and hoops.
And his perjured father defrauds
Friends and family,

Piling up gold no one will
Deserve at his death. Stolen riches
Grow, oh yes, but there's always something
Missing, it's never complete, it's never right.

III, 25

Where are you pushing me, Bacchus, hurrying me
To what groves of new inspiration, what
New grottoes? From what deep caves is my voice
To rise, trying to tell the immortal

Stars, and Jove's great council, that Caesar
Too is immortal, and matchless?
Let my song be noble, and never
Sung before—as the sleepless

Worshiper at your shrine, Bacchus, stands
Dazed on mountain tops, staring at
Hebrus, and snow-covered Thrace, and
Barbarian Rhodopé—as I

Follow my feet, delighted, down
Rivers and into empty woods. O Master of
Naiads, Lord of Bacchantes who
Tear up trees with their hands, I will sing

No mortal song, nothing humble, nothing
Slight. Bacchus! How sweetly
Dangerous, this worship of the god
Crowned in green wine leaves.

III, 26

I lived love's warfare, once,
And fought for glory, and won it;
But now this wall that shields
Sea-born Venus will wear

My sword and shield, my lyre, all done
With fighting. Let the glowing torches
Burn themselves out—here, here!—and all
The axes, and the rams, for beating in doors.

O queen and goddess of rich Cyprus and of
Memphis where Thracian snow can never
Fall, flick your whip, just once, just
Once, on proud Chloe's back!

III, 27

Let the wicked guide their lives
By omens like these: an owl's piercing
Shriek, a red she-wolf or a pregnant bitch
Running down Alban hills, a fox and her new-whelped

Litter! Let snakes leap across their path
Like arrows, as they begin a journey, let their horses
Rear in terror! But I, farsighted
Prophet of the Muse, protective, fearful,

Invoke for *her* the raven croaking
From the east, he who
Foreshadows storms, before he
Returns to stagnant pools.

Be happy, Galatea, wherever
You go, and live with memories of me;
Let no wandering crow, no woodpecker
Flying from your left, keep you!

Yet Orion rages, sinking low:
You see it. The West wind
Can blow up evil, the Adriatic
Turn fierce: I know it.

Let our enemies' wives, and their children,
Feel the dark wind roar, hear
The churning sea, shake like the
Shore beaten by waves!

Europa trusted her snow-white
Loveliness to a treacherous bull, and brave
As she was turned pale at the ocean
Deep with danger, filled with monstrous

Creatures. Fresh from flowery meadows
And garlands fit for Nymphs, night's
Dark shadows showed her, now,
Just waves and a handful of stars.

And landing on Crete, mighty
With cities, she cried, "O father:
Fallen from duty, now, daughter only in
Name, swept up in frenzy,

"Where have I come to? Where am I going?
A single death could not punish me
Enough. Am I dreaming or awake,
Am I repentant as well as guilty,

"Or am I only mocked by phantoms
Escaping the ivory gates? Was it better
To ride the wide waves, or rest
At home, gathering fresh flowers?

"Could anyone bring me that horrible
Bull, I'd chop off his horns,
I'd axe him to death,
Oh that monster I stupidly adored!

"How shameless I left my father's
Shelter! How shameless to stay alive!
O gods, if you hear me, send me
Naked among the lions!

"Before these lovely cheeks wither
Away, before my blood drains out and
My beauty is gone, oh let me be
Food for tigers!

" 'Worthless Europa,' my distant father instructs me,
I hear him, 'Why wait to die? Here on this
Ash tree you can hang yourself:
Luckily, you wore a belt!

" 'Perhaps a cliff and sharp rocks below would please you
Better: come, step out on the wind
—Or are you, daughter of kings,
Ready to cringe like a slave,

" 'Carding wool, ordered about by barbarians,
    Even a concubine!' " Ah, but Venus
    Appeared, smiling, and Cupid her son
    With his unstrung bow.

  "Enough of your anger, enough complaining!" she directed
    When her laughter was done. "Your loathsome
    Bull will give you his horns,
      You can tear them to your heart's desire.

"Invincible Jove has taken you for his wife
    —Fool! No tears: learn to be
    What Fate has made you, mighty and
    Famous, and a part of the world called by your name."

III, 28

The best thing to do on Neptune's
Feast day? Out with our stored-up
Caecuban, Lydia, let's
Storm wisdom's stronghold!

You see the sun dropping and yet,
As if Time and his wings stood still,
You hesitate. That jar, it dates
From Bibulus' days!

We'll sing in chorus, I of
Neptune and green-haired Nereids,
You of Latona, mother of Apollo,
Mother of huntress Diana,

And then we'll sing of Venus,
Ruler of Cnidos, who visits
Paphos drawn by swans. And at last
We'll sing a song that belongs to Night.

III, 29

O Maecenas, son of a
Son of a son of Etruscan kings,
The wine that's waiting for you, here in my house,
Is long since mellow, and there are roses

For your hair, and balsam. Come soon,
Do not sit waiting for Tiber
To run dry, do not stay staring at high
Green fields, sloping to the river, and those hills

Where Telegónus killed Odysseus, his father.
Too much is too much; give up
Great Rome, rich Rome,
Smoky, noisy, brawling Rome.

Simple food, on a bare
Table, under a plain board
Roof, is a useful taste
For a rich palate. The dog-star

Is burning, and Andromeda's glowing
Father, and all of Leo is lit
In the sky, and the sun
Is full, and the fields are dry;

And sleepy sheep and tired
Shepherds crawl under trees and into
Bushes, along the riverbank where woodgods
Roll and no breeze blows.

You carry Rome in your heart
Wherever you go, thinking, dreaming
For Rome: what's China doing? and Persia?
And the civil war in Russia?

But the gods are wise:
They cover the future in darkness,
And they laugh if men try
Too hard to know. Take

Calmly whatever comes to you:
Everything else runs away
Like a river down to the sea, quiet
One minute, the next whirling rocks

And trees and cattle
And houses around and around
As mountains roar, and forests,
Watching the fierce flood

Chew up ground. A man is his own
Master, is happy, Maecenas, saluting
The sun and saying "Today I've been
Alive." The gods can let tomorrow's

Sky glow or be black with clouds,
But tomorrow's tomorrow, I've got what I've got,
Nothing I've had in my hands will be nothing,
Though time takes it.

Fortune is stubborn, and proud,
And cruel; she shuffles
The world this way, that way;
I'm up, I'm down; he's king, he's slave.

I praise her if I have her: if she shakes
Her wings I let her go, let everything
Go, and walk with naked
Virtue, poor if an honest man can only

Be poor. When ships stagger
In an African storm, no begging prayers,
Thank you, no bargains with gods
For Greek glass and Asian

Pots: not me, I'll ride
The storm, safe
In my rowboat,
Blown home by the wind.

III, 30

The monument I've made for myself will outlast
Brass, reaches higher than Egyptian
Kings and their pyramids; nothing can corrode it,
No rain, no wind, nor the endless years
Flying past. I'll die, but only be
Partly dead: the goddess of death
Will take a part, but leave a mighty
Part untouched, a part forever
Young, green in men's praise for as long
As priests and silent virgins climb
To the Capitol. My name will be heard where Daunus
Ruled a land of water-hungry
Farmers, and the wild Aufidus River
Roars in winter, a land where I,
Poor, was born, and made myself famous,
The first Apulian singer of Greek
Music. You won my honor, Muse:
Accept it, now, raise the laurel
Of Delphos as a crown for my head.

IV, 1

Venus, you're stirring up battles
I haven't fought in years: mercy, I beg you, I beg you!
Whatever I was when my sweet Cynara
Ruled me, I am no more. O cruel

Mother of gentle Cupids, at fifty
I ought to be immune, leave me dumb
To your soft urging! Go
Where young men call on you, pray to your name;

Go to Paulus Maximus, ride your gleaming
Swans to his door, rejoice decently
In his willing heart
If you need a heart to whip up,

For Paulus is noble, and handsome, an eloquent
Lawyer defending anxious men, accomplished
In a hundred arts, a man who'll wear your glove
And carry your flag far and wide,

And when next he wins a famous victory
He'll laugh and set you a statue,
A marble statue, under a roof of citron,
There beside Lake Alba,

And kindle you fires of incense
And play you music on lyres
And double-reeded flutes
And shepherds' pipes

And twice a day boys and girls
Will sing your praise and dance
Your praise on bare white feet,
Dance processions and parades in your name.

O Venus, no girl, no boy,
Could delight me, now, I refuse to be tempted
By mutual love, I can't drink
My share of wine, I'll never bind flowers in my hair.

But why, Lirius, why am I
Crying? What holds
My eloquent tongue, stops its flight
Even as I stand pouring out words?

At midnight, I dream I'm holding you,
I dream I'm flying after you
Across the meadows, out over the sea,
Flying after you and your hard, hard heart.

IV, 3

O Muse, someone you've smiled on
No Olympic labor
Can turn aside, can make him a famous
Athlete, a boxer, a racer

Of swift Greek chariots,
No battle can bring him
Crowned with Delian laurel
To the crowded Capitol,

Hailed as a conqueror of kings.
Sweet flowing rivers and
Thick green groves will make him
Immortal in Aeolian song.

And now the Romans, from the queen
Of great cities, are pleased to
Call me a poet—and envy snaps
Less vicious at my heels.

O Muse, who bends the lyre's
Gold strings, you who
Could fashion even fish
Singing like dying swans,

You and you alone make me
A Roman singer, worthy to be heard,
My life and my art, if my songs are artful
Enough, are all your gift.

IV, 5

Augustus, born of the gods, Rome's
Best guardian, you've stayed away
Too long. Return, as you promised
Our pious Senate, come swiftly.

O noble prince, light up your country!
Whenever your face, like the Spring,
Shines on your people, that day is better,
That sun shines with more warmth.

As a mother calls to her son,
Kept far from his beloved home
By the jealous South wind, holding him
A year and more, far

Beyond the Carpathian ocean,
Calls with prayers, and promises, consulting
Omens, her eyes forever watching,
So loyal Rome longs for Caesar.

The ox tramps safely in our fields,
Ceres and Faustita nourish our corn,
Sailors glide on a tranquil sea,
Good faith shrinks from blame,

Families stay chaste, undefiled,
Law and morality prevail over sin,
Women's children resemble their fathers,
Punishment chases after guilt.

Who could fear Parthians or frost-bound
Scythians, who could worry about Huns,
While Caesar lives? Who cares about
Wars in savage Spain?

Every Roman walks his own hills,
Marrying vines to widowed elms,
Then feasts at his own table, rejoicing,
Pouring a libation to Caesar as if

To a god. He worships Caesar, with prayers
And wine poured from bowls, Caesar
Joined with his household gods—as the Greeks once
Did in honoring Hercules and Castor.

"Let Italy celebrate in your name,
    O blessed leader!"—our sober prayer
Each morning, with day to come, our prayer
Each night, as the sun sinks away.

IV, 6

Apollo, known to Niobé's children
As the revenger of boasts, who punished
That rapist, Tityos, and Achilleus,
Almost triumphant at Troy,

A noble warrior but a man,
Though sea-born Thetis was his mother
And he shook Troy's towers
With his terrible spear.

Like some pine tree gnawed by an
Axe, some cypress toppled by the wind,
He fell on his face, his neck
Rolling in Trojan dust.

He'd never have hidden in that
Lying horse, pretending worship of Minerva,
Falling on festive Trojans, on Priam's
Court, dancing in joy,

But he would have burned prisoners, babies,
Even unborn, still in their mothers' wombs,
In Greek fires—oh evil, oh horror!—
Had not Jove almighty

Heard you, Apollo, and lovely Venus,
And promised prince Aeneas
A better fate, walls blessed
With kinder omens.

O Phoebus, minstrel, teacher,
You who dip your hair in Xanthus,
O Apollo, make Roman
Singers worthy of you!

Whatever breath blows through my poems
He gave me, and my poet's name.
Noble virgins, noble boys,
Born of noble fathers,

All wards of Artemis, goddess
Who cuts down deer and lynx with her bow,
Sing! Keep the Lesbian measure
My hands teach you,

Sing of Apollo, sing of that goddess
Of Night, ripener of grain,
She who pushes the months
Swiftly along!

Married, you will say: "Horace taught me
How his poems should move, I sang his hymn,
Welcome to the gods, when the year swung
Round and we celebrated how it came, how it went."

IV, 7

Snow is gone, fields grow green,
Trees open with leaves;
The earth shakes and changes, Spring
Rivers shrink, flow still,

Nymphs and Graces dance, naked.
Expect nothing to last,
No hour, no year, no gracious day
Fading away.

Warm winds blow away Winter,
Summer drives off Spring—
Then dies itself, as Autumn pours out
Harvest, and dead Winter is reborn.

Whatever the skies lose, quick-running
Months repair—but men, good Aeneas
Or rich Tullus or Ancus king of Rome,
Die and turn to shadows, to dust.

Who knows if the gods will add tomorrow's
Hours to your time today?
Whatever you give yourself, here, now,
No greedy heir can clutch at.

Torquatus, once you're buried, once
The Lord of Death has judged you,
Nothing will bring you back, no ancient
Name, no noble words, no one's love.

Even Diana can't take Hippolytus
Back from the darkness,
Even Theseus can't rip chains
From his friend, belovèd, dead.

IV, 9

No, these words I frame and the lyre
Sings, with arts unknown
Before me—I, born near far-sounding
Aufidus—these words will not die!

Homer may be first among poets,
But Pindar's Muse still sings,
And Alkaios' threatening odes, and Simonides',
And the noble songs of Stesichorus,

And time preserves Anakreon's
Lovely playing, and Sappho's
Love, confided to her lyre,
Still breathes and lives.

Spartan Helen was hardly the first
Or the last to burn for shining
Hair and gold-embroidered robes
And a prince's splendor, and his servants,

And Teucer, Telamon's son, shot mighty
Arrows, but there were other archers. Troy
Was encircled more than once, and even
Idomeneus, a magnificent warrior,

Deserves one song among many. Hector
Was strong and brave, but never
The first to suffer for his wife's
Virtue, for his children.

There were heroes before Agamemnon
Was born—but who knows them? Unmourned,
They lie buried in eternal darkness,
Sung by no sacred song.

Deep in the tomb, heroes and cowards
Can't be told apart. But you, Marcus Lollius,
My poems will honor, my poems
Will preserve; jealous silence

Will grope in vain for all your
Mighty works. Skilled, experienced,
Poised however fortune may
Turn, your mind seizes on greed, and fraud,

And punishes, itself immune to
That infinite magnet, money.
Consul year after year, an honest,
Impartial judge, you choose

Honor over advantage, you scorn
Bribes from the guilty,
As a soldier you fight
Always triumphant.

Happiness is more than wealth:
To earn that title
A man must use Heaven's gifts
With wisdom, with reason,

Must be able to be poor, and endure,
Must dread dishonor more
Than death, must die for his country
Or his friends without fear.

IV, 10

Ligurnus, young and vain and rich
With Venus' gifts, when those tender cheeks
Begin to bristle, that long waving hair
Falls out, that rosebloom lovelier than rosebloom
Fades, that cruelly beautiful face goes shaggy,
Rough, and you stare at the mirror, and you sigh:
"Oh where was ambition, when I was only a boy?
And where is that lovely face, now that I have it?"

IV, 11

Phyllis, I've a jar of Alban wine, nine
Years old, my garden is ripe
For the weaving of garlands,
And I've ivy all over,

Just right for your lovely hair, and to make you
Still lovelier. My house smiles
With silver, my leaf-wound altar
Longs for lamb blood;

Everyone's bustling, my slaves
Run back and forth,
The fires quiver, smoke rolls
Under my roof.

And why this invitation?
To celebrate sea-born Venus,
Born this day in the middle
Of April, even more

My day than the day of my birth,
For April gave me
Maecenas, this day opened the roll
Of his years.

You hunger for Telephus, too rich
For you: but some greedy
Golden girl has tied him
With pleasant chains.

Remember ambitious Phaeton, burned
To the earth, and Bellerophon, who needed
A goddess to help him mount
His winged horse:

Always do what you can, what you should,
Don't hope for more than the gods
Allow you! Come, last love
Of my life

—How could I burn
For another woman?—and learn to sing,
Use that lovely voice. Songs
Can drive off sorrow, singing can help.

IV, 12

Ships are blowing in the Thracian winds
Spring always brings;
Meadows are soft, now, frost melted
Away, rivers go quietly, all snow

Gone. Weeping for Itys, the swallow
Builds her nest, forever afflicted,
Cruel revenger of kings'
Barbarian lust.

In the new grass, keepers of fat
Sheep pipe songs,
Delighting the god of flocks
And Arcadia's dark hills.

Virgil: it's the thirsty season—
But for a cup of my wine
Pressed at Callés the price
Is a sprig of spikenard.

Bring the herb, and I'll roll out a cask
From Sulpician cellars, a cask of
New hope, a cask fit to wash away
Bitterness and worry!

Hurry, sell me your wares, if your throat
Is dry enough: wine
Is taxable, here, though rich men
Can pour it for free.

Don't linger, don't stop to be sensible,
Let a little folly mix with your wisdom,
Be aware of death's dark fires:
Frivolity is sweet, in season.

IV, 13

They've heard me, Lisa, I've prayed
And the gods have heard me: you're growing
Old, you want to be
Young, and beautiful, you run around

Laughing and drinking too much and singing
Drunken songs to Cupid: Come, O Cupid, come, oh
Come. But he's busy with lovely young Chia,
Plucking her delicate harp.

He wrinkles his nose at withered old oaks,
And staggers when he sees you—
Yellow teeth, sagging cheeks,
Ash-white hair.

Purple robes, those heavy diamonds:
Nothing brings back hours, days
Time has written out, locked away
In tomes the whole world reads.

Where did your loveliness run to?
That gentle skin? Your soft walk? What's left
That once, once you shared with her
Who breathed love, who stole me from myself,

You, alive and happy when Cynara
Was dead? The fates were kind to Cynara,
Gave her a very few years, but you,
Lisa, they pickled you in time,

Stretched out your life like some ancient
Crow, so hot young lovers
Could bellow and laugh, seeing this torch
Burned away to ashes!

IV, 15

I've tried to sing of battles and wars
And conquered cities, but Apollo god of my music
Scolded me, striking his lyre, ordered me
To float no paper sails on Tyrrhenian seas.

O Caesar, this time, your time, is a time of fields of grain;
You've pulled down Roman flags hanging on
Persian doorposts, you've brought them home to Jove;
Quirinus' temple, sacred to war, is closed

For lack of worshipers; morality's become a proper
Noun; Rome knows nothing of crime
Or criminals; and Romans have begun
To remember Roman ways,

Ancient virtues which made us famous
And strong and great, known
And obeyed across the world, from where the sun
Rises to where he sinks in the west.

As long as Augustus guards this Empire
We'll know no civil war, no riots, no hatred
Forging new swords, setting cities at each other's
Throats: peace will continue, will remain.

No one will break your Law, no Germans from the Danube,
No Greeks, no Tibetans or Chinese, no scheming
Rotten Persians, no Russians
Born near the River Don.

Every day, and on holy days, let us draw
Our wine and praise the gods,
We and our wives and our children,
As Romans have prayed from the beginning of time.

Then sing as our fathers sang, to the sound
Of flutes, celebrate Roman heroes and Troy
Fallen and Anchises, who fathered Aeneas,
Who sailed to Rome and fathered us all.

EPODES

1

Maecenas, my good friend, you'll go in
Liburnian galleys, sailing in and out and around
Caesar's great ships, ready to risk yourself
With every danger he deals with.
But what about us, delighted when you return,
Miserable if you do not?
You tell us to stay, to wait, to enjoy
Ourselves, but how be happy without you?
Or should we experience this hardship, act
Like men, stay close at your side?
          We will come, we will follow you
Bravely, if you climb the highest Alps,
The savage Caucasus, if you sail to
The farthest corners of the world.
          But how can I help you, you wonder, neither
Strong, nor trained for war, nor warlike?
Fear is worse at a distance:
I'll be braver, Maecenas, staying near you,
The way a bird worries more
Leaving her young alone, though some silent snake
Could do as it pleased
With her in the nest or absent.
I'll tackle this war, and any war,
Cheerfully, hoping to please you—not
So I'll earn more oxen
To plough up these fields of mine,
Not so my cattle can come from Lucan
To Calabrian pastures, when the dog-star burns,
Not to acquire a gleaming villa
High in the Tuscan hills—
No, your generous hands have given me more
Than enough: Miser Chremès
Can hide his gold in the ground, spendthrifts can throw it
Away, but I need no more treasure!

2

"How good never to worry about business,
  To plow the ground your father plowed
  And his father before him,
  Turning the soil like men at the beginning of time,
  Your oxen your own,
  Free of grubbing money, of all getting and lending.
  It's good to be deaf to trumpets,
  Indifferent to crashing seas,
  To leave the Senate to Senators
  And rich men alone
  In rich men's houses,
  Counting up power.
  It's good to marry tall poplars
  With climbing vines,
  Or watch cattle grazing in your fields,
  Wandering in far-off valleys,
  Or trim woods that bear nothing
  And splice on fruit-bearing branches,
  Or pour clean honey in deep clean jars,
  Or shear fat soft sheep—
  Or when Autumn pokes up his head,
  Crowned with reddening apples,
  How good to harvest purple grapes,
  More royal than dyed Imperial robes,
  To pluck pears grafted in rows,
  All for you, Priapus, god of bellies, once,
  Now god of gardens, and you,
  Our Father Silvanus, keeper of fences and borders.

"It's good to lie under some ancient oak,
  Or deep in the tall grass,
  While brooks run between high-piled banks,
  And birds sing sadly in trees,
  And fountains flow up, cool,
  And the murmuring sound brings sleep.
  But when Jove thunders winter, sends
  Rain and snow, then, then
  How good to drive wild boars into snares,
  This way, that way! with hounds baying,

Or trap hungry thrushes with nets
Spread on polished poles,
Or catch hares in a noose,
Or far-flying cranes—sweet
Game for the winning!
Who can remember love, and its miseries,
Surrounded with pleasures like these?

"But a modest wife, tending
House and cheerful children, like some Sabine woman,
Some sunburned mate of a poor
But sun-sweated Apulian—
A modest wife, piling good dry wood
High on the sacred fire, waiting
For her bone-weary husband, penning
Leaping sheep behind split-stake fences,
Milking their swollen udders,
Drawing sweet new wine from jars,
And fixing food at her own hearth—
Ah, give me no oysters fresh from Lucrinus, no,
No parrot-fish, no tender turbot
(If winter winds drive them to our shores,
Blow them from the thundering East),
No, give me no African pheasant,
No woodcock trapped in Ionia,
Nothing would tickle my palate
More than olives plucked from some thick branch,
Or sorrel pulled from my own fields,
Or soft squash (so healing to the sick),
Or a lamb killed and roasted in honor of Terminus,
Lord of boundaries,
Or a bleating goat saved out of the wolf's jaws.
And savoring such food, what delight
To watch fat sheep hurrying home from pasture,
To see weary oxen dragging home the plow,
Blade turned to the sky, their huge necks drooping,
And to find all the domestic slaves, born
Where they work, gathered around the household gods!"

As soon as Alfius, famous around the world
As a skinflint lender of gold, had spoken

These words, he was ready to
Turn to the soil. He canceled his loans,
Took up his money: that was on the first.
On the fifteenth he lent it out all over again,
At the usual rates.

3

Were there ever a man so sinful
He could snap his old father's neck, sentence him
To eat garlic, deadlier than hemlock!
Oh peasants' bowels, constructed of iron!
What poison rages in my belly?
Who boiled some hidden viper blood
In these herbs? Has that witch
Canidia handled my cursed food?
Medea, when she longed for Jason,
Loveliest of Argonauts, anointed him
With this when he yoked Aetés' fire-breathing
Bulls, and before she fled on her winged dragon
She soaked her presents in this and burned
Her rival to death. No dog-star heat
Like this has burned Apulia;
Nessus' poison burned less savage, though fatal,
On Hercules' shoulders.
        Maecenas, bring such stuff again and
I pray your sweetheart push you
Away, cover her face with her hands,
And hide at the edge of the bed!

4

As the lamb was made to hate the wolf
So I hate you—you,
Your back scarred by Spanish whips,
Your legs scarred by irons:
You strut in expensive purple
But Fortune changes purses, not breeds.
You can't see the stares, can you,
When you parade the sacred road with
Your robe three yards thick,
Every face bursting with indignation?

"*This* ploughs a thousand acres of
Falernian land? *This*, which was whipped
Till the triumvir's arms ached?
This wears out the Appian Way with his horses?
This sits, illustrious, important,
Foremost, and despises noble Otho?
Oh why send such strong-beaked
Ships against pirates and runaway
Slaves, such massive ships, when *this*
Is a tribune and commands men?"

6

Cur, why snarl at harmless strangers
When you run from wolves? Coward,
Try threatening me, if you dare:
I'll bite you back! Like
Molossian hounds and Lacon mastiffs,
Shepherds' friends, I'll track you in
The deepest snow, my ears ready;
I'll catch any beast I follow.
Oh you howl, the woods ring with your awesome
Yelps, but you eat scraps thrown
To keep you quiet. Careful, careful: I've horns
For spitting evil, as Archílochus attacked
His wife's cheating father, as Hipponax
Cut up the sculptor who mocked him.
Let anyone sink a poisoned tooth in my hand
And see if I sulk and whimper like a child!

7

Villains, where, where are you running? Why
Are those swords in your hands again?
Has there been too little Roman blood
Poured in the sea, spilled in the fields?
And not so Romans could burn the towers
Of jealous Carthage, not so
Rebel Britons could be led
In chains along the sacred road,
No, but just as the Parthians prayed, so this city
Could die by its own right hand.
No wolves turn on themselves, no lions:
They fight with other beasts.
Are you mad? Guilty? Drugged?
You act like blind men. Answer me!
Silence. Their faces grow pale,
Conscience strikes them dumb.
Indeed: indeed: a bitter fate haunts us,
A brother dead at his brother's
Hand, innocent Remus, murdered by
Romulus, his blood run out in the ground!

8

Old bitch, stinking
Old hag, asking *me*
"How come you can't get it up?"
You, with your black pit of a mouth,
A forehead time plows with wrinkles,
And a gaping ass, putrid between dried-up
Haunches, gaping like a sick cow-hole!
But what really turns me on
Are your horse-hung tits
And your sagging belly, your dry-bone thighs, those
Sloppy fat legs—agh!

My blessings, dame: when you go to your grave
May it be behind a line of
Exultant wax Priapuses,
And as long as you stagger about
May no one wear longer ropes of pearls.

What? Because you've got handsome Stoic books
Lying happy on your silk pillows,
Should my nerves go less rigid
And my prick
Less limp, just looking at you?
For *you* to lift my pride
Into action, your tongue needs to stop wagging
And get down to serious work.

10

A ship that sails with slimy Mevius
On board sails with an evil omen.
O South wind, remember to bash her
With horrible waves, fore and aft!
East wind, you dark-browed gale, scatter
Her broken oars, her torn-up ropes, on the face
Of the sea! North wind, blow with the fury
That smashes bending oak trees, high in the mountains!
Let there be no friendly stars, when gloomy
Orion goes down, let the night stay black,
And let the sea be exactly as smooth and gentle
As when the Greeks sailed home from Troy
And Pallas Athena spun away from the ashes
And turned her vengeance on Ajax's ship!
Ah, how the sailors will sweat,
How you'll turn pale, and
Wail like a woman, and pray
To deaf-eared Jove,
When the Ionian bay, roaring,
Bursts the boat open!
Yes, but when you're stretched on the shore,
Fat carrion meat, if the gulls enjoy you
I'll offer a frisky goat and even a lamb
To the gods of the storm.

12

Good lord, woman! You're better fitted for a big
Black elephant than for me. Why send me letters
And presents? I'm no adolescent, I still have taste:
I can sniff a growth or a goaty stink
Under hairy armpits as fast as a boar-hound
Smells out a hidden pig.
Oh what a ghastly stench, what a sweat
On her shrivelled arms and legs when, open like a cave,
She tries to scratch her endless itch!
The crocodile shit that dyes her skin,
The damp cosmetic chalk on her face, slide off—
And grunting like a hog she rips up the mattress.
She dislikes my dislike, it provokes her:
      "Hey, Inachia don't tire you like this! Yeah,
She gets it three times a night, I'm lucky if I
Get it once. The hell with Lesbia, damn her,
She sent you over, you limp stick. I need
A goddamn bull—and I had that Amnytus,
He pumps it straight and tight like a tree
Stuck in a hill. Oh he really has it!
      "What's all that wool dyed in Tyrean
Purple? Oh yeah, so all your friends'
Wives can think you're really something,
Chase you instead of their husbands.
You make me cry, running like you do, like a lamb
Scared of wolves, a deer with a lion on his heels."

13

A savage storm pulls the sky down on us, rain
And snow drop out of Jove's hands, the sea, the woods,
All ring with Thracian wind. Friends, take what
The day brings us: while our knees still bend easily
And time is our own, let age and wisdom be forgotten.
Pass that jar sealed when Torquatus was consul,
Talk of nothing serious! Some god may mend our sagging
Fortunes. Or not. But now anoint our heads
With Persian perfume, lighten our hearts,
Drive off anxiety, with this Cyllenian lyre.
As that famous Centaur sang to his adopted son, great
Achilleus: "O invincible son of Thetis, mortal,
Troy waits for you, where tiny Scamander
Flows cold as ice, and swift-gliding Simois,
And there your fate will be cut, the thread hangs short,
Your sea-blue mother will never bring you back.
Ease all evil, at Troy, with wine and song—
Those sweet consolations, protection against ugly sorrow!"

14

Honest Maecenas, you kill me, harping
Away at my laziness, forever asking
How I can seem exactly like a
Thirsty soul that's drunk deep of
Lethé's cups and lost all inner sense.
It's the god, not me, the god
Who blocks me, stops my iambics,
Silences the poem I promised you
So long ago! Wasn't Anakreon
Charred as I am, loving Samian
Bathyllus, composing love-wails
To a discordant lyre, singing out of tune?
And you're in love: but if you burn
No worse than Troy, count your blessings!
My love is for Phryne, and she loves
Everyone, and it eats me up.

15

Night, and a cloudless sky, and the moon
Bright among smaller stars,
And you, your arms tighter around me
Than ivy wound on an oak, you
Soon to offend the holy gods of heaven,
Swearing to be faithful,
Swearing our love would be shared
As long as wolves stalked cattle,
As long as Orion whipped up wintry seas
And sailors hated his light,
As long as winds flared
In Apollo's long hair.
O Naera, what a man you've lost!
If Flaccus is half, just half a man
(Old flaccid Flaccus),
You won't be lying, night after night,
In arms you like better than his,
Or he'll find himself another woman,
And stay so angry that even your beauty
Won't stir him, he'll hate you so hard.

And you, whoever you are, happy to be
Where you are, happy that I'm not there,
You may be the richest of ranchers, a baron
Of cattle and oil, and the rivers of gold
May flow to your lap, and Pythagorus
Come back to life may whisper wisdom in your ear,
And you may be handsomer even than Nireus—but friend,
Friend, whenever her love takes her to some other bed
You'll weep.
But me, I'll laugh.

16

Another generation, another! ground down in civil
War, and Rome wrecked
By her own strength—Rome,
Whose neighbors never destroyed her,
Or Porsena's Etruscan army,
Or proud Capua, or Spartacus
And his fierce slave-soldiers,
Or the treacherous Allobards, or wild
Germans and their blue-eyed sons,
Or Hannibal, hated by Roman mothers—
Rome, Rome, brought down
By an evil generation, a cursed
Roman race—and our land a wilderness
Again, ruled by lions and tigers!
O Gods: barbarians will dance
On our ashes, shaking their spears,
And horsemen beat our stones under hoof,
And holy Quirinus pulled from his temple
And thrown—oh horrible—like dust
To the winds, dry bones in the sun.

Maybe you're thinking, some
Of you, the best of you: how
Can we save our country and ourselves?
Let Ionian Phokéia show you,
Abandoned to wolves and wild boars
And Persians—fields and holy places
And temples, everything, cursed and
Abandoned, rather than surrender: and why not
Us? Let us walk where our feet take us,
Sail where the wind blows us,
Or the hot gale from Africa. Why not?
Has anyone a better idea? If the omens
Are good, and they are, we can sail today—
But first, all of you, swear:
   when stones float, we'll return
   when rivers climb mountains, we'll return
   when mountains swim in the sea, we'll return
   when monsters mate in the woods,

        tigers and deer,
        doves and hawks,
        lions and sheep,
    and goats grow scales and dive like fish,
        we'll return!
And having sworn, being ready,
Go, all of us—all of Rome, or any part
Of Rome wiser than the stupid mob,
        or the despairing,
        or the weak,
Who can stay rotting in their beds.

No more woman's tears:
All brave Romans, sail! out past Etruria,
Out on the great Ocean.
Sail, O Romans, toward Elysian Fields,
Lands of the Blessed, where wheat
Sprouts, year after year, from unplowed ground,
Where vines grow by themselves, hang heavy with grapes,
Where olives blossom, year after year after year,
And figs flower ungrafted,
And honey pours from hollow oaks,
And clear water runs, leaps, splashes
Down from mountains—
Where goats run out of
Mountains, udders leaking, eager to be milked,
Cattle roam free of blight,
No stars burn down at sheep,
And no bears growl in the darkness
Around the sheepfold, and grass
Never ripples with vipers—
Where we will stare at marvel
After marvel after marvel: where
Rain never sweeps down, ruining young wheat,
Where seeds never char in dry hard ground,
The gods controlling heat and cold
With even hands. No sweating Argonauts ever
Landed on these shores, no shameless
Medea, no Sidonian sailors,
Nor Odysseus' oarsmen.
A place Jupiter saved for honest, god-fearing

People. He blended brass in our Age of Gold,
But saved this place—brass, first,
Then iron, to harden this
Brittle time. But we can escape,
We can still
Be happy, if you'll listen,
Romans,
If you'll listen to me.

17

Horace:
"Canidia, I yield, I surrender to your mighty
Science, I beg you, on my knees, by Proserpiné's
Realm, by Diana's pure majesty,
By your own books of spells, able
To call down the stars from Heaven,
Oh stop your magic and turn the wheel
Back, oh turn it! Telephus defied
Achilleus, sought to defeat him in
Battle, threw poisoned spears, but softened that
Hero's heart with his terrible wound.
Trojan women wept for Hector
When the manslayer fought without walls to
Protect him, and fell prey to dogs and vultures,
They begged his pitiful body of hardhearted
Achilleus, knelt and moved him. Circé took pity
On Ulysses' sailors, turned them from pigs
To men, gave them men's tongues, men's minds,
And the dignity of men in their faces
Again. You've had your revenge, and more,
O beloved of sailors and salesmen.
You've taken youth and my rose-colored cheeks,
My skin hangs sallow on my bones,
Your potions have whitened my hair,
Nothing can stop the pain, no rest,
As night turns quickly to day, and day to night;
Even my breath wheezes in my lungs.
My misery makes me believe what once I
Denied, that witch-spells confuse the heart,
Witch-songs can split the skull.
What more can you want? O earth, O oceans,
I burn worse than Hercules, covered with
Nessus' black blood, I burn hotter than
The flames of Aetna! And you, you
Roll out Colchian poisons, jar after jar,
Char me to a cinder the winds can carry
Away. Where will it end, what final tribute?
Speak: I will pay what must be paid,
I swear it, I'll expiate my sins, ask me for a

Hundred bullocks, ask for a song from
My lying lyre. O chaste, O righteous,
I'll sing you to Heaven, a golden constellation!
Great Castor and Pollux his brother, angry
At an insult to Helen, blinded the poet
—But prayers brought him back his eyes.
Release me, oh free me, for you know you can!
You are no hag with tainted blood,
You are no public witch, scattering
Ashes on poor men's graves.
Your heart is warm, your hands pure,
You have a son, you bore him yourself,
The midwife washed your blood from the sheets
Though you rose and walked like a goddess."

Canidia:
"Why waste prayers on ears unable to hear them?
The winter ocean, lashing rocks with its waves,
Is no more deaf to shipwrecked sailors.
Can you mock our mysteries unavenged?
Prate about Cupid's rites and laugh at them?
High priest of the safe aristocracy, talk boldly
Of me, unpunished, immune? Never!
Am I to labor for nothing, make my country
Sisters rich in vain, invent swift poisons
And be afraid to use them on a fool
Like you? O ungrateful wretch, you'll live
And live long, but only so you can suffer new
Tortures. Tantalus, father of that traitor Pelops,
Longs eternally for rest, rest,
And Prometheus chained to the vulture begs for it,
And Sisyphus struggles to set his rock
On the mountain, but Jove's laws forbid it.
You'll long to leap from some tall tower,
You'll try to split your heart with a Noric
Sword, you'll tie a noose around your neck—
In vain! A sorrow that loathes life and itself
Will hang on you. And I will climb on your
Hated shoulders and ride you, show all the world

My power. I, who can breathe feeling into wax
(As you've learned to your sorrow!), I who can pull
The moon from the Heavens with my spells,
And raise the cremated dead, and mix
Potions that create love, *I* lament
That you're exempt from my art, and only you!"

SATIRES

I, 1

Maecenas, why is no one living
Happy where he is, whether he chose for himself or fate
For him? Everyone wants to be someone else.
"O blessed merchants!" cries the stiff old soldier,
His body broken by years of hard campaigning.
But the merchant, as the West wind tosses his ship,
Cries, "War is better. And why? There's a battle,
In a moment you're either dead or a hero."
The lawyer swears he'll return to the land, when
A client drags him out of bed at dawn.
The farmer who's signed a bond and is forced to travel to town
Swears the city's the only place.
      Well, I could wear out Faubius himself, who jabbers like an ape,
With more of this, but enough is enough.
Listen: suppose a god appeared, declaring:
"I'll do exactly what you say, here and now. You who
Were just a soldier, you'll be a merchant. Lawyer, you'll be
A farmer. Go, quick, it's all arranged. Well?
Why stand here?" They wouldn't. And yet they're able
To be happy. Tell me why Jove, deservedly angry,
Shouldn't puff out his cheeks and promise
Never to listen to their prayers?
      And then—I've no interest in journalism, or making jokes
On serious subjects—though why can't one tell the truth
With a smile? Teachers coax children to love
Learning by giving them cookies.
All right, no jokes, I mean to be sober and truthful.
      He who cracks the hard earth with his plough,
And this wine-watering innkeeper, and soldiers, and sailors
Who plough every ocean on earth, all of them say
They work for one thing only: to be able to live, to eat,
When they're too old for work. Like the tiny,
Industrious ant—their model, they say—who drags off whatever
She can find, piles it all up, always
Thinking of tomorrow, forever planning ahead.
Yes, but when winter descends she stays
At home, wise little creature, and lives
By what she gathered in summer. Not you,
Gentlemen! No heat, no winter, neither fire, nor sea,

Nor sword can keep you back, while anyone alive
Is richer. What pleasure can you find in a horde
Of gold and silver that you hide in a hole in the ground?
"But divide it up, it would come to nothing."
Oh Lord: unless you divide it, what's lovely about it?
Thresh out a hundred thousand bushels and still
Your belly holds as much as mine, not more.
The slave who carries bread for the work gang
Tires his shoulder, but eats no more than the slave
Who carries nothing. Live reasonably and why
Should you care if you plough a hundred acres
Or a thousand? "Ah, it's lovely to feed from a full
Trough!" If we eat as much from our small ones,
What difference does it make? Suppose
You needed a pitcher of water, or just a glass,
But declared, "I'd rather have drunk
From a mighty river than this miserable fountain."
Well, wish for too much and swift Aufidus
Will wash you away, storehouse and all.
But wish for what you need, no more, and your water
Is free of mud and your life is free of waves.
        Too many men, bewitched by false desire, insist that
"Nothing is enough: people value you by what you own."
What can I say? Let him be miserable, that's how
He wants it! As the Athenian miser
Is said to have answered, when citizens
Mocked him: "They hiss me, but at home I
Applaud myself, counting the coins in my safe."
Tantalus, forever thirsty, lunges for rivers
That run from his lips. You laugh? Change
The name, and it's your story too! You sleep, gaping,
On your bags of gold, adore them like hallowed
Relics not meant to be touched, stare as at gorgeous
Canvases. Money is meant to be spent, it buys pleasure:
Did you know that? Bread, vegetables, wine, you can
Buy almost everything it's hard to live without.
Is it pleasant, lying half dead with fear,
Day and night dreading thieves, and fire, and slaves
Who might rob you and run? With wealth
Like that, I'd choose to be poorer than poor!
        "But when a fever strikes, when you're twisted

In pain, when something pins you to your bed, with money
You can buy help, someone to sit beside you, fix medicine and food,
Call the doctor to cure you, bring you back to your family and friends."
        No, your wife does not wish you well, nor your son. Everyone
Hates you, neighbors, acquaintances, little boys and
Little girls. Why not, when money is always
First? Should people offer you affection
You've never deserved? Would it waste your precious time
To try to keep what Nature gives you,
Family, friends? As much of a waste
As training a donkey to run races? In a word:
Enough of this endless acquiring! You have more
Than you had; fear poverty less, begin
To rest. You have what you wanted: don't
Act like Ummidas—it's a *very* short tale—
A man so rich he used a yardstick to measure
His money, but so cheap that he dressed like a slave,
Dreading to the moment of his death
That poverty might strike and he'd starve. Well,
Some woman chopped him in half with an axe.
        "What's *your* advice? Live like Navius, throwing
Gold away like water?" Why go from
Ice to steam? Don't be a miser: does that mean
Live like some good-for-nothing, waste it all?
There's always a middle road. Find it.
There are limits to everything, right and
Wrong are never wholly relative.
        I'm back where I started, asking why greedy man
Is never happy with himself, always envies others,
Sees his neighbor's goat with a heavier udder
And dies, never thinks of those with nothing at all
But scrambles to catch this one, and that one, and then the next.
The rich man always blocks the road for someone
Less rich. It's like chariot-racing:
The driver worries about those ahead of him,
Never about those behind. And therefore it's hard
To find a man so happy with his life
That he's ready to leave what he's thoroughly enjoyed,
Like a guest who's had all he could want.
        That *is* enough. You'll think I babble like some
Professional poetaster if I add another word!

I, 2

Female flute-players, beggars, quacks, clowns,
Actresses, and all the rest, they're mourning
The death of Tigellius, a singer and wonderfully
Free with his money. But here's a fellow, rich
Enough, afraid to give to a starving friend, cold
And hungry, because he might be thought careless
With his cash. And *him*, ask why he stuffs his gullet,
Stripping his father's and his grandfather's estate away,
Buying up goodies with borrowed money:
"Well," he says, "who wants to look like a
Miser?" He has his critics, he has his supporters.
Fulfidus, who owns a million acres, and makes a thousand
Loans at once, at ruinous interest, is worried they'll think him
Wasteful: he chops the interest away from the principal
To start with, and the worse you want the money the worse
He treats you. He hunts for very young men
With very strict fathers. "Lord! Surely he does all right
By himself?" A natural assumption, yes?
No. It's hard to believe how nasty
He is to himself: that guilty father in Terence's
Play, punishing himself for exiling his son,
Lived like a king, compared to Fulfidus.
        All right, what am I saying? Just this:
Fools who run from vices, run vice versa.
Malthinus drags his robe on the ground; some fop
Tucks his clothes as high as his waist (gross, but true).
Rufillus stinks of perfume, Gorgonus stinks like a goat.
Nothing runs down the middle. Some men meddle only
With women in trailing gowns, even the ankles
Decently hidden. Some find excitement in dirty
Whores. One of those whore-hounds, returning to
Civilization, was greeted by wise old Cato: "Continue, continue,
This is virtue! Better to ease that passionate swelling
Here, young man, than seduce other men's
Wives." Cupennius, lover of many men's wives,
Longtime lecher, excuses himself from such praise.
        Listen: if you'd rather adulterers did badly,
They're all in trouble, these days,
They get their pleasure liberally salted

With pain—and not much pleasure, and oh, at what
A price! Here's one who jumped from a roof, head first.
Another was flogged to death. That one ran from a hot bed
Into a den of thieves. Him, he bribed his way out.
That one the slaves got, and worked him over. And oh,
Him! They cut him like a steer, balls
And all. "Right!" everyone says (except Galba).
     But second-class seduction, now that's a safer
Story. Freedwomen, I mean—the ones Sallus
Chases, wild as any wife-diddler.
He could be decent, and even generous,
As far as reason and his inheritance dictate,
He could pay well and properly
And feel no shame. But he's crazy proud
Of himself, just loves his own way: "Now me, I never
Mess with a married woman!" Wonderful.
Like Marseus, Origo's lover, who gave
His father's house, and his father's farm, to an actress:
"I never screw another man's wife!" Holy, holy.
And your name loses more than your estate.
All very legalistic—but moral? Well, what's morality
Anyway, what's in a name? Lose it, friend,
And see. *And* your father's estate. Married woman, slave,
Whore: it's the sin that matters, not the title.
     Villius, Sulla's son-in-law, crawled into bed
With noble Fausta, and suffered more than sufficiently.
Noble? She had him beaten, and kicked, and stabbed
While her door was locked and another lover inside it.
If he'd asked himself, wondering what his passion
Wanted: "Just what are you hunting? A whore
Born of a duke, wearing an evening gown?"
Maybe he'd have answered: "Her father was noble."
Her father! But Nature has a richness
Of her own, totally different, and recommends it
Freely, if only you're ready to work *with*
And not *against* her. Pain is a different matter
If you make it for yourself or if it simply happens.
Avoid repentance by avoiding married women;
Success is unpleasant in that line of work,
The reality is pain and misery, not pleasure.
You won't agree, Cerinthès, but pearls and emeralds

Make no woman softer or lovelier: in fact
The prettiest I know are whores.
And a whore is what she is, advertises honestly,
Displays her good points and her bad
Without pretending, without boasts, all open and
Above board. So rich men buy horses, inspecting
Unsaddled beasts: a supple back
Can stand on a damaged hoof; fine buttocks
And a stately neck, a streamlined head,
Can deceive. They're wise. Don't calculate beauty
With too fine an eye, better be blind
Looking at deficiencies. "What a leg, what arms!"
Say nothing of feet too long, waist too short, huge nose,
Flat ass. Unless it's Catia, a married woman
Shows her face, the rest is covered.
If you hunt forbidden charms—and you hunt them because
They're forbidden, right?—it becomes an obstacle course:
Servants, hairdressers, all sorts of parasites,
Robes down to her ankles, even a veil:
Who can see through a thousand layers?
The others make it easy, the sheer silk they wear
Shows you everything: no ugly legs, no clumsy
Feet, can escape you, it's all right there. Which
Is preferable, a well-laid trap, money on the line,
Without a look at the goods? "Hunters love
The chase, not a rabbit caught in a snare,"
The rake responds, "and I love like a hunter:
I want what no one has, I avoid what's available."
Does stuff like that free you from sadness
And pain and all human suffering?
            Better look for Nature's boundaries,
What appetites she permits, what she denies,
And understand the solid and the insubstantial!
Who hunts for golden cups, when thirst strikes?
Hungry, do you starve except for peacock
And salmon? When passion afflicts you
Would you rather do nothing, and suffer, than leap on
Some serving wench, some slave-boy, who happens
To be near? Not me: give me a mistress who gives in!
No "Pretty soon" and "Wait a minute" and "First let my husband
Leave": that's for eunuchs! No dallying, please,

No extortion, no haggling. Let her be reasonably
Pretty, no humpback, and decent enough
Not to pretend to more than Nature gave her.
When I've got her in my arms she's as good as
Any noble lady: I call her anything, who cares?
Her husband's not hurrying home from the country,
Either, no one will break down the door, with dogs
Yapping, the whole house shaking, an incredible
Racket, wife leaping out of bed, her slave-girl
Weeping for fear, the lady afraid for her dowry, and me afraid
Too. I'd have to run off barefoot, clothes flapping,
Worrying about my money, my ass, and even my reputation.
Getting caught is no fun: and *that* I can prove!

I, 3

Singers, they're all alike: ask them to sing
For friends, and no, they can't, but uninvited
They start and never stop. Sardinian Tigellius
Was just like that: Caesar himself, who could have
Forced him, could beg by his father's friendship,
And his own, in vain. But if he felt like singing he'd roar
From first course to last, first high as a woman,
Then low as the voice goes: "Hail Bacchus!" over
And over. No balance: one minute he'd run
As if someone deadly were after him, and then he'd walk
Like a priest to the altar. His house had two hundred slaves
—Or else ten. Sometimes he'd talk of kings
And emperors, everything magnificent, and then, "A simple
Stool for a table, friends, a shell of salt, and a robe—
Coarse—to keep off the cold." Give him a thousand
Dollars, this frugal fellow, content with so little,
And five days later he'd have nothing. He'd sit up
Till dawn, he'd snore all day. No one was ever
Less consistent.
              "And you? You have no faults?"
I do, of course, but different ones, maybe smaller.
Manius was running down Novius—in Novius' absence—
And was asked: "You, sir! Don't you know who you are?
Do you think you can fool us, like some stranger?" "Oh, I forgive
Myself!" That is foolish, and brazen, and worthy of censure.
              Investigating your own faults with weak and runny
Eyes, why stare at your friends' failings like an eagle
Or some sharp-eyed snake? To be sure, it's turn
And turn about, they're hawkeyed with you:
       "Him? He's bad-tempered, yes, polished chat is
Beyond him, true, you might laugh at his country-cut
Hair, his robe's too loose, his shoes flap
As he walks—but he's a decent fellow, all in all,
A good friend, there's real genius, somehow, somewhere
Under that rough exterior." Shake yourself, see if
Nature, or some nasty habit, gave you a vice or two
Of your own, the way fields left fallow too long
Develop weeds—which have to be burned.
              And note: lovers are blind

To their ladies' flaws, they even love them,
As Balbinus adored Hagna's warts.
I wish we did as much for friends:
Ethics should have a name for it!
Anyway, we ought to deal with our friends like fathers
With their sons, not disgusted by a fault. A squinting
Child gets called, fondly, "Blinky"; a dwarf (like
Misbegotten Sisyphus) is "Chickie";
This crooked-leg wonder is "Crookshanks," and
That one, almost unable to stand on twisted ankles,
He's "Curlylegs." He's stingy, your friend? Let's call him
Thrifty. He has no taste, no tact, talks of himself
Too much? He'd like to be thought a wit. He's rather
Rough and outspoken? He's frank and unafraid.
He has a temper? Call him spirited, or energetic.
This keeps friends friendly, I think. And yet
We see things upside down, we look for smudges
And dirt on a clean bowl. A friend is honest,
Deeply modest: we call him slow, or even stupid.
Another dodges traps, makes himself
No man's victim, understands how envy
And slander pervade the life we lead—
And instead of praising his common sense
We call him false, and sly. And someone
A bit naive—as I've often seemed
To you, Maecenas, blundering in when you're reading,
Interrupting some special thought: "No tact,
No tact at all!" we say. Ah! How casually
We condemn ourselves, condemning others unjustly!
No man living is perfect: the best of us
Have fewer faults. A friend, true friend, should set
My virtues against my defects. That's only fair, weighting
The good more heavily—if there's enough of it! He'll
Be weighed in the same indulgent scale.
If you want a friend to ignore your warts, forgive
Him his pimples. Reason requires
He who is pardoned to pardon in return.
        In short, since most men are fools (myself included),
Subject to anger and other faults, and impossible to cure,
Let Reason work with her own tools and measure
A punishment fit for every crime. Would anyone

Crucify a slave caught licking a plate,
Fresh from the table, thick with half-eaten
Fish and gravy? Wise men would call that, wisely,
Insane. But more insane than this?
Your friend offends you, something minor, slight,
The sort of thing only a lout could fail to excuse.
Your friendship turns to hate, you avoid him (like Russo
The bill collector, from whom debtors run in panic,
Knowing they'll have to listen to his poems, be his literary
Prisoners, if they can't scrape up his money!).
My friend gets drunk, soils my sofa, almost breaks
An antique bowl. So? For that, or because he snatched
A bit of chicken, served on my side of the dish,
Before I could grab it myself, am I supposed
To hate him? He was hungry! What would I do if he stole
Or broke his word or betrayed a trust?
Stoics tell us that sin is sin, and all alike, but
Life's not Stoic: every instinct, every custom
Protests, too practical, too real. Justice is useful, not Stoic.
        When living creatures crawled on the new-made earth,
Shapeless, mute, they fought for caves and acorns,
Used fists and nails, learned about sticks, and little by little
Invented knives and swords, because they needed them,
Then invented names, words, gave meaning to their grunts,
Began to express themselves. And then they learned
Not to fight, to fortify towns and formulate laws
So no one would steal, no one commit adultery.
Until Helen's time the worst wars were over
Women—but those who fought for some fickle love,
Like animals, died unknown, unsung,
Ground down like bulls in a herd. History
Is clear, you have to admit it: justice and laws
Were born of the fear of injustice.
Nature knows nothing of right or wrong,
Only what's useful, what's not. Reason
Can never prove that he who steals cabbage
From a man, and he who steals sacred vessels
From the gods, are equally guilty. Punishment
Needs to be just: what deserves the strap
Never deserves the scourge. Swing the cane
When the whip's required, make petty thieves

Into highway robbers, threaten to cut away crime
With the same fierce blade, all crime the same,
No great, no small, and you're likely to wait for the world
To put you in power.
                    If wise men are rich,
And are also shoemakers, and terribly handsome, and are also kings,
Why bother to wish for perfection? "You don't understand
The Stoics. The wise man himself fashions no shoes—
Yet the wise man's a cobbler." How? "As Hermogenes,
Forever silent, is the greatest singer
Alive. As clever Alfenus was still
A barber when his stock was sold, his shop
Was closed. So the wise man, and he alone, is an artist
In all arts—and thus a king." Oh, the boys will pull
Your beard, and you'd better hold them off with your stick,
And the crowd that's milling around you, while you yell
And scream, O wretch, O king of all kings!
What can I say? King, go off to your penny bathhouse
(Only crazy Crispinus goes with you),
And my friends will forgive me, a poet and no philosopher,
If I've insulted anyone, and I'll be delighted
To bear with their faults—and this private citizen
Will be happier than Your Majesty can ever know!

I, 5

A dozen miles out of Rome, magnificence
All behind us, we stopped at a quiet inn
In Aricia, Helio and I: professor of oratory,
Most learned of Greeks, and I, a poet.
And then Appia, where the canal begins,
Crowded with bargemen, lousy
With barmen squeezing pennies. We were lazy,
It took us two days to get through: better travelers
Make it in one. But that Appian Road
Jars your bones, if you take it hard:
We took it slow. My stomach and I fought a war,
Here—the water was foul—and I waited,
Restless, while everyone else ate.

Then twilight, almost dark across
The earth, stars ready to appear, and slaves
Curse at sailors, and sailors at slaves:
"Here, here! Put it here!"
"That's three hundred more than she'll carry!"
"Stop, stop, enough!"
Then an hour dribbles away, paying
Fares, harnessing a mule to the barge.
No one can sleep, for the damned gnats
And the marsh frogs; the drunken
Bargeman, soaked in rotgut wine, bellows
His girl's beauty, and some dimwit passenger
Tries to outshout him, finally
Wearing himself (at least) into sleep.
And then the bargeman, disinclined to hurry,
Lets the mule graze on the bank, ties the harness
To a stone, flops on his back,
And he snores too—almost till dawn,
When some hothead realizes we're not moving
And jumps out, grabs a willow branch,
And bangs on bargeman and mule, back
And head and back. So we get there,
At last, about ten. And wash faces
And hands in water sacred to you,
Feronia. Then breakfast and a three-mile

Crawl up to Anxur, high on white rocks
Bright in the sun. Maecenas was to meet us,
Here, and Nerva, noble men, ambassadors
On important business, old hands
At settling quarrels among friends. My eyes
Gave out, I rubbed them with black muck
And was better. Maecenas came, finally,
And Nerva, and Fontus Capto, Antony's
Best friend and as good a man as exists.

Fondi was a lovely town
To leave, with its pompous mayor, Aufidius Luscus,
Decked out like a savage, purple stripes
On his coat, and sacred charcoal carried
Burning in front of him (in case he could sacrifice
A goat, or at least a chicken,
For Maecenas, friend of Emperors).
Weary, weary, we lay up in Formia,
Where Murena lent us his roof and Fontus
Capto fed us from his own kitchens.
We rose happily, next day, knowing we would meet
Plotius, Varius, and Virgil, the clearest,
Noblest souls ever put on earth, friends
No one can claim more love for. Oh
How we hugged them, and they us,
And the laughter, the pleasure, the joy!
Nothing delights me more than a good
Friend, a truly good friend; nothing
Will ever please me as much,
Unless my mind fails me.

Near the Campanus Bridge there's a state
Inn, and we slept there, and the innkeepers supplied
Salt and wood, as the state requires.
And then to Capua, where we
And our mules rested. Maecenas
Was off to play ball, Virgil and I were off
To bed: people with sore eyes
And weak digestions should leave ball fields
To the healthy. And then to Nerva's well-stocked
Villa, up above Caudium.

Quick, Muse: describe the battle
Between Sarmen, Maecenas' buffoon,
And Cirrus, a native clown, and tell us
Who was the father of whom. Cirrus
Could cackle in Oscan, that ancient tongue;
Sarmen was born a slave, and in Rome, where
Maecenas had freed him,
But the lady, once his owner, still lives.
Sarmen begins:
            "A horse, a wild horse, that's you!"
We laugh, Cirrus nods and tosses his head:
            "A horse, exactly."
Then Sarmen:
            "How wild, even without the horn
They cut off your head. What a fighter you'd be,
If only you still had your horn, poor horn."
(Cirrus' hairy forehead was scarred
All down the left side.) Sarmen pulled his leg
And begged him to dance a Cyclops ballet—he'd need
Neither costume nor mask.
And Cirrus poured insults back:
That chain he used to wear, had he offered it up
To the gods? He could write, now, and copy papers,
But his old mistress could press him back
Into service whenever she itched for his
Service. And why, really, had he run
From so gracious an owner? He was easily small enough
To do quite well on a pound of grain.

Ah, that was a meal we relished to the end.

Than straight to Benventum—and there
Our innkeeper, rushing around, almost
Burned the place down, spinning some spitted
Skinny birds on the fire—flames spat out the smoke hole
And the roof began to burn—and how
Hungry guests and frightened slaves ran
In circles, protecting their dinner
And quenching the fire.

And then I could see Apulia, and those hills I know
So well, where the sirocco burns: we'd never
Have made it over, except a farmer near
Trivicum took us in. And stuffed his stove
With wood so green it had leaves on it: the smoke,
The smoke! We sat and cried at our supper. And then,
Till midnight, I sat waiting for a girl
Who never came. And then I slept
Badly, and came in my sleep, all over
Bedclothes, bed, and my bare belly.

And then in carriages, twenty-four fast miles,
To a village with a name I can't mention
In Latin hexameters; if you've been there you know
What I mean. Water needs to be bought, there,
Though everywhere else it's the cheapest item
In the world, but the bread is the best
There is, and wise travelers stock up
For the next leg of the trip—in Canosa
It's hard as a rock, and the water is just
As bad, though brave Diómedes built the place.
And Varius leaves us, here, and we weep at his going.

And then to Rubi, weary after a rain-wrecked
Road. The sky was clear, next day,
But the road was worse—from there all the way
To Bari, a fisherman's town. And then Gnatia,
A waterless hole, amused us: they tried to tell us,
By god they did, that in their great temple
Frankincense melts
On a magic stone, and never needs a fire!
People who scream at black cats can believe it,
Not me. I know the gods can't be bothered:
Miracles aren't dropped on our heads,
Rolled off the roof of high heaven, by surly gods, but by simple
Nature, all by herself. And then Brindisi,
The end of the road, and the end
Of this endless story.

I, 6

No one is nobler born than you,
Maecenas, in all the Etruscan
Lands; your mother's family, your father's
Family, gave Italy mighty generals—but no one
Is less
Of a snob
Than you,
Indifferent to a man's unknown father, or
To a bourgeois father
Like mine.

You say, and you mean, that a slave is a slave
But everyone else is a man, and you know that
Before Servius Tullus, King of Rome
And son of a slave, men with fathers no one
Could name lived honorably
And held honored office.
But highborn Valerius, descended from that family
Which drove Tarquin
From the throne,
He was dirt even
In the mob's eyes—the mob that stupidly honors
The dishonorable, is tied to fame's tail,
Is dazed by glorious titles
And ancient estates.
The vulgar herd
Knows this much: and should we,
So far
Above them, know less?
Suppose the herd preferred Valerius,
Even Valerius, to Decius, lowborn,
Unknown, who charged to his death, and Rome's
Victory, on enemy swords—and that bugger Appius
Would cheerfully blot out my name (as he did to others)
Since my father
Was born unfree.
All right, agreed: no Ass
In a Lion's skin can hope to be
A Man in a Man's skin. And that's how

It is: Vanity
Pulls everyone behind her shining chariot,
Senators and freemen, everyone,
Tied tight to pride's turning wheels.
Tillus: they tossed you out of the Senate,
And you ran for tribune
And got in again
Through the back door.
And the mob mocked, and threw mud;
You could have been quiet, happy, immune.
What drove you back, what drove you on?
But anyone who isn't forced to, anyone who wants
To wear the Senate's uniform
Is mad. The minute they see him, it starts:

"Who's that? Who's he to be
In the Senate? What did his father
Do? What's
His father's father's father's name?"

Like Barra, ugly and insane, but sure
No one was ever handsomer, begging girls
To ask for details, for proof: his face, you see?
His foot, his ankle, his teeth, his hair,
And all the rest of him: here, here—like Barra,
O friend, you make mobs determined
To know you, to poke your parents' bedsheets,
If you stand on a platform
And promise to care for Rome
And Romans,
Our City, our Empire, our Gods.

"You, son of a slave, of two slaves mated in a ditch,
Who
Are you to discipline Romans,
To order Romans hanged for crimes?"

"But—but: take Novus, there. He has
To sit behind me, you see? He's only
As good as my father, my ex-slave father,
He's not as good as *me*."

"And that makes you
Aristocratic?
Hah! If a hundred carts invade
The Forum, and another hundred, and then
Three funerals too, Novus can shout
Them down, bugles and trumpets
And all. That's real speechifying.
That's *something*, now; we can honor *that*."

But back to me, Maecenas,
A freeman's son
And barked at for being
Only
A freeman's son
And your friend—
Just as they barked,
Before,
Because Brutus made me a tribune
And I commanded a legion
And was still
Only
A freeman's son.
It's not the same thing, then
And now. A tribune's a mighty
Man, and I was nobody
Mighty. But why should they
Bark at your friends—you,
Maecenas, who pick and choose
Friends you want, friends worthy
Of friendship, friends
Interested in friends,
Not favors.
Luck had nothing to do with it:
We came together
When Virgil praised me, bless him,
And then Varius told you who
And what I was. I said almost
Nothing for myself; you called me to you
And I stuttered and stood silent, much
Too shy

To speak much. Whatever I said
Was only the truth; I told you no tales
Of my famous father or my fabulous
Farm and the wonderful nag
I rode around and around it. And you too said
Nothing much; you never say much.
I left. And nine months later
You called me again and asked
For my friendship. And I'm proud
That you, who look for virtue
And decency, who know good
From bad by good and bad, not by
Whatever a father was or did, you,
Maecenas, chose me, and honored me
In that choosing.
Whatever faults I have are standard
Faults, few and not flourishing,
Like moles on a handsome face.
And if no one can call me greedy
Or vicious or mean, if everyone admits
My innocence, my friends' love—I praise
Myself, but mean to praise another: listen—
Then my father's the only
Cause. He had no money, his land
Was half-exhausted. Beefy retired sergeants
And beefy retired captains
Sent their beefy sons to a local school,
Satchels and tablets on their shoulders, tuition pennies
In their hands at the middle of the month.
But me, I was brought to Rome, trained
Like a Senator's son. Seeing my clothes,
My faithful slaves carrying books, Roman
Style, Romans must have thought me
An aristocrat, living off ancient
Estates. And my father, a true
Guardian, went where I went, saw all the teachers
I saw. Why spell it out?
He kept me honest in every way, chaste
In name and fact, free
Of scandals, not frightened that someday
I might be an auctioneer, or a tax collector

Like himself, and people would scold him
For spending money and time
For nothing.

And how could I feel shame
For such a father? Never, as long as my mind lasts.
I've no excuses for my birth: people
Can cry that their fathers are no fault of theirs;
They do; but I don't. I think
And I speak
Very
Differently. If Nature forced us to live
Our lives again, and gave us the chance
To pick our parents, as noble as we pleased, I'd pick
The father I had, happy to live
Without honors and offices. The mob
Would say I was mad—but not you,
Maecenas, not you, I think. Why make myself
Miserable with a life I've never known
Or wanted? I'd need money, a lot
Of money; I'd need
To open my doors to many more people;
I'd have to hire companions,
And then travel—oh, never alone—with men
Beside me, for a trip abroad
Or a trip to the country. I'd need
Coaches
And horses
And grooms, I'd need
A caravan of carriages. But as it is,
Now, I can ride a bobtailed mule
Almost as far as Sicily, if I want to,
My bags shoving down his tail,
Me sitting up on his shoulders.
You, Tillus, you take five servants
And a case of wine
And a portable privy
And you travel down the Tiber Road
And everyone says you're a miser.
You're a Senator, yes, and you're famous,

Yes, but here my life is better,
And over and over again my life
Is more comfortable, over
And under and in a thousand
Ways.

I go out alone, if I want to.
I price vegetables, and flour; at twilight
I stroll the Circus Maximus, where liars
And cheats feed on fools, and I walk to the Forum.
I watch the fortune-tellers telling
Fortunes. I ramble home
To a supper of onions
              and peas
              and flat biscuits,
Served by three boys,
Served on a slab of white marble,
With two cups, and a ladle,
And a cheap saltcellar,
And a clay jug on a clay dish.
And then I go to sleep, and my mind's
At peace, no need to wake early and walk
Through the Forum and see the same satyr statue
Guarding his wineskin and scowling down at that usurer
Novus, sitting and squeezing his
Brass. I can rest till ten, then
Walk if I want to,
Or read
Or write
Something to please me, later, when everything
Is quiet. And I rub myself with oil, ready for games—but not
The kind that dirty Natta rubs with, no,
The kind he steals from lamps. When I'm tired
And the sun burns and I need
A cooling bath, I leave the park
And the games I play there
When the sun is calm. I eat
Enough lunch to say I've eaten
And I rest at home, doing
Nothing.

Only a man with no ambition, no miserable
Ambition, can live as I live. And I like
The idea that I live better,
Living like this, than if
My father had been a judge,
And my father's father,
Not to mention my uncle on my mother's side,
Once-removed.

I, 7

Everyone who's ever sat in a barber's chair or bought
Drugs from a druggist, knows this story: how half-breed
Persius was revenged on Rupilus Rex, the outlaw, for his filthy
Tongue. Persius was rich; he did lots of business
In Clazomen, and he had lots of lawsuits with old Rex.
Persius outdid even Rex in boasting and bragging
And blistering hides—he was rough and tough and he had a nasty temper.
Even Barros, even Sisennas, couldn't touch him for general meanness.
        Well, as for Rex: when their lawsuits got too tangled
To unravel (which is how lawsuits go: they turn into
Single combat to the death—like Hector, Priam's son,
And angry Achilleus, who hated each other so hard
That death was the only resolution—and why?
Because both were brave, and brave men don't run:
Take two cowards, or one hero, one coward, mismatched
In combat, like Glaucus and Diómedes, the weaker
Surrenders in advance, he even sends presents to the certain
Winner, if they ever met)—anyway, when Brutus was Asian
Praetor, Persius and Rupilus met head-on,
Like gladiators perfectly matched and eager as hell. And they rushed
Into court, ready to fight, to die (but not to pay).
        Persius opens; everyone laughs. He sings
Brutus to the skies, and all his friends, calls him the Son
Of Asia, his servants health-giving stars—except
Old Rex. Rex, he says, is a dirty dog-star,
Farmers hate him—and on and on he runs, like some winter
Flood racing down a mountain. Then Rupilus
Roars in his turn, so glib, so savage, vinegar
Of vinegars, like some barnyard bull used to
Butting, banging it in straight and stiff.
        But half-Greek Persius, drenched in Italian vinegar,
Responds: "O Brutus, I beg you by all the gods!
Since chopping the heads off kings is just your line,
And this is one Rex that really needs it,
Chop him down: it's what you do best!"

I, 8

I was the trunk of a fig-tree, once, a worthless log,
When the carver hesitated between a stool and a Priapus
And the god prevailed, and I became a god, watchman of gardens,
Terror of thieves and birds. My right hand watches for robbers;
This pole, protruding red from my indecent middle, warns them
Off; and a reed, set in the middle of my head, frightens
Birds, keeps them afraid to land in Maecenas' huge new garden.
This was a cemetery, once, for criminals and slaves,
For bodies dumped out of coffins and buried bare;
It was where paupers came, and no-good Pantolabus,
And Nomentantus who threw away a fortune. And a pillar
Informed the world that no one was to inherit this land,
Which ran a thousand feet in front and three hundred deep.
And now, where once men walked and looked out, sadly, on a field
White with bones, now houses stand, healthy and also beautiful,
And an embankment has risen, and a moat dug all around.
The carrion-hunters and criminals who haunted this place concern me
A little, but mostly I worry about the witches,
Twisting human minds with their spells, and with their poisons:
Once the wandering Moon shows her gleaming face
They emerge, plucking up bones and noxious herbs,
And there's nothing I can do to stop them, to drive them away.
        I have seen Canidia stalking in her black robe, her hair
Disheveled, her feet bare, she and that hag Sagana
Shrieking as they went, terrifyingly pale. They'd dig at
The earth with their nails, and tear a black lamb apart
With their teeth, pouring the blood in a trench, to pull out
Spirits, dead souls to torment with questions.
They'd set up a pair of images, a great one of wool,
A small one of wax, and make the wool punish the wax,
Keep it in order: it stood there, the littler one, like a slave
Awaiting death, a mute beggar hoping for mercy.
One witch cried to Hecaté, the other
To murderous Tisiphoné. Snakes and hellhounds
Ran loose, and the shy Moon, afraid to watch,
Hid herself behind the tallest tombstones. If I lie
With a single word, let crows shit my head white,
May that thief Voranus, and that freed slave Julius, and Pediata
Who was a soldier and now is who knows what, piss me to tears!

Why bother with details? Should I tell how the ghosts and Sagana
Spoke back and forth, sad and shrill, or how
They secretly buried a wolf's head and the tooth of a spotted snake,
How the wax image burst into a great blaze,
And how I trembled, seeing, hearing these two Furies
—But not without striking back. Suddenly I let
My fig-wood ass crack—and it blew out a noise
Like a bladder bursting—and they ran for their lives.
Ah, it was beautiful, seeing Sagana's piled-up hair
Falling, and Canidia's teeth, and all their herbs
And magic love knots scattered to the winds!

I, 9

Walking down the Via Sacra, minding
My business, thinking hard about nothing
Much, but lost in my thoughts, my hand
Was grabbed, suddenly, by some fellow
I hardly knew.

"O Quintus, dearest Quintus! How good
To see you! How *are* you, my friend?"

I answered :
        "Good enough, as well
As possible. May things go well with you."

I tried to leave, but he hung on my arm,
He followed in my footsteps. I stopped:

"Is there something you want?"

"Surely you know me, Quintus. We're both
Writers."

"All the better," I said, "I'll think
Much the better of you."

I was desperate to shake him off
And walked as fast as I could, then stopped
Suddenly, then whispered in my slave's
Ear, sweat trickling down to my ankles.
("O Bolanus, my lucky friend!" I said to myself
Over and over, "O Bolanus, blessed with a fierce
Temper!") And all the time the fellow rattled on,
Jabbering whatever struck his tongue,
Praising the city
And the city's streets.

I said nothing; he finally noticed.

"Ah Quintus, you want to move on,
I see it, yes, I do. I saw it at once.

But not without me! It just won't work.
I'll stick like glue, wherever you go I'll go
Too. And where are you going?"

"Don't trouble yourself: I've got to visit a man
You've never met. He's sick in bed,
His house is all the way over the River Tiber,
Down near Caesar's Gardens."

"That's nothing, my time's my own, my legs
Are strong. I'll walk with you
To the end."

I listened and drooped
Like an angry donkey, loaded
To the ears. And then it started:

"If I know myself, and I think
I do, I'm as valuable a friend as Viscus
Or even Varius—for who
Can write more
Than me,
Or faster?
Who dances lighter
On his feet? Even Hermogenés, with his poems
Pasted on every wall in Rome, might envy my songs!"

He took a breath; I took the chance
And interrupted:

"Have you a mother, or
Any relatives, whose lives depend
On your well-being?"

"None, none whatever. They're all
In their graves."

"Oh how lucky they are! I'm
Still here. Finish me off: my fate
Is on me, prophesied by a Sabine hag
In my childhood. She shook her magic urn

158 SATIRES

And sang, 'No ghastly poison will kill
This child, no enemy's sword,
No rotten lung, no broken gut, no gout
Creeping along his legs, but only a clattering
Fool, talking him to death. This child
Will keep talkative dunces at a distance,
If he grows up wise.' "

We had crossed the Forum, come to Vesta's
Temple, and a quarter of a day was gone.
My guest was due in court, he was being sued,
He had to appear or lose it all.

"O Quintus, if you love me, dear, dear friend,
Come to court with me, help me!"

"It would kill me to stand for hours. I know
No law—and I need to hurry,
And *you* know where!"

"What a decision: to give you up
Or give up my case!"

"Oh, me, please!"

"No, no," he said, "I'll stay
With you." He walked on. How do you argue
With a conquering
Bull? You don't.
I walked on
Too.

"Are you really in with Maecenas?" he began
Again. "A man of rare good sense and damned
Few friends. How lucky he's been, how well
He's played his chances! I'd play
Your second fiddle, and play it hard,
If you'd drop a word or two
In my favor. Lord, with me behind you
You'd push the others out!"

"It's not like that, no one's like that
   With Maecenas. There's nowhere in Rome freer
   Of scheming, no simpler, purer household.
   And anyone richer than me is richer; I never
   Mind. Anyone better read is better read—
   That's all. Everyone does what he does,
   Is
   What he is."

"Ah, you're pulling my leg. Quintus,
   I can't believe it."

"And still it's true."

"You make me fairly pant to get near him:
   What a man he must be!"

"It's up to you. You're brave enough, and strong
   Enough, you'll win him over. He's easy
   To win—if once he knows you well.
   But he's hard to meet."

"I'll do it, I'll do it! By god, I'll bribe
   His slaves, I'll never give up, I'll get
   My foot in his door, somehow. I'll watch,
   I'll wait, I'll catch him in the street,
   I'll follow him home. Nothing worth doing
   Is easy, here on earth!"

He went on and on—and then Fuscus,
   Old friend, dear friend, came walking by.
   He knew my guest, oh he knew him!
   I stopped.

"Horace: are you coming from home?
   Where are you off to?"

I pulled at his cloak, I snatched at his arms
   —He pretended to notice nothing. I winked,
   I rolled my eyes, bugged my eyes, begging him
   To rescue me. My funny friend, playing

A vicious joke, saw nothing, felt nothing.
My liver began to burn.

"Fuscus," I said, "what was it you needed
  To tell me, some secret affair
  Needing the strictest privacy?"

"Oh yes, but it can wait, there'll be better
  Occasions. Besides, today's the thirtieth
  Sabbath—and you wouldn't want me to fart on
  Our half-pricked Jews, would you, talking business
  On a holy day?"

"It's not my religion, I couldn't
  Care less."

"Ah, but *I* care! I'm not as strong
  As you, I'm one of the lesser herd.
  Excuse me: we'll discuss it
  Some better time."

A golden sun gone black!
The evil-minded villain ran, left me
Under the knife.

And then my guest met
The man who was suing him.

"You! you thief! Where are you running?"
  He shouted at my guest, and grabbed him.
"Can I call you as a witness?" he asked.

I was glad to say yes. He hurried
The fellow to court, everyone running
To see the fun, and shouting—and so
Apollo, God of Poets, saved me.

II, 1

Horace:
People think me a vicious satirist, sometimes pushing it
Past where satire should go. And the rest of them think it's
Flaccid stuff, that anyone could spin out poems
Like these, a thousand a day. O Trebatius, learned lawyer,
Counsel me, prescribe.

      Trebatius:
             Do nothing.

    Horace:
Write nothing, is that your advice?

      Trebatius:
                Yes.

    Horace:
By God, it might be best! But I have trouble sleeping.

      Trebatius:
                        If it's sleep
You're after, coat yourself with oil and swim across the Tiber. Three times,
Back and forth. And then, at night, soak yourself in wine.
And if passion for poem-making sweeps you away, why, sing praise
To our Caesar, his invincible victories. It might pay.

    Horace:
Oh I would if I could, believe me! But whatever it requires,
I haven't got it. You aren't born able to deal with
Battalions bristling with javelins, or Gauls dropping next to
Their broken spears, or wounded Parthians falling from their horses.

     Trebatius:
And why not write of Caesar himself, brave and just
At once? Wise Lucilius did it, in poems about Scipio.

    Horace:
I will, I will, as soon as I can! But my words
Must slip through Caesar's ear when it's open: flatter him

Too early, too late, too hard, too soft, and he'll only ignore it.

Trebatius:
Much better, really, than those bitter, nasty lines about
"No-good Pantalobus and Nomentantus who threw away a fortune."
Everyone's afraid of you, and hates you, even before they're attacked!

Horace:
Is it *my* fault? Milonius starts his dance as soon as wine
And heat meet in his brain, as soon as it's dark and the lamps burn bright.
Castor's in love with horses; his twin brother's crazy about
Boxing. Take a thousand people and find a thousand
Prejudices. My own is for words marching in well-made
Feet—as Lucilius arranged them, a nobler man than either of us!
He told his secrets to his books, like trusted friends,
And never looked elsewhere. For good or ill, that was it.
And now we can see his life, spread out for viewing, that good
Old man, like a funereal painting.
                                   I follow him—and no matter whether I'm Apulian
Or Lucan. Who knows which? Those old settlers ploughed
Up to the borders in both directions. That was their job,
They were sent to the frontiers, the story goes,
After the Sabines were driven out; no enemy was to break
Their settlements and drive at Rome, no Apulian rebels,
No violent Lucans. But this blunt pen of mine
Attacks no one before he attacks me.
It's like a sword, I keep it for protection, I keep it
In its scabbard. Why draw it, why swing it, as long as
I'm safe? O Father Jove, king of kings, let
My weapon rust unused, let no one assault a lover
Of peace! But attack—it's better not to, believe me—and live
To regret it, your name paraded all over Rome!
        Get Cervius angry and he threatens with lawyers and lawsuits;
Offend Canidia and she reaches for poison; make Turius
Your enemy and he reminds you, quick enough, how costly you'll find
His courtroom, when next you appear there. Everyone flexes
His particular muscles, to frighten you off—exactly as Nature
Arranged it. Wolves bite, bulls butt—and why?
They have to, it's what they are. Let even that rake Scaeva
Guard his old mother; he won't lift a hand against her. Wonderful, eh?
Be surprised the wolf doesn't butt and the bull won't bite!

She'll die in her sleep, hemlock in her honey.
Let me be brief: whether I end my life ancient,
Peaceful, in bed, rich or poor, or whether Death with his sable wings
Is waiting, even now, here in Rome or perhaps in exile,
However it happens it will find me writing.

Trebatius:
                                        Son, you won't
Live long! One of your powerful friends is sure to chill you down.

Horace:
Good Lord! When Lucilius took his life in his hands and wrote
Satires, the first Rome saw, pulling off masks
And proving that a shiny outside could conceal a foulness
Within, was Laelius offended at his wit? was Scipio,
Conqueror of Carthage? Did anyone mourn for Metellus,
For Lupus, smothered in vicious verse? And yet
He hit at everyone, heads of state, and any
Citizen in any state: only virtue was immune,
And virtue's friends. Lord! When wise and gentle
Laelius retired, and virtuous Scipio, left public life
For private, with whom did they play and fool about,
With whom make jokes, everyone in easy undress? This same Lucilius.
They boiled their beans together, and then ate them. I'm no Lucilius,
But whatever I am, whatever I'm worth, even stubborn
Envy will admit I've always lived with great and powerful:
Let her bite for something soft, she'll knock her teeth
On steel! But perhaps my learned friend takes issue?

Trebatius:
        How could I possibly argue? But be it however
It may be, let me warn you, as a lawyer, that libel
Is a law of the state, and ignorance of that law could threaten you.
No man is allowed bad verses against another man.

Horace:
        Well, yes, bad verses—to be sure! But what if they're good,
What if Caesar himself pronounces them good? What if the attacker
Is good, and attacks someone bad, someone worthy of abuse?

Trebatius:
They'll dismiss the case with a laugh; they'll send you
                                        back to your desk!

II, 3

Damasippus:
Four rolls of parchment a year: that's all you use!
You're always revising, unweaving what you've woven.
And you're angry with yourself: you sleep enough, drink
Enough wine—but you write almost nothing. Eh? And *this* is where
You hide, when Rome celebrates the Saturnalia? Well, while you're still sober
Say something sensible, make some promises. Begin!
                                            Nothing?
Don't blame your pens! Does banging on that innocent wall
Help? Poor wall, fashioned by angry gods, and angrier poets.
You seemed so full of promise, once, sheltered
At long last under your country roof.
But what good has it done, dragging Archílochus and Menander,
And all those worthy Greek dramatists, down there with you?
Perhaps your plan is to escape unpopularity and virtue
Together? O miserable Horace, how they'll mock you! Shun
That wicked Siren, Laziness, or give up whatever glory
Your better days earned you.

Horace:
                              Philosopher Damasippus, my friend,
May the gods give you, in gratitude—a barber for that goat-beard!
Anyway, what gives you such intimate information?

Damasippus:
                                            Washed away
By Fortune, wrecked on the Exchange, I spend myself watching
Other men's business. Once I peeped and pried
Into bronze vases, looking for the tracks of sly old Sisyphus,
Investigating carvings, testing how well the brass
Had been poured. I put prices on statues: a hundred thousand here,
Less for that other one. I knew gardens and houses and how best
To buy them. They called me Mercury's pet: I had the knack
Of money-making.

Horace:
                    Indeed. I'm surprised to see you
Cured of it.

Damasippus:
All that's surprising is how a new disease
Replaced the old—the way a pounding head
Becomes a stomach ache, or a patient with sleeping sickness
Wakes up, turns boxer, and beats his doctor senseless.

Horace:
Do as you please—but don't do *that*!

Damasippus:
My friend,
Why fool yourself? You're as mad as the rest—and most men
Are idiots, if Stertinus speaks truly. I learned my lessons
At his feet, wrote out his words. He soothed my soul, told me
To grow this wise man's beard, and sent me home happy, free
To leave Fabricius' bridge, from which, I admit it, I planned
To throw myself into the river. He stood at my side, touched my hand,
and said:

"Be careful, do nothing unworthy of yourself. Your anguish,
Your shame, are both false: you're afraid to seem mad
In a world of madmen. And let me ask you, to start with,
If you know insanity when you see it? What is it? If you *are* the only
Madman, then jump, I'll be silent; die as bravely as you can.
"We Stoics, following Chrysippus, say this: all men
Driven by folly, perverse and blind and ignorant, are mad.
Whole nations are mad, in this sense, and great kings are mad, and only
The wise man is sane.
"Listen: here is why everyone
Who calls you mad is just as senseless himself.
It's like a forest, where people wander this way and that,
Hunting the path and never finding it, not right, or left,
Or center, all confused, all equally lost, but all
Lost in different directions. Believe yourself mad,
If you like, but as sane as the man who laughs at you
And never sees the tail tied behind him.
"One kind of fool is afraid of everything—that is,
Of nothing real. Fires and rocks and rivers stop them from running
Free, they cry! Another kind, different but equally dense,
Rushes through fires and rivers. A loving mother, a virtuous
Sister, a father, a wife, a whole family, can call to them:

'That ditch is wide, that cliff is steep, watch out!'
But they hear as much as that drunken actor, Fulfius, who slept
So soundly that players and audience together couldn't wake him—
More than a thousand voices! Most men—no, the entire
World!—are equally mad. I'll prove it. Listen.
          "Damasippus, admittedly, was mad for buying up ancient statues.
Are your creditors sane, Damasippus? Perhaps. But consider:
If I offer you money and assure you I don't expect it back,
Are you mad if you take it? Or madder still
If you turn it down, a gift from Mercury?
Fill out a dozen moneylender's bonds—no, more: add
A hundred lawyer's knots, add a thousand clever nooses.
No matter, a good Protean villain gets out of them all!
Drag him to court, he'll laugh in your face, wagging his jaws;
He'll be a boar, or a bird, or a stone—or a tree, if he feels like it.
If managing money badly is the mark of a madman, and managing
Money well proves you're sane, well, believe me, Perellius
Extracting a useless bond from you is pretty well addled.
          "Ahem: students: arrange your robes, open your ears:
Anyone whom ambition turns pale, anyone enamored of money,
Anyone feverish for luxuries, sad with superstition, or suffering
From any disease of the mind: come closer, pay attention, I'll prove
You mad, each and every one of you: come closer!
          "Avarice requires the largest dose of medicinal hellebore;
It might be best, I suspect, to send the greedy-insane to Phocia, where
It's grown. Consider. Staberius' heirs were obliged to engrave his bequest,
In dollars and cents, on his tomb: otherwise, supply a hundred
Gladiators for his funeral, and a feast for thousands, and all the corn
Africa can grow. 'Don't argue,' he wrote in his will,
'Just do it. It's *my* will, not yours.' He understood, I think,
How odd they would feel: how prudent he was! 'But why,' you ask,
'Why carve dollars and cents on a tombstone? What good does it do?'
Ah: all his long life he thought poverty the worst
Of evils, he ran from it furiously till the day he died—
And had he died owning even one cent less, he'd have thought himself
Wicked. Virtue, fame, honor—everything human,
Everything divine, is illuminated by money, shines only (to his mind)
In the beauty and glow of wealth. He who is wealthy will be famous,
Brave, and just. 'And wise?' Oh wise, and a king too
—Anything he wanted. He expected his gold to bring him immense
Renown, like something won by incredible virtue.

"Can we compare
Staberius to Socrates' pupil, Aristippus, who was crossing
Libya and ordered his slaves to abandon his gold? It made them
Travel too slowly, he said. Which is the greater madman?
Impossible to decide: a puzzle never solves a puzzle.
Suppose a man buying harps, and harps, and more harps, piling them
High in a storeroom—but indifferent both to music and the harp.
Or someone buying cobblers' lasts, but ignorant of shoemaking.
Or someone buying sails for ships, but afraid of the ocean.
We'd call him crazy, all of us, and we'd all be right.
Is the man who piles up silver and gold any different, totally
Ignorant of how to use it, afraid even to handle the sacred stuff?

"Imagine a man lying beside a huge granary bin,
Forever on guard, his club ready, but forever afraid
To ease his hunger with a single grain, though he owns it all,
Feeding himself, instead, on bitter herbs.
Imagine a man with a thousand casks of old Falernian
—No, that's nothing: three hundred thousand!—who drinks
Vinegar. Imagine an eighty-year-old with velvet
Blankets molding away in his storeroom, while he
Sleeps on dirty straw, shivering. How many
Would think him mad? Few, few: most men
Lie on their beds, rotting with the same fever.
O godforsaken old fool, are you afraid your heir
Might drink some, is that why you hoard it? Are you afraid none will be
Left for you? Put a bit of good oil on your lettuce! And on
Your scurvy head! How much would it matter, a penny
A day? Having enough, why do you cheat and lie and steal
At every chance, right and left? And *you* are sane?

"If you started throwing rocks at pedestrians, or even at slaves
You owned yourself, bought and paid for, cash on the line,
Every boy and every girl would call you crazy.
If you strangle your wife with a rope, if you poison your mother,
Is your head in good order? Why not? You're not at Argos,
You're not that mad Orestes, killing his mother with a sword.
Don't think he went mad *after* he'd killed her: oh no,
It wasn't the wicked Furies who drove him to it,
Forced him to warm sharp steel in his mother's throat!
But then, once he was thought insane, Orestes
Did nothing worth condemning, did he? Electra's husband, Pylades,
Was never touched by his sword, or his sister herself:

He called Electra a Fury, that's all, and called Pylades
Something obscene—obliged by his irrational bile, to be sure.
     "Opimius—poor in spite of his gold and silver hoard—
Would drink cheap wine from a cheap cup—on holidays.
On working days he drank wine gone sour.
He dropped into a coma, once, so deep that his heir
Ran around and around his keys and his lockboxes, almost hysterical
With joy. But his quick-witted doctor, who was also his friend,
Revived him with a trick. He had a table brought
And bags of money poured out, and men came
To count it. That brought him back, all right! 'Now,'
The doctor warned, 'Guard your money, or your greedy heir will get it.'
'While I'm alive?' 'Wake up, if you intend to live!' 'And how?'
'Your veins are collapsing, you're weak, you need some meat,
Some brandy, food for your failing stomach. How can you
Hesitate? Here, take this bowl of rice.'
'It cost?' 'Piddle!' 'Exactly how much?' 'Eight cents.' 'Ah!
Does it matter if I die of disease or by the hands of thieves?'
    'But *who* is sane?'
               Whoever's no fool.
                      'And the miser?'
Is a fool and a madman.
               'Well, if you're not a miser, then plainly
You must be sane?'
          Of course not.
               'But why, good Stoic?'
                     Listen:
Here's old Doctor Crateris. 'This patient's heart is sound
As a dollar.' He's well, he can get up and work? 'Not at all.
His lungs, or maybe his kidneys, are full of pus.'
Here's a man, no miser, no liar either. He sacrifices pigs
To the gods. But he's also ambitious. And stubborn. Reach for the
Hellebore! Does it matter if you drop your gold in a pit
Or simply never use anything you own?
     "They tell about Servius Oppidus—rich by the old standard—
That on his deathbed he divided his two Canisium farms
Between his two sons, called them to his side, and said:
'Aulus, ever since I saw you careless with your toys,
Giving them away, betting with other boys—and saw you,
Tiberius, counting yours, and hiding them away,
I've worried for you both. You, Aulus, be careful not to be

Another Nomentantus, waster of wealth—and you, Tiberius,
No moneylender Cicuta. Swear, both of you, by our household gods,
Never to lessen, never to increase, what your father
Declared sufficient, and what Nature herself limits.
Never let glory or ambition tempt you. And I solemnly
Vow: if either of you becomes a magistrate, a commissioner,
A general, he shall be both abominated and accursed!
How insane you'd be, wasting your wealth, giving it away
For favor and for votes, strutting in the Arena, cast in bronze,
But stripped of your land, stripped of the money your father left you!
Oh yes, you'd get as much applause as Agrippa, married to Caesar's
Daughter herself—a sly little fox aping the noble lion!'
    "And I'd say to Agamemnon: 'Why not bury Ajax? Why forbid it?'
                                                'I am king.'
'And I, a common man, will say no more.'
                                        'And my command is a proper one.
Yet anyone who thinks me wrong is free to speak.
Say what you think.'
                    'King of all kings, may the gods
Grant you and all your fleet your homeward voyage, when Troy
Has fallen. If I ask, will you answer?'
                                    'Ask.'
'Ajax is second only to Achilleus. Why should he
Lie rotting, unburied, for Priam's people, for Priam
Himself, to gloat over, he who killed so many sons
Of Trojans, left them unburied in their native land?'
'That madman killed a thousand sheep, shouting
It was Odysseus he killed, and Meneleus, and me.'
'Were you sane, Agamemnon, when you brought your beautiful
Daughter to the altar at Aulis, your daughter instead of a calf,
And sprinkled her head with salted grain? Oh monster!'
                                                    'And?'
'What did mad Ajax do, slaughtering sheep with his sword?
He killed no wife, no child: he cursed your family, and you,
But he hurt no one, not his brother Teucer, not even Odysseus.'
'My decision was to free my fleet from that hostile shore.
Release was bought from the gods, properly, wisely, with blood.'
'Yes—but your own blood, madman!'
                                'Mine. But I am no madman.'

    "But a mind which confuses false ideas and true ones,

Which heaves and whirls in a maelstrom of sin, is no normal mind,
Whether disturbed by anger, like Agamemnon, or by folly,
Like Ajax—does it matter which? Ajax slaughtering sheep
Is mad. Agamemnon, his heart swollen with pride, chooses to commit
A crime, and for an empty glory: is that sane? Is *that* a pure heart?
Anyone who dressed a lamb like his daughter, drove it
All over Rome in a carriage, gave it servants, and presents,
And gold, arranged a marriage with some soldier husband—
Well, the judge would order him confined, stripped of his rights,
And his sane relations would be forced to care for him. Eh?
A man who sacrifices his daughter, instead of a lamb,
Is *he* right in the head? Never! Perverse folly
Is the very peak of madness. A wicked man
Is always a maniac; caught by the transient glow of fame,
You're always a frantic spiller of blood—even your own!
        "And now, my students, let us accuse extravagance and Nomentantus:
Reason proves that foolish spendthrifts are always madmen.
Nomentantus inherited his money and invited everyone
He bought from (the riffraff of Tuscan Street) to be at his door
In the morning—fishmongers, grocers, chicken-pluckers,
Perfumers, sausage-cooks and clowns, butchers
And cheesemakers. And why? They came in crowds to find out.
A pimp spoke for them: 'Anything I have, anything anyone here has
At home, believe me, it's yours if you want it. Just ask, anytime at all.'
And that thoughtful, considerate young man responded: 'You sleep
In your boots, high in frozen hills, so I can eat boar
For dinner. You, you sweep the winter ocean for fish. Me,
I'm lazy, I don't deserve this money. Take it, take it!
Take a million—you too—and you, whose wife comes running
At midnight, when I call her, you take three million!'
        "Clodius Aesopus pulled a precious pearl from Metella's
Ear and, wanting to drink down a million in one swallow, dissolved it
In acid. Would it be more insane to throw a million
Down a sewer, or into a swift-flowing river?
Quintus Arrius' two sons, oh a noble pair,
Like twins in their vices, their love of stupid things,
Ate only nightingales for breakfast—nightingales!—and bought them
At crazy prices. Sane? Should we write their names in chalk, or in charcoal?
        "Any old fool who builds dollhouses, yokes mice
To tiny chariots and bets on their races, and rides a hobbyhorse
Himself, is permeated with madness. But suppose, for a moment,

That love is even more childish than this, and Reason can prove it,
That it's all the same—making sandcastles at the shore, age three,
Or whining with tortured love for a whore.
Let me ask you: *if* it's true, would you do as Polemon did,
Converted from love? Would you give up love's badges, its ribbons,
Its garters, its cloak? He became a philosopher, afraid
Of his virtuous teacher's voice, and even drunk with wine
Heard and obeyed, unwound garlands from his neck and discarded them.
Offer apples to a pouting child, he'll refuse them.
'Here, my pet.' 'No!' Try not asking: he'll want them desperately.
Is the lover any different, turned away from her door, debating his direction,
To stay, to go, knowing he's uninvited, but hanging on in front of
That angry door? 'If she calls me, now, should I go?
Or should I end it all forever, here and now? She shut
Me out. She calls me. Should I go? No, even if she begs!'
But his slave knows better: 'My master, no method, no reasoned
Thought will work with no room for discretion, no chance for moderation.
Love contains these intrinsic evils: one minute war,
Then peace the next, both almost as changeable as the weather,
Ruled by blind chance. No one can make them stable,
Certain: if you loved by logic and rule you'd seem
Like a logical madman, raving according to regulation.'
What? Playing she-loves-me, she-loves-me-not,
You find yourself loved. Are you sane? Are you master of yourself?
What? An old man lisping, prattling of love, is wiser
Than a child building with blocks? Add blood to foolishness
—And stir the fire with a sword! When Marius murdered his girl friend,
Just the other day, then threw himself from a cliff,
Was he mad? Or shall we call him sane—but a criminal,
Excusing his whirling brain and convicting his hands?
Custom imposes different words, but the things are the same.
        "A freeman, once, when he was old, and when he'd been fasting,
Would wash his hands and run around Rome at dawn, crying, praying,
'Save me, save me, just me!' ('It's not asking much,' he'd add.)
'Keep me from death, the gods can do anything!' His eyes and his ears
Were healthy—but who could have guaranteed his mind
And stayed out of court? My master Chrysippus ranks this crowd
Of superstition-mongers with Menenius the insane.
'O Jupiter, who gives disease, who takes it away,'
Cries the mother of a boy five months in bed, 'let
These chills leave my child—and the first morning

Of your first feast day he'll stand in the Tiber,
Naked!' If luck or a doctor should cure the boy
His crazy mother will kill him, freezing him on the river bank
And restoring his vanished fever! Just what disease
Afflicts her brain? Superstitious fear of the gods."

      Stertinius, eighth of our wise men and my friend, gave me
Those weapons to keep myself safe from name-callers. Call me
Mad, whoever you are, and I'll give you back
As good as I get.

      Horace:
             O Stoic, may you sell your wares for better prices, bankrupt,
Than you did before! But tell me: you see so much madness,
Which kinds afflict *me*? I feel myself disgustingly sane.

      Damasippus:
      What! When Agavé, Cadmus' daughter, carries her son's
Poor head in her hands, cut off by herself, does she think herself mad?

      Horace:
      I'm a fool, I admit it! I'm probably mad, too—truth
Is all-powerful. But *explain* my folly, O wise man. Where
And how and from what has my mind become so diseased?

      Damasippus:
      Listen. You're putting up buildings on your farm: that's first!
That means you're aping men taller than yourself—you almost-dwarf!
And you laugh at Turbo, strutting around in his armor!
He's small, but his spirit is large. Are you any less ridiculous?
And Maecenas, you ape him too: is that right? Whatever he does,
You try to do—though he's a better man than you'll ever be.
      A mother frog went out hunting, and all her children
But one were crushed by a careless calf's foot. The survivor told her
The tragic tale. 'How big a monster?' she asked him.
She puffed herself out. 'This big?' 'Bigger, bigger!' 'As big
As this?' and she blew herself fatter. 'This big?' 'You'd burst,'
He assured her, 'before you could swell as big as that!'
It strikes me, Horace, there's an excellent metaphor for you.
Now toss in your poems—I mean, throw oil on the fire!
If anyone was ever sane, and bothered composing poetry, I suppose

That's you. But your terrible temper—

> *Horace:*
>
>   Stop!

> *Damasippus:*
>
>   The way you live

Beyond your means—

> *Horace:*
>
>   Damasippus, mind your own business!

> *Damasippus:*

And your thousands of love affairs, with girls, with boys—

> *Horace:*

O greater madman, spare this lesser lunatic!

II, 4

Horace:
Where to, Catius?

Catius:
              I'm sorry, I can't stop, I have some lecture notes,
Here, I need to write down, new rules greater
Than Pythagoras, greater than Socrates, greater than Plato!

Horace:
       Your pardon for this awkward interruption: I apologize.
And yet, anything which escapes you, now,
You'll catch later, I know you will. Whether
It's art or training, your memory's a marvelous thing.

Catius:
       Precisely my problem: oh, a subtle discourse,
On a subtle theme, and ever so subtly delivered!

Horace:
       A Roman lecturer? or a foreigner? Tell me his name.

Catius:
       I can tell you his rules; I cannot publish his name.
       First: oblong eggs are whiter, have better flavor
Than round ones, and should always be served in preference: their tough
Shells are wrapped around a male yolk.
Cabbage grown in dry fields is sweeter than irrigated stuff
Grown near Rome—watered gardens grow ghastly, tasteless greens.
       An unexpected guest with no affection for ancient
Fowls will thank you if you water some good Falernian
And let the bird soak—before it's slaughtered, of course.
       Meadow mushrooms are best: beware of others!
       Summers can be salubrious if you complete each midday meal
With black mulberries—but picked before the sun
Is high.
       Old Aufidius diluted Falernian with honey—
Not a good notion. Empty veins should receive nothing
Except what's mild. Flood your bowels with mead—
The mild variety. For stubborn constipation

Try mollusks, or any ordinary shellfish, or sorrel—always
With white Coan wine. That loosens things up!
       Slippery shellfish swell under a new moon
—But the best kind can't be found everywhere. The Baian cockle,
For example, is distinctly worse than the Lucrine mussel,
And oysters are best from Circei, crayfish from Misenum,
And ah! the lovely scallops of Tarentum!
       And who can claim—oh rash!—to truly master the art
Of eating, before he knows the delicate theory of essences?
No, it's not enough to sweep up fish from the dearest
Stalls in the market: what sauce goes with them, eh?
Which should be broiled, to properly tempt your tired guest?
       Boars fed on Umbrian acorns—now *there* is meat
Fit to bulge your platter! Nothing flabby there!
The Laurentian boar—ugh, it's fattened on water weeds!
       She-goats bred in a vineyard can prove inedible.
A knowing diner asks for the flesh of a pregnant hare.
       But fish and fowl—well, no palate except mine
Has ever known their secrets: the ripe season, the right
Taste. Call yourself a connoisseur—and all you know is *pastry*?
Ah: there's no genius in knowing only one thing.
Suppose wine absorbs your attention, only wine—
And any oil will do, poured on your fish!
       Take Massic wine. It's coarse, the bouquet is rough
—But set it under a cloudless sky, at night, and the air
Filters it sweet and light. But strain it through linen . . .
It rots, the flavor's gone. Now Surrentine needs
A dose of Falernian dregs, and a bit of pigeon's egg,
And all the sediment gets trapped by the yolk,
Dragged to the bottom: you have to *know* such things!
       Stewed shrimps and African snails: if you've drunk too much
They'll snap you to attention. Lettuce just floats, you know, in a stomach
Made acid with wine; the soured stomach craves ham, and craves
Sausages—Lord, anything brought round, smoking
Hot, from a delicatessen, pleases it best.
       Study the nature of sauces. There are several basic
Varieties. The simple sauce starts with sweet oil (olive,
Of course), is mixed with thick wine and pickle juice—
But only the sort drawn from Byzantine jars.
Boil it, adding a dose of chopped herbs, sprinkle on
Corycian saffron, let it settle, then add—this is

Important—liquid left from pressed Venafran olives.
    Apples from Tiber have a noble appearance, but the Picenian
Are sweeter, finer. For pickling, use Venuculan grapes;
For smoking, the Albanian grape—indeed, my table
Was the first to offer smoked Albanians and apple, set out
On shining white plates, with white pepper chopped
In black salt, and with caviar. How stupid some men are!
They spend their thousands in the market, bring home glowing
Fish—then cramp them in tiny dishes! And how
It turns the stomach, seeing a slave with greasy
Hands fumbling with your glass (he's been stealing forbidden
Food) or an antique bowl mouldy with dirt!
Sawdust, and brooms, and napkins, and mats—how much
Can they cost? And yet, neglected, they create scandal.
Sweeping expensive tile with a dirty palm-leaf broom—
Covering filthy beds with rich Tyrian carpet—
How awful! Common cleanliness costs so little
That such filthy habits deserve double blame: better a bare
Table than a dirty one bent with noble dishes.

    Horace:
    O learned Catius, I beg you in the name of our friendship and your love
Of the gods, let me be at your side when the next lecture comes!
Your memory is astonishing, yet even so eloquent an interpreter
Can never delight like the original. And you're lucky enough
To have seen his face, his bearing. It seems to you
Like nothing—but I, less fortunate, long to approach
That hidden fountain of knowledge, bask in its light,
And drink in its rules for a life so delightful, so good.

II, 5

Odysseus:
Just one more question, Tiresias. You've told me of mighty
Matters, but not how my ruined fortune can rise
Again. You're laughing?

Tiresias:
                              Schemer, trickster: what more
Can you ask than return to Ithaca and your household gods?

Odysseus:
O you who forever speak truth, and can see the future,
See how ragged and poor I return, exactly as you said.
Nothing that was mine is left, the suitors took everything.
And nobility is nothing without money, it's less than seaweed.

Tiresias:
You're afraid of poverty, to put it plainly: very well,
Listen, these are the ways of growing rich.
      Given a thrush, or some other dainty, don't eat it,
Let it fly where fortunes live, and old men.
When your farm sprouts up succulent fruit, delicious apples,
Give them to some rich man, more useful and worthier than the gods.
He may be a convicted liar, with no father, no mother,
He may be a runaway slave who's killed his own brother,
But let him walk on the inner side, if he asks you to walk.

Odysseus:
My body a shield for some filthy Damas! At Troy
My only competitors were kings.

Tiresias:
                              Stay poor, then.

Odysseus:
I'll force my soul to bear this, as bravely as possible.
I've lived through worse. Continue, O prophet, teach me
The ways of piling up money, piling it higher and higher.

Tiresias:
And as I have said, I say again. Hunt
Like a fox for old men's wills; never give up, even
When a few escape you, nibble at the bait and run.
Abandon hope before you admit defeat.
Eventually a law suit will come, large or small, it hardly
Matters, and the plaintiff will be old, and rich, and childless, perhaps
A rascal pursuing some better man (but a man, alas, with a son
Or a childbearing wife!), and you will turn your back on virtue
And take up the rich man's case, embrace it body and soul.
"Quintus," you'll say, or maybe "Publius"—they like to be flattered
On a first-name basis—"your virtue has made me your friend.
I know the knotty points of the law, I've argued them all.
Rest assured, I'll let them pluck out my eyes before
They insult you, or rob you of a single nutshell. Your cause is mine,
You'll lose nothing, no one will laugh at you." Tell him to go home,
Nurse his precious skin: you'll take on his case.
Then keep yourself at it, even when the dog-star burns so red
That statues split with its heat, even if sloppy poets
Cover the wintry Alps with a yard and a half of snow.
"Eh, see"—someone's sure to say, nudging his neighbor
With an elbow—"how patient he is, how loyal, how he helps his friends!
What a mind!" And fish will swim to your fish ponds. And more. And more.
        And then, if a rich man's rearing some sickly brat,
And you're worried that chasing childless bachelors could make you look bad,
Why, creep into second place, give the grateful father
Reason to make you an alternative heir. Then something
Kills the little snot—disease, accident, anything!—and you're
The heir. A *very* successful game, by the way.
        If they show you their will, newly subscribed, pretend
To push it away, pretend to avert your eyes—
But sneak a sideways glance, get the name
Of the heir (first page, second line, as a rule), so you know
If you've won or lost—or maybe inherited only a part.
It pays to be alert: finger in the dike,
A stitch in time—if you see what I mean.

Odysseus:
You're mad—or mocking me with these muddy predictions!

Tiresias:
Laertes' great son, Apollo's gift enfolds me:
I see the future, I see the past, all is as I say!

Odysseus:
Explain that fiddle about fingers and stitches: please!

Tiresias:
It's a common tale—and a nasty one. There was Nasica, you see,
Head over heels in debt to old Coranus
(Who thought himself a gay young blade). So he pushed
His daughter, tall and lovely, into marrying Coranus—
Expecting, of course, the fortune to go to his grandson
And the debts to go up the chimney. Well, Coranus made
His will, and Nasica finally agreed to read it—
And found himself left with nothing but those same old debts.
      And then consider this: if some cunning woman, married
To an ancient fool, or maybe some clever slave, ties the old man
In knots, join them—tell the graybeard how good they are (they'll say
The same of you)—it's all to the good, but the best approach
Is a direct attack. The idiot scribbles poetry?
Praise it. He's a rake? Don't wait till he asks:
Give him Penelopé—the least he deserves!

Odysseus:
                                        Really?
She's chaste and discreet, you know—the suitors got nowhere.
Do you think she'd go along? Pure Penelopé?

Tiresias:
      Ah: the suitors were young, and miserly. They thought
Much more about eating your herds than bedding your wife.
Penelopé's chaste, of course—but let her taste what a rich
Old fool can produce (half and half with you, remember)
And she'll hunt with the best of your hounds!
      I recall a grisly story. A Theban hag, rich
And wicked, willed herself a special funeral:
Her body, well oiled, was carried on her heir's bare shoulders.
She wanted to know, at last, if dead she could escape him;
Living, he followed her about with his nose to the ground.
      Be cautious: eager, but not too much; attentive, but not

Too much. Twitchy ones, and glum ones, don't like talking. But silence
Is risky, if protracted. Act like Davus in the play—you know,
Tilt your head like someone awed by a Presence.
And flattery above all. If the wind blows, warn him to cover
His precious skull; push him a path through a crowd,
Use your shoulders; open your ears when he wants to prattle.
Praise, and more praise, is wanted? Give him gusts of it,
Blown hot from a swelling bladder, until
He lifts his hands to heaven and cries, "Enough!"
     When finally your bondage is done, when he sets you free
With these words—"one-fourth of everything goes to Odysseus"—
Keep ploughing the field, scattering such seed as, "Ah! my old friend
Damas, gone, quite gone? Where shall I ever find
His equal?" Manage a tear or two and it goes down
Better. You can hide your pleasure, it won't be too hard.
Build him a massive tomb, if he leaves you the choice;
Be sure the neighbors notice the elaborate funeral.
And if any other heir, especially old, especially sick,
Covets a house or some land that's come to you,
Assure him it's his for a song, you're glad to oblige.
     But Queen Proserpiné summons me: live—and live well!

II, 6

Oh this, this was what I prayed for!
A bit of land, a garden, a spring
Running forever next to the house,
And trees up above. The gods
Have given me this and more,
And better. It's good, it's good: Mercury,
God of Luck, I need nothing
Except the right to keep
What I have.

    If

        I've done nothing dishonest
        to make this place greater

    If

        I do nothing stupid
        to make it smaller

    If

        I never pray, foolish,
       "Oh give me, only give me
        that corner there, which ruins
        the line of my farm! O
        Hercules, God of Treasure,
        find me a pot of gold, like that slave
        who bought the land he'd plowed,
        once, for his master, after you, O
        Hercules, showed him hidden silver
        and gold!"

    If

        I'm happy with what I have

Then
Mercury, fatten my sheep,
Fatten everything except my head,
And stay my guide and protector!

And once I've left the city, come to this castle
In the hills, what better subject
For my Satires, for the fame of my
Prosy Muse? There's no ambition,
Here, to sicken me, and no heavy

Sirocco blowing from the South, and no pale
Sick Autumn, feeding and honoring
The goddess of funerals.

O Father of Dawn, O Janus if
Janus pleases you better, O Morning, you
Who bring the beginning of men's day
And their labor—as the Heavens have decreed—
Be thou the beginning of my song! At Rome
You sweep me off: Quick, quick!
No one should be working before you! And North wind
Blowing, or snow dragging days in a narrowing
Circle, I go, I have no choice. I'm a pledge
In some suit: I speak my piece
To the court, tell my troubles, then
Fight for my life in the hurrying
Crowds, pushing, shoving.

"Hey, idiot! What's your hurry?" some city
Bandit shouts. "Running off to
Maecenas, eh? You'd knock down anyone in your way!"

I like the sound of that, all right,
It's honey out of the hive.

But then I pass the cemetery
(Where you've planted your garden, Maecenas)
And they all start shoving petitions
In my face, and in my ribs, and my head buzzes:
    "Roscius wants you to meet him
        Tomorrow at seven, near
        The Wall."
    "The clerks at the Treasury, of whom
        You once were one, want you
        To visit, again, on new
        And important
        Business."
    "Maecenas needs to sign these: here."
If I say, "I'll try," he urges me on:
"If you want to, Horace, you can!"

It's seven years, now—no, it's almost eight—
Since Maecenas made me his friend,
Someone to sit beside him in his carriage,
Someone to ask, "What time is it?" or
"Will that Thracian gladiator beat
Syrus?" or "It's cold, these days,
If you wander out early and without
A coat," and such trivial stuff
As leaky ears can be trusted to hold.
And for every hour of every day
Of every one of those years
People envy me more and more. The latest
Plays? Oh Horace sees them all, Maecenas
Takes him. They play together
In the Park, you know. The lucky
Son of a nothing! A rumor
Runs down the streets, everyone asks me
What I think:
                    "Good Sir, you know,
Of course you know, knowing the great
And mighty as you do. What about the Dacians,
Which side are they on?"

"I don't know a thing. Nothing."

"Ah, witty Horace, always joking."

But by all the Gods in Heaven, I've heard
Nothing!

"Now, where will it be, in Sicily or here
Near Rome that Octavian is giving his soldiers
Land?"

I swear my ignorance and they stare,
They wonder: this Horace is a marvel
Of silence and secrecy. Oh yes. Oh yes.

And I waste the day with nonsense
Like this, praying all the time:
O my Sabine farm, when will I see you

Again? When can I forget
This fretting existence, reading ancient books,
Sleeping, resting, doing nothing
If there's nothing to be done? Oh when will I eat
Beans, green Pythagorean souls,
And cabbage and bacon? Oh nights,
Oh feasts fit for Gods! My friends
And I, eating under my own roof, and feeding
My stubborn servants our half-eaten
Food—everyone drinking little
Or much as they please, a weak drink,
A strong drink, no crazy social games
With forfeits and rules. And then
We talk—not about houses, or rich men's
Villas, or the pantomime actors, but things
More relevant, important, dangerous
To ignore: if goodness or money
Is worth more, in happiness; if friends
Are friends out of selfish pleasure
Or some better reason; and what real Goodness
Is, and if we can find it, and where.

And Cervius, my neighbor, rambles out a moral
Story, if someone envies Arellius, too rich
To know peace: like this old fable:

"Once upon a time a country
  Mouse, living poor in his hole in the woods,
  Had a visitor from the city.
  A rough old mouse, the country
  Fellow, tightfisted, but for all that glad
  To see an old friend, and generous, too.
  Indeed, he dragged out peas, dry
  From years in the ground, and oats, and carried in
  A raisin, very very dry, in his own mouth,
  And bit off bits of bacon, and tried
  To serve as many different dishes
  As he could, seeing how his guest squirmed
  And hardly ate. Meantime he slept on straw
  And ate hard corn
  And weed-grass (all he had left).

And finally the city mouse cried:

" 'My friend, old friend, how can you live
  Here on the edge of a jagged
  Forest? Men and cities
  Await you: why not be happy?
  Trust me: come to my city, for no one
  Lives forever, not on this earth, and everyone
  Dies, rich and poor alike. So
  Be happy, live well, while you can.
  Remember, it's not for long!'

  "The country mouse leaped to his feet, ready
  To leave, eager to start. They reached
  The city, crawled under the walls
  In the dark.

  "And there, in the silent night, they came to a palace,
  Ivory couches covered with rugs, gleaming
  Red rugs, and food all over, piled in
  Baskets, left over from a feast. The city mouse
  Stretched his friend on a purple cloth and rushed
  About like a waiter, carried in dish
  After dish, running like a slave (and tasting
  Everything first). And the country mouse ate
  And rested and beamed and was a happy, happy guest
  Until
  Suddenly
  Doors banged
  And they ran
        and ran
        and ran,
  And everywhere huge dogs
  Barked, and the walls rang.
  And the country mouse trembled and shook and said:

" 'This is
  Not
  For me.
  Farewell, friend:
  My hole in the wood

Is quiet
     and safe
          and there
               at least
I can enjoy my dried
Beans.' "

II, 7

Davus:
I've listened, and listened, and wanted to speak—but a slave
Must be careful.

Horace:
　Davus?

Davus:
　　　　Davus, yes, a faithful
Slave, and reasonably honest: the good may die young
But I'm as good as I need to be, no more.

Horace:
　　　　　　Well, it's Saturnalia
Time; men were all equal, in Saturn's time: speak, tradition permits it.

Davus:
　　There are men who love to be wicked, and work at it; most men
Hesitate, sometimes able to be virtuous, sometimes
Unable to keep from evil. Senator Priscus, now,
Would wear three rings—or none; his life was so irregular
He'd change his costume, and the style of his costume, every hour.
He'd walk out of a mansion and suddenly hide himself—and in places
Where a respectable freeman would lose his reputation, on sight!
He'd be a rake in Rome, then a philosopher
In Athens—born in the sign of the changing year,
Cursed with change. That clown, Volanus, once gout
Crippled his fingers (and he worked to acquire it!), hired
A man, paid him by the day and paid him well,
To shake the dice and throw them for him. Work at your vices,
I say, and be happier, and better, than the man who pulls
Against a rope slack one minute, tight the next.

Horace:
　You rascal, do you need all day to get to the point?

Davus:
I'm talking about *you.*

Horace:

Me? You scoundrel! How?

Davus:

You're always praising tradition, and the ancient ways
—But let some god arrange to transport you back
In time, you'd dig in your heels, squealing you'd changed your mind,
Because virtue's only talk to you, or maybe because
You'd rather plant your feet in the mud and stay there.
In Rome you long for the country; in the country you sing
Of glorious Rome! If no one invites you to supper
You praise your plate of greens, and if they make you go
You drag your feet, thanking your lucky stars
No one called to take you out drinking! Maecenas sends
Around, he needs an extra guest at dinner, it's late,
It's lamplighting time. You bellow for oil: "Is everyone deaf?"
You stamp and roar—and then you hurry off, obligingly.
Mulvius and those other parasites expect you to feed them; you don't;
They leave, with nasty curses. "Well, yes," he'd admit, that Mulvius,
"My stomach leads me around, I follow this sensitive nose,
I'm lazy, yes, I'm weak-willed, and sure, I drink too much.
By god, you're just as bad, Horace, and maybe
Worse! Don't condescend to me, don't varnish your vice
With those pretty words." And maybe, my master, you're more
Of a fool than I am, I, a bargain-basement slave! Don't try
Staring me down, I'm not afraid. Keep your hands and your temper
To yourself: listen, here's what Crispinus' doorman taught me.
      Davus chases a whore, you chase another man's wife.
Which of us ought to be hanged for our sins? When Nature
Burns at me and I lift up that sheer dress, and she's naked
Underneath, and I plough right into her, well, she sends me
Off happy, and there's no dishonor—and who am I
To worry, afterward, if someone richer, or better
Looking, gets to use her the same way I did?
But you, when you put away your uniform, all your rings,
Every sign of rank, and you sneak along, dressed
Like some slave, your cloak hiding that perfumed head,
Aren't you *really* what you pretend to be? The woman's servants
Let you in, your knees knocking, passion and fear fighting
For your heart. Maybe they'll throw you into the arena, a gladiator,
To be whipped and killed, or maybe your lady's maid,

Afraid for her mistress, locks you in some filthy clothes-box,
And your head pushes into your knees. The law lets
Her husband punish her—and you too! Or maybe
Only you: the seducer is worse. She doesn't change
Her costume, or pretend to be something different. She's afraid
You're fooling her, with your fancy words; she can't trust you.
You risk everything, fortune, reputation, even
That carcass of yours, and you do it willingly, your eyes open!
　　　　You escape. You ought to be warned by experience, afraid, on guard.
In fact, you'll try to terrorize yourself again, try to die
A second time, O slave many times over! What beast
Could break its chains and then, perverse, return to them?
"I'm no adulterer." Oh no, by Hercules—and I'm no thief
When I watch myself and leave your silver where it sits. Remove
Danger, and restless Nature leaps, all bounds broken.
And *you're* my master—you? Slave to so many circumstances,
So many men? Freed from bondage over and over
You remain enslaved, miserable, afraid. And more:
Consider this, equally important: whether a slave
Who obeys a slave is still a slave, or a colleague,
Whatever he is, what am I, Horace, to you?
You rule me—but you are ruled, you serve others in misery,
Pulled like a puppet on wires you can't control.
　　　　Who is truly free? The wise man, ruler of himself,
Unafraid of poverty, or chains, or even death,
Courageous enough to resist himself, to despise ambition,
In all things dependent on himself, a perfect whole, so rounded,
So smooth, that nothing external can obstruct him, and Fortune
Barks uselessly at his heels. But is any of this
A description of you—*any* of it? Your mistress begs
For money, abuses you, slams her door in your face, dumps cold water
On your head, then—sweetly calls you back. Throw off your chains,
Cry out, "I'm free, I'm free!" Go on. You can't:
Your master's a slave driver, dimming your mind, tormenting
Your weary flesh, forcing you on, and on.
　　　　Madman: when you gape at a painting by Pausias, how
Is your sin any smaller than mine—I who marvel
At posters of gladiators, painted on walls, charcoal
And red chalk, as lifelike as champions in real combat, swinging
Swords and spears, parrying, striking hard?
I'm called a rascal, yes, and a lazy oaf—but you, oh you're

A connoisseur, an exquisite critic, a true judge of art.
    If a smoking pie tempts me, I'm worthless—but you,
Does your great virtue, your heroic determination, resist rich suppers?
Why is it worse when it's *my* stomach that's pleased?
I'm whipped for it, yes, but aren't you punished too,
Lusting for all these ridiculously expensive dainties?
Endless guzzling ruins your guts, you know,
And your failing feet will refuse to hold up that wasted
Body. Is a slave guilty, swapping a stolen brush,
In the darkness, for a bunch of grapes? When you sell your inheritance
To stuff your belly, is that slavery? And you cannot stand
Yourself for an hour, you throw away your time
And your leisure, you avoid yourself like some runaway slave,
Trying to soothe your spirit with wine, or sleep,
But in vain. Your black partner follows you everywhere.

Horace:
A stone, where can I find a stone?

Davus:
                                For what?

Horace:
                                            Or maybe arrows.

Davus:
He's either insane—or composing poetry.

Horace:
                                Leave me!
Or off you go, the ninth laborer on my Sabine farm!

II, 8

Horace:
You dined with rich Nasidus: how was it? I sent you
An invitation, yesterday, and heard you'd been there since noon.

Fundanius:
Nothing has ever pleased me better. Nothing!

Horace:
Tell me, please, what dainty dish
Led things off, soothing your savage appetites?

Fundanius:
We began, dear Lord, with a Lucanian boar—caught when a gentle
Southern breeze was blowing, as our host kept informing us. Arranged
Around it were pungent turnips, lettuce, radishes, spices
To tickle the taste buds and tempt the stomach—caraway, anchovies—
Everything! Then the table was cleared—the best maple wood, by the way
—And a slave wiped it down with a purple napkin,
And another swept up the leavings and left us tidy
And all in order—and then, exactly like those Greek
Vases, where they carry in symbols of the harvest, an Indian slave
Brought us Caecuban, and Alcon, and Chian so fine it was served
Unmixed. And our host announced: "Maecenas, there's Alban, too,
And also Falernian, whatever your palate prefers."

Horace:
How wretched to be rich! But tell me, my friend,
Who ate this feast with you? I'd love to know.

Fundanius:
I sat at the head of the table, with Viscus next to me,
And Varius at the foot, I believe. Servilius Balatro was there,
Of course, and Vibidius: they go wherever Maecenas goes.
Next to our host was Nomentantus, and Porcius on the other side,
Making us laugh by gulping cheesecakes whole.
Nomentantus made it his business to point with his finger,
In case we overlooked a dish: we less knowing
Diners ate oysters, and fowl, and fish—
Tasting, believe me, unlike anything any of us knew.

I knew that right away, as soon as he handed me flounder liver,
And a kind of salmon utterly new to me. The honey apples,
He explained, were red with that special glow, picked
By the light of a waning moon. If it matters: he could speak
To that himself, I suppose.
                              Well, Vibidius said to Balatro:
"We'll die to no purpose, unless we drink him bankrupt."
So he called for larger cups. Our host turned pale:
He was worried by such determined drinkers, people who talk rough,
Too—And more: a ton of wine can blunt a delicate palate.
Vibidius and Balatro emptied whole decanters
Into their cups, and everyone followed suit—except
The guests on the lower couches, who were moderate drinkers.
        In came a lamprey eel, stretched on a platter, shrimps
Swimming all around it. "This," announced our host,
"Was caught pregnant. They're not as tender, later.
The sauce—do try it—starts with Venafrum oil
(First pressing, of course), and blends in juice from Spanish mackerels,
Wine five years old—Italian, mind, not Greek—
Poured in as the mixture boils—once it's cooked, you know,
Chian goes best—with white pepper, and vinegar, to be sure,
Fermented from the best Lesbian grapes. My chef and I,
Indeed, invented this wonderful method of boiling in green slugs
And bitter herbs: Curtillius, I admit, invented the addition
Of unwashed sea urchins—much better than salt pickles, after all."
        And then the wall hangings fell in the food, with a mighty
Splash, flinging as much black dust around
The room as the North wind howling on Campanian fields.
We thought the whole house was falling—but finding nothing dangerous
We tried to seem cheerful. But Rufus, he bent his head and wept
As if his son had died. Who knows what might have happened?
But philosopher Nomentantus was up to the occasion, bucking up
His friend: "Ah, Fortune! Is there a crueler god?
How you love to toy with us, playing with our lives!"
Varius just managed to hide his laughter, lifting his napkin
To his face. But Balatro, who loves to sneer (when he can),
Observed that "Life's like that, eh? You never
Get the fame you work for. Never. Just think:
To feed me well, to pull off this feast, you've been forced
To suffer, to worry—is the bread burned? is the sauce
Seasoned properly? are all the slaves in uniform?

Are they clean and neat, are they trained and obedient?
And all these other problems—those wall hangings tumbling
Down, just now, or maybe some slave slipping,
Smashing a dish! But giving a banquet is like fighting a battle:
A general's real talents show when he's losing, not winning in a walk."
And Nasidus answered: "May the gods give you everything
You pray for, for speaking such kind and gentle words! A courteous
Guest indeed." He called for his slippers. Everyone all over
The room was whispering, mouths to ears everywhere.

> *Horace:*
> Oh I wish I'd been there! Nothing in the theater could be better.
> And then? What tickled you next?

> *Fundanius:*
> Vibidius was heckling
The slaves, asking if all the bottles were broken—
He'd called for more wine and hadn't gotten it—and all of us
Pretended to be enjoying an excellent joke (Balatro was really working at it),
When Nasidus returned, his face shining, as if
Bad luck was about to yield to skill. His slaves followed,
Holding high a great platter, wooden, with a roasted
Crane all sprinkled with salt and meal, and the liver
Of a snow-white goose (fattened up with figs),
And cut-up rabbits—more flavorful, I suppose, than rabbits
Eaten whole. And they brought in roasted blackbirds,
Delicately scorched, and ring-doves (but not the rumps)
—Delicious stuff, in truth, except that our host
Lectured us on everything. We took our revenge, running
Off without tasting a bite, as if his table
Reeked of Canidia's breath, worse than African snakes.

EPISTLES

I, 1

Maecenas, sung in my first songs,
To be sung in my last, you'd like
To lock me into the same old game
I played so often, once, and won
The prize for. I'm not as young,
Now, my heart beats to another
Tune. Old gladiators hang their swords
On the war-god's door,
And hide in the country to keep
From begging their lives, down on
Their knees in the dust. And in my ears
I always hear: "Let the ancient
Horse run free, or he'll stagger
And fall and burst his sides, while the mob
Laughs."

So I've put away poetry
And other games. I study
Right and wrong, and all I study
Is right and wrong. I store up,
Now, what someday I'll need, I lay
It all out. Whose lessons
Do I take? No one's: I'm a stranger
Everywhere, I follow where the wind
Blows. Today I'm an activist,
Civic, stern, a follower of
Virtue; tomorrow I'm a Socratic
Sensualist, bending the world to me,
Not me to the world.
As nights are long for a cheated lover,
As days are long for a wage slave,
As a year drags by, for children
Pushed and pressed by parents,
So time flows slow and worthless
If it keeps me from understanding
What I need, what I want
To understand, keeps me from knowledge
That blesses poor and blesses rich, knowledge
That no one neglects without paying

A thousand times over. I know almost
Nothing; I need to understand exactly
That nothing, and live as it tells me.
Your eyes will never see as Lynkeus
Saw, riding with Jason, but when your eyes
Hurt, you rub them with salve. Olympic
Winners are stronger, alas, than you
Can ever be, but you too protect
Yourself from the wringing pain of gout.
It pays to go as far as our feet will take us,
Though there's farther to go,
And we can never go that far.
Does greed burn in your heart? The pain
And swelling can be eased with magic
Words. Are you puffy with ambition? There's a book
Of charms for washing your soul, if you'll read it
Once, and again, and again. Jealousy,
Anger, laziness, drunkenness, lust: everything
Can be cured, nothing is so wild
That patient teaching will ever fail you.

Running when vice runs after you
Is the beginning of virtue; shaking
Foolishness off is the beginning
Of sense. Men
Sweat and strain, afraid of poverty,
Afraid of shame, of losing elections: they think
Such things the darkest horrors.
Devoted merchants rush to the Indies,
And beyond, running
From poverty, dashing through seas, rocks, through fire
Itself—but to learn
Not to want
What fools want, to learn
Not to love
What fools love, you need
To listen to someone wiser.

Take a village wrestler, sweating
At fairs, grunting in the grass,
And offer him an Olympic palm

EPISTLES   199

For no work at all: how many
Would refuse? And surely
Gold is better than silver, goodness
Is better than gold. "Citizens, citizens:
Money comes first, first
Get rich, then
Get virtue." Bankers parade these slogans,
Young and old sing them in the streets,
Carry them to school with their slates.
You're
      wise,
          good,
              eloquent,
                    honorable:
No matter, you've less than
Four hundred thousand in cash, so
You're less than one of the four hundred.
Yet boys bawl out in their games,
"Be good, and you'll be king."
Let a man stand
Behind this bronze wall:
Never guilty,
Never pale with sin, and fear
Of sin.

The law gives front-row seats
To the ripe four hundred. Children
Make good men
Kings. Which is better,
Which helped Romans be heroes?
Who gives better advice, a man urging you
"Get rich, get rich, honestly
If you can, but rich, that's the thing,"
So rich you can sit close to Pupius' tear-jerking
Plays—or
A man who helps you
Stand by yourself,
              free,
                strong,
Unafraid
Of Fortune's proud eyes?

Let Romans ask, if they want
To ask, why I walk in Rome
And refuse to think
What Romans think, all Romans,
Refuse to love
What they love,
Hate what they hate.
My answer (like the cautious fox
Refusing a lion's invitation): "All
These footprints
Frighten me. All
Go to your den,
None come back."
Rome is a many-headed monster:
Who should I follow, and *what*?
Romans
Who bid on public buildings?
Romans
Who hunt for widows,
Old women squeezing
Old gold, and bait their traps
With candy, and fruit, and trapped
Old men, stocked like fish in a pond?
Romans
Who grow money
With that silent fungus,
Interest
On gold?

All right: men are different, want
Different things. For one long unbroken hour,
One single hour, can Romans
Love the same thing?
"The Bay of Campanis shines brightest in the world."
A millionaire speaks. And
Builds. And the sea and
The lake
Are ruined.
Then another morbid fancy tickles him.
"Off to Teáno!" he cries. "Workmen, builders.

Ah Teáno, Teáno!" If he's married,
"To be a bachelor is heaven itself!"
He's single?
Only marriage is sane.
He's Proteus, shifting his face: how
Can I hold him? And the poor, what
Of the poor? Laugh:
They move from attic to
Attic, bed
To bed, bath
To bath, barber
To barber. They rent
A boat and turn as green as rich men
Rocking in a yacht.

If a bad barber mangles my head,
You see me
And laugh. If my shirt's ripped, but my tunic
New, you laugh. But
If my understanding fights with itself, wants
What it said it was tired of, tires
Of what it wanted,
                    shifts
                        and
                            floats
Like a tide?
If my mind never squares
A corner, rips out here,
Builds up there, turns
Straight lines curved, and curved lines
Straight? That's a madness you know,
All Romans have it: you never
Laugh or think I need
A doctor, or a court-appointed guardian
—Not even when it's your job to watch over me, no,
Though you scowl
If my nails are poorly filed,
No matter how I love you, need you, respect you.

In a word:
Wisdom raises a man

Almost as high as Jove,
Makes him
        rich,
            free,
                handsome,
                    honored—
Oh a king of kings,
And sane,
And sound
Except
When
He
Catches
A
Cold.

I, 2

Lollius, while you're at Rome, studying rhetoric, I've been
At Pranesté, rereading Homer's poem of the Trojan War.
He tells us what's good, what's bad, what works, what doesn't,
And tells it plainer and better than Stoic Chrysippus or that other old
Philosopher, Crantor. And here are my reasons: listen, if you can.
    His story is the fierce passions of countries and kings:
How Greece survived a long war, in a foreign land,
Fought for Paris' love. Trojan Antenor advised
Handing Helen back to the Greeks—and Paris?
Nothing can force him, he says, though life is impossible
And the throne totters. Nestor anxiously soothes
First Agamemnon and then Achilleus, one burning
With love, hatred burning in both of them. Kings
Commit folly, and all the Greeks pay the price.
Everything goes wrong, inside and outside Troy's walls:
Mutiny, treason, evil, lust, and always: anger.
    And to show us what virtue can do, and wisdom, he offers us
Odysseus: a pattern we can learn from—conqueror of Troy,
Voyager in many lands, watcher of many men
And their ways, wise, struggling to bring himself and his shipmates
Across the wide sea, enduring endless suffering
But never drowning in Fortune's angry waves.
The Sirens' songs, Circe's magic: you know them.
Suppose Odysseus like the others—foolish, greedy;
Suppose he'd become, like them, brainless pawns of a sluttish
Queen, living like a dirty dog, wallowing in filth
Like a pig. Men are nothing, made to eat and die,
Like Penelopé's worthless suitors, Alkinos' followers, young,
Worried about their pampered bellies, stupidly proud
Of sleeping till noon, fond of soothing fear
And responsibility with the soft sound of the lute.
    But robbers rise in the dark, to kill their victims:
Won't you arise, to save your own life? No—
Exactly as you refuse to exercise, until a swollen body
Demands it. Either you wake before dawn and work
At your books, struggle for an honest profession, or jealousy
And restless longing torture you awake all night.
You run to the doctor, if anything sticks in your eye,
But leave your sick soul to be cured some other time,

Some other year! To begin a job is half the labor: be brave
Enough to be wise: begin! The fool waits
For the river to run by, so he can cross, but it runs forever,
On and on, and always will. Now is the time.
          Money—and a wife with money, and children free of charge:
That's what we hunt. And we tame the forests with our ploughs.
But having enough we should never want more. No house
In town, no land, no piles of gold and bronze,
Have ever freed a man's mind, or eased the fevers
Racking his body. To enjoy treasure you must be sound
In mind, stable in body: a miser, or a man endlessly
Greedy, enjoys his mansion, his rolling meadows, as much
As a sore-eyed man takes pleasure in paintings, a gouty man relishes
Hot cloths, a man with pus-filled ears loves music.
If the cup isn't clean, everything you drink is dirty.
          Pleasure is worthless: pleasure bought with pain
Is worse. The greedy never have enough: never want too much
For yourself. The jealous man grows thin as his neighbor grows fat;
No Sicilian tyrant could invent a fiercer torment
Than envy. Let your temper rule you, let anger run wild,
And you'll wish you'd never done what it made you do,
Your violence eager, your bitterness unchecked, your vengeance accomplished.
Anger's a transient insanity: check your passion or your passion
Checkmates you. Rule it like an unruly horse—chain it, if you must.
          A good groom trains a colt, teaches it obedience,
Before its neck grows too strong; a hunting hound
Works in the woods from the day it finds a deerskin
In the yard, and barks at it. You're still a boy: drink
My words with a boy's pure heart, trust in men who know.
The first scent you pour in a jar stays there
For years. Go as fast as you like, go as slow:
My pace is my own, now, indifferent to the world around me.

I, 3

Julius Florus, tell me on what distant shores of this world
Tiberius, the Emperor's stepson, leads his armies.
Are you surrounded by Thrace and the River Hebrus, with its icy
Chains, or at the Hellespont, between Sestos and Abydos,
Or crossing Asia's fertile fields and mountains?
What are you learned officers writing? This too interests me.
The Emperor's great battles: who shapes them in words fit
For eternity to read? His wars—and also the peace
He has fought for. And Titus, meant to be a name in every mouth,
And soon, what has he done—unafraid of the pure Pindaric fountain,
Brave enough to turn his back on artificial pools?
Is he well? Does he think of me? Is he courting the Muse,
Coaxing Theban melodies into our Latin song?
Or has he roared and puffed to a tragic tune?
And my Celsus? I've warned him—and he needs to be warned—
To hunt in himself, to be careful of those great treasures
Stored in Apollo's library, on the Palatine hill:
Some day those beautifully colored birds might claim
Their plumage—and he, poor crow, stripped to his skin,
Would make the world laugh. And you, what are you writing?
What lovely flowers are you fluttering around? Your gift
Is a real one, you've trimmed it well, groomed it with care.
Whether you sharpen your tongue for the law, or shape
Charming poems, you'll earn yourself laurel wreaths.
And yet, if only you could give up more, put aside
Worry—that ice pack that ruins inspiration!—Heaven's
Wisdom would lead you as far as your genius could go.
Noble and commoner alike, we owe that task
To our country, if we want it to love us—and we owe it to ourselves.
And tell me, when you write, if you love Muntius as much
As you should—or if the friendship you patched together
Has ripped apart? Remember, my friend: driven
Across the world by your ignorance of the world, propelled
By rash young blood, both of you wild, unbroken stallions,
You're both too virtuous to break that brotherhood: wherever
You are, I'm fattening a heifer for the day you return.

I, 4

Tibullus, who reads, and enjoys, and understands my Satires,
How shall I say what you're doing, now, off in the countryside?
That you're writing something to outdo old Cassius
Of Parma? Walking peaceful, silent, in those healthful
Woods, meditating as a good man, a wise man, meditates?
You were never mere flesh, always soul embodied: the gods gave you
Beauty, and wealth, and the gift of relishing both.
What more could a nursemaid want for her ward—that he thought,
And said what he thought, and said it well; that fame came to him,
And a good name, a good health—all in abundance—and that
He lived as well as he needed to, and wrote as well, and as much, as he could.
       Live with hope and with fear, with worry and with angry passion,
But expect every hour to be your last:
Days come even more delightful, unexpected.
And when it's laughter you're looking for, come this way: you'll find me
Fat and happy, like a hog from Epicurus' herd!

I, 5

Torquatus, if my tiny couches can hold you, and my herbs
And greens—and not too much of them—can satisfy your stomach,
I'll wait for you, here at home, when the sun goes down.
Our wine will be from marshy Minturné, near Petrinum,
And only as old as Statilius Taurus' second consulate:
If you've anything better, send it—or drink what I give you.
The fire has been bright and hot, for you, and my furniture's clean.
Forget ambition and the making of still more money, forget
Your famous clients: tomorrow is Caesar's birthday,
Everyone's allowed to relax and to sleep. No one will mind
If we stretch a summer's night with pleasant talk.
        What good are Fortune's gifts, unused? Worry
For what your heir will have and you're halfway along
The road to madness. I'll take the first cup, I'll wear
The first flowers: who cares—not me!—how it looks?
Wine was made for miracles, and makes them: it reveals secrets,
Our hearts go leaping high, and higher, cowards run
Into battle, anxiety lifts from our backs, even art opens
Itself. Whose tongue can resist hot wine? Even grinding
Poverty falls away, and a man feels free.
        My duty (cheerfully assumed) will be to keep you
From dirty napkins, which wrinkle your nose, to save you
From faded couches, which offend your eyes, to offer you cups
And plates bright as a mirror, to let no one in who would carry out
What good friends say inside: equal with equal,
Equally met.
        Butra will come, and Septus,
And Subinus too—if no one offers him better, no woman
Offers herself. Bring anyone you like, I have room
—Though too many sweating guests can turn into fragrant goats.
Write me, tell me how many, then leave law and lawyers—
And escape from that client, waiting to ambush you out in the hall!

I, 6

Let nothing astonish you. Numicius, if there's any way to make
A man happy, and keep him happy, this I think is that way.
There are men who can see the sun above us, see the stars,
Who can consider the seasons forever fixed in time,
And feel no fear. What do you think of earth and its gifts,
Or the endless ocean, bringing gold to far-off Arabs
And Indians—or our average Roman, with his games, his applause, his smiles?
How do you see all this, how do you judge it, what do you feel?
          Wanting or fearing—these things, or their mirror images—it's all
The same, it's the excitement that injures you, either way,
The unexpected springing out at you, awful, terrifying.
· Pleasure or pain, desire or fear, it makes no difference:
See something worse than you expected, or something better,
And you gape, eyes wide, mind and body paralyzed.
Call a wise man mad, even a just man unjust,
If he pushes virtue past where virtue should go.
          Go, stare at antique silver, marble statues, and bronze,
And jewelled cups rich with Tyrian pigment, and paintings;
Be happy that a thousand eyes hang on your lips, as you lecture;
Hurry, eager to be rich, and reach the market early,
Be home late, worry because Mutus might make more with what
He acquired by marriage (oh shame, he was born to less!)
And you might end up astonished at him, not he at you.
Whatever is under the earth, time will dig out;
Whatever shines, sooner or later, will lie buried in darkness.
Fashionable Rome may love you, today, but tomorrow
You too will descend where even Roman kings have gone.
          If disease attacks your kidneys, or your lungs, consult a doctor,
Seek relief. You want to live decently? Who doesn't?
Can anything but virtue give you what you want? Then forget pleasure
And work to be good.
                    Is virtue a matter of words for you, are the sacred
Groves just trees for burning? Watch out: don't let competitors' ships unload
While yours are at sea, you might lose your Asian markets.
Make a thousand dollars, and then another, and then
A third thousand, and add enough to heap it high—
For golden keys unlock all doors, don't they? A dowry
Fit for a king, unlimited credit, and friends, and family, and beauty: oh yes,
Venus and that fast-talking goddess of Persuasion come when gold calls!

That Asian king, rich in slaves, poor in gold:
Don't walk in his footsteps! Rich old Lucullus, asked
To lend the theater a hundred cloaks, answered:
"A hundred? Who could have so many? I'll lend you whatever
I can find at home." And then, a little later, he wrote:
"I find five thousand. Take them all, or as many as you want."
But any decently wealthy house is rolling in luxuries,
And more, and the master loses a lot to his sticky-fingered slaves.
If wealth is your key to happiness, and only wealth, work at it, oh yes,
Work at it early, work at it late, never give up!
        If fame brings happiness, and putting ourselves on public display,
Let's all buy slaves to rattle off names, to tell us when the great
And useful appear, to nudge us into leaping across streets for the shaking
Of hands: "Him, he pulls the Fabians behind him. This one's got the Velines.
That one can make or break you, if it's office you want;
He does what he pleases. Please him." "Ah Brother! My Father!"
Adopt the world, when the world is worth it, each according to his age.
        If decent living is decent eating—hurry! it's dawn,
Off where appetite leads us! Let's fish, let's hunt—like old
Gargilius, a mighty hunter (in his own eyes, at least), who marched
His hunting crew through the middle of crowded Rome, in the morning,
So a boar he bought in the market, and hung on a mule, could come home
In triumph. Stuffed like pigs, bloated, let's bathe our bellies
In public, indifferent to decency, citizens worthy to be struck
From the rolls, fully as depraved as Odysseus' evil
Sailors, who would rather have pleasure than their native land.
        And if, as Mimneurus tells us, love and laughter
Make for lasting happiness, then live with laughter and love.
        Farewell: live long! Have you better rules for living?
Teach me, if you do. If not, follow me in mine.

I, 7

I promised you a week, one week, would be my country
Stay, and I broke my promise, I stayed all August.
And yet, if you wish me well when I'm here, indulge me,
Maecenas, as much when I'm afraid of illness as when I'm ill
In act—now when heat and new-blooming figs
Grace our undertakers and their black-robed men,
When fathers and mothers feel fear for their children,
And all our society business, our petty affairs
In the Forum, bring us fevers—and frequently break wills.
When winter spreads snow across Alban fields
Your poet will go down to the shore and, bundled in blankets,
Careful of his health, he will study his books and revisit you,
Dear friend—if you let him—with the spring winds and the year's first swallows.
         You've made me rich—but not the way a Calabrian
Host pushes a guest toward pears. "Have some, have some!"
"Thank you, I'm full." "Take some home. As many as you like."
"No thank you." "Little children adore them as gifts."
"I'm as grateful, believe me, as if I'd left you loaded down."
"Whatever you say. Everything that stays gets fed to the pigs."
         A fool wastes what he never wanted, he gives it away:
Sow such a field and reap a crop of ingratitude. So it has been,
So it will be. A wise man is ready, he says, to help the deserving
—And yet he knows there are gold coins and false ones.
I propose to prove myself worthy, and worthy of you.
But you, if you choose to chain me to your side, must give me back
My good strong lungs, the black locks that hung on this narrow
Forehead, the lovely voice I had, my easy laugh, those sad
Laments we shared over wine, mourning shamelss Cynara.
         Once, a skinny fox crawled through a crack
And into a bin of corn, and stuffed his belly,
And found the hole held him tight, now.
A weasel explained: "Come to that little hole,
Escaping out, as skinny as you came in." If the fable
Applies to me, I give you back everything: no belly full
Of dainties will ever make me praise the noble mob;
My freedom can't be bought for all the gold in Arabia.
You've called me modest, and I have called you patron
And father—to your face and behind your back, both the same.
Test me, see if I can give up your gifts, and smile, and mean it.

Telémachos, son of long-suffering Odysseus, answered well when Meneléus
[offered
Him gifts: "Ithaca's no place for horses, it has no level
Fields, it grows only a little grass. I leave your gifts
Here, son of Atreus, they're better for you than for me."
A humble man should live humbly: what pleases me, rather
Than mighty Rome, is quiet Tibur, peaceful Tarentum.
        Our famous Philippus, that vigorous lawyer, a brave old man,
Was coming home from court, one afternoon about two,
And grumbling about the distance between his home
And his work—when he saw (the story goes) a close-shaven
Man, sitting alone in a barber's empty stall,
Cleaning his nails for himself, knife in hand.
"Boy!" he ordered his slave, who hopped when Philippus
Barked, "get me that man's name, and where he's from, and what
He does, and who his father is or who's his patron."
Off he goes, and comes back saying it's Volteus Mena,
An auctioneer, an honest man and not a rich one, well known
For working hard, when he has to, and resting well, when he can,
Delighting in humble friends and a home of his own, enjoying
The theater and games in the Arena when his work is done.
"I'd like to hear it from his own lips: ask him
To dinner." But Volteus can't believe it, he sits
And thinks it over, and then, in a word, says "No, thank you,
I can't." "He says no to *me?*" "Indeed, the rascal! He's either
A snot or afraid."
                Next morning Philippus comes on
Volteus selling trinkets and trifles to common folk
And greets him warmly. Volteus explains that his work and his business
Contacts kept him from coming to Philippus' house, that morning,
To acknowledge what he couldn't accept, and he apologizes because
The greater man greeted the lesser. "Nonsense! But you're forgiven
Only if you come to dinner today." "To be sure." "After three, then.
Go, make yourself money as hard as you can!"
He comes to dinner, he jabbers like an ape, and finally gets packed
Off to his home.
                And when he's been seen, over and over,
Running like a fish to some hidden hook, a client
In the morning, and a constant guest, he's invited to come
To the country, at festival time, to celebrate at the lawyer's
Estate. Sitting in the carriage (pulled by expensive ponies) he praises

Sabine soil, and Sabine air, on and on. Philippus observes,
With a smile—and wanting some fun, not caring how he gets it,
He gives him seven thousand, promises him seven thousand
On loan, and talks him into buying a little farm. He buys one.
To make the story decently short, to move it straight
Ahead, this Roman sophisticate becomes a farmer,
Chatters about furrows and vineyards—and nothing else. He prunes his elms,
He struggles, he toils, he tries so hard to get rich that, instead,
He gets old. But when his sheep are stolen, and his goats get sick,
And die, when his crops won't grow, and his tired ox drops dead
In its tracks, he worries himself ill, then jumps on his horse at midnight
And rides like a fury, angry as a lion, to Philippus' house.
Philippus sees him—unshaven, dirty, his hair to his shoulders—and cries:
"Vulteus! You're working too hard, you're hurting yourself!"
"By god, patron, call me miserable
If you want the right name! I beg you, by all the gods,
By your own right hand, please, please, give me
Back the life I used to lead!"
            Anyone who sees how the things he's left behind
Are better than what he has, let him go back, let him resume
What he was. We all must measure ourselves by ourselves.

I, 8

Celsus: my greetings, my warmest wishes! Muse,
Bring this message to Nero's secretary and friend.
Tell him, if he asks after me, that my resolves have been noble
But my life neither pleasant nor good—not that hail
Has crushed my vines, or heat shrivelled my olives,
Or my herds sicken and die in distant pastures,
But only this: my mind is distinctly weaker
Than my body, and I want nothing—nothing!—to cure me.
I quarrel with my faithful doctors, I'm angry with my friends
When they try to shake me out of this awful blackness:
I insist on doing what hurts me, I refuse to do myself good,
I'm fickle as the wind, wanting Rome at Tibur, wanting Tibur at Rome.
        Then ask about him, how his duties go, and himself,
How the prince and the prince's people like him. If he says,
"All's well," first wish him joy, then later warn him,
My dear good friend, with words like these: "As you deal
With your fortune, Celsus, your friends will deal with you."

I, 9

Tiberius, only my other friend, Septimius, realizes how well
You think of me. And when he asks—no, forces me
To tell you about him, to recommend him as worthy
Of a man and a family like Nero's, all of them virtuous
—When he thinks of me in such intimate terms, he both sees
And knows better than me what I can do.
I told him, many times, that I could not, and should not
—But I was also afraid of making myself seem littler
Than I am, less potent with you, only interested in myself.
To keep myself from a greater sin I rely, now,
On the privilege of urban impudence. If you approve
My putting modesty aside at a friend's importunity,
Make him one of your own, and believe him both worthy and good.

I, 10

Fuscus, who lives in town and loves it, greeting from one who loves
The country, and lives there! But however different we are
In our dwelling, we're almost twins, with brothers' hearts,
In virtually everything else: when you say no and yes, I say
No and yes, we nod like a pair of ancient doves.
    You stay in your nest, I sing my lovely rural
Rivers, and trees, and moss-grown rocks. Why drag out
Our differences? I live here, I rule here, as soon as I leave
Those city pleasures celebrated with such noisy gabble:
Like a professional cake-taster I run looking for good plain bread,
Just crusty bread, no honeyed confections, dripping sweet!
    If life in harmony with Nature is a primal law,
And we look for the land where we'll build our house, is anything
Better than the blissful country? Can you think of anything?
Where are winters milder? Where do cooling breezes
Blow away the dog-star's fury and calm the summer
Lion, when he roars back at the sun and its piercing arrows?
Where can we sleep, safer from biting envy?
Is grass less fragrant, less lovely, than your African tile?
Is your water as clear and sweet, there in its leaden pipes,
As here, tumbling, singing along hilly slopes?
Lord! You try to grow trees, there in your marble courtyards,
And you praise a house for its view of distant fields.
Push out Nature with a pitchfork, she'll always come back,
And our stupid contempt somehow falls on its face before her.
    An incompetent weaver, unable to match fleece
And dye, so Sidonian purple and Acquinian color
Can blend, will lose no less, and no less drastically,
Than a man unable to tell true from false. If Fortune's been kind
—Too kind!—loss will seem more than loss, will seem
Catastrophe. Whatever you like is the hardest of all
To lose. Try for nothing grand: kings and the friends of kings
Can be excelled, even under a humble roof.
    There was a stag, once, who could always defeat a stallion
And drive him out of their pasture—until, tired of losing,
The horse begged help of man, and got a bridle in return.
He beat the stag, all right, and he laughed—but then the rider
Stayed on his back, and the bit stayed in his mouth.
Give up your freedom, more worried about poverty than something

Greater than any sum of gold, and become a slave and stay
A slave forever, unable to live on only enough.
A wrong size fortune is like a wrong size shoe:
Too big, it makes you trip; too little, it pinches your foot.
　　　　Live happy with what you have, Fuscus, and live well,
And never let me be busy gathering in more than I need,
Restlessly, endlessly: rap me on the knuckles, tell me the truth.
Piled-up gold can be master or slave, depending on its owner;
Never let it pull you along, like a goat on a rope.
　　　　These lines come to you, my friend, from behind the Sabine goddess'
Crumbling shrine, and they leave me happy—except for your absence.

I, 11

Bullatus, what did you think of Chios and famous Lesbos?
And beautiful Samos? And Sardis, where Croesus built his throne?
And Smyrna? And Colophon? Better or worse than you expected,
Were all of them like nothing compared to our Arena or Tiber's
Swift flow? Did you leave your heart, perhaps, in Attalus?
Or are you sick of the sea, and of roads, and longing for Lebedus?
Well, you know Lebedus: it's lonelier than Gabii, and Fidenae
Too—but I'd like to live there, forget my friends,
Let them forget me, just stand on that quiet shore
And watch Neptune boil up the waves—from a distance.
      But a traveler on the highway from Capua to Rome, rained-on,
Splattered with mud, couldn't live forever in an inn,
And after catching a chill no one claims
That stoves and hot baths are all we need to be happy—
And you, tossed by a fierce wind from the South, won't sell
Your ship, off on the other side of the Aegean.
      To a man in good working order, Rhodes or lovely Mitylene
Is like a heavy coat in summer, a wrestling-apron
In the snow, a stove in August, or the Tiber in December.
While Fortune smiles, and we have the chance, let Samos
Be praised at Rome—and also Chios—and far-off Rhodes!
Take your happiness at God's hand, however, whenever it comes,
Be grateful, suspend nothing good to some other time.
Wherever you are, wherever you've been, live as well
As you can: knowledge and wisdom drive off worry,
Not some city looking out to sea. Rushing
Across the ocean changes your climate, not your mind.
Brisk inertia blocks us: we run after happiness
With carriages and boats. But whatever you're hunting, it's here,
Right here, if only you'll look with a balanced mind.

I, 12

Ixus, if you're enjoying Agrippa's crops, there in Sicily
—And you should, even collecting them for him and not for yourself—
Not even Jove could give you more. Stop complaining!
No one is poor who has enough of all he needs.
If your belly is full and your health is good and your feet
Don't hurt, why would an emperor's wealth be worth having?
If you choose to live on herbs and prickly pears,
And leave what you might have had, you'll live the same
If Fortune gilded you over with a flood of gold—
Your nature immune to money, or else the most valuable
Of everything on earth, to you, just virtue.
         Why wonder that Democritus wandered abroad, in his mind,
And left his fields and meadows untended, and his cattle destroyed them,
When you, living in the middle of money and money-grubbers,
Still hold your standards, still think of things sublime:
What keeps the oceans in place, what makes the year go round,
If stars roam the sky of their own free will, or according
To rule, what darkens the moon, then lights it up again,
What the discordant harmony of things will do, can do,
If Empedocles made mistakes, if Stertinus failed to understand.
         But whether you butcher fish, or only onions,
Let Pompeyus Grosphus be your friend, and give him, please,
Anything he asks: he'll ask for nothing unreasonable.
Friendship's worth little in the market, when good men are forced to go lacking!
         And just to keep you informed, here's how Rome stands:
Agrippa has conquered Cantabria, Tiberius has humbled
Armenia, the Parthians, down on their knees, have kissed our feet
And shouted hail to Caesar: prosperity pours out
Her horn of gold and plenty on Italy.

I, 13

      Vinius, as I lectured you at length, and often, before you left,
These well-wrapped volumes go to Augustus—*if* he's healthy,
If his mood is good, *if*—bluntly—he wants them.
God help me if you try too hard, thinking to push me
Ahead, and your irritating zeal reflects on my innocent poems!
If these books become too heavy, throw them away, I mean it,
Rather than thump them down, there where I've told you
To bring them: you'll make all Rome bray at your father's
Name of Asina, you and your father the joke of the town.
      Be strong, scale the mountains, swim the streams, ford
The fens! When you've reached the emperor's palace, carry
Your bundle carefully, don't let it—for example—look
Like a lamb lugged on a peasant's arm, or as drunken
Pyrra in the play totes her bale of yarn, or some poor
Shepherd holds his hat in his hands, if you ask him to dinner.
And don't announce to the world that what's been making
You sweat is a load of poems designed to please
Caesar himself. Let anyone ask, but answer no one. Push on, go,
Good-bye! Don't trip, don't drop your bundle, do just as I've told you. . . .

I, 14

Bailiff of my woods and the little farm that makes me myself
Again—though you despise it, it houses five full families
And sends five votes to Varia—let's try our strength, see
If I am better at plucking thorns from my mind or you at rooting them
Out of the land, let's test if Horace or his farm is healthier.
        I'm held here by concern for Lamia, my inconsolable friend,
Grieving for his brother's death, endlessly lamenting,
Yet mind and emotion both carry me there, longing
To break these barriers which keep me away. For you
The city man seems happy, for me it's the country, only
The country. If you envy others, inevitably you loathe yourself.
Both of us blame the place which holds us, but the place
Is innocent, it's the mind that's guilty, unable to escape itself.
        Once a city slave, you used to sigh (in secret)
For the country—and now, promoted to bailiff, you long for everything
Urban, games, baths—everything. I never change, I go to Rome
Reluctantly, to do what needs to be done, I leave sadly.
We see things differently: that's the source of our disagreement.
You see a hostile wilderness, a desert, but anyone who agrees
With me sees loveliness and loathes everything that's beautiful
To you. The whorehouse, the greasy food-shop, I gather,
Draw you to the city; we grow pepper and spices,
Not grapes, in my farm's hard ground. You miss the tavern,
Where they serve both wine and flute-playing whores: *that's*
The music you love to dance to! Nothing pleases you
In the country, you say—and yet you're always ploughing up
Fields left fallow for years, and you groom the unyoked
Ox, and you feed him well, with leaves you've stripped off yourself.
And irrigation keeps you busy, constructing dams
When it finally rains, channels to keep the meadows green.
        And *this* is why our two-part song is discordant: listen.
I dressed in fine clothes, before, I oiled my hair, greedy
Cynara loved me (though I was poor as a mouse), I drank
The best Falernian for lunch, and loved it—but now I relish
A simple meal, a rest alongside a brook. Folly is fine
In its place, but only a fool prolongs it. No one
Envies me, there where you live, ruins my pleasure
With nasty looks and secret talk and poison in their hearts:
My neighbors laugh, seeing me lugging sod and stones.

You'd rather chew your cud in town, with the other slaves,
You love the mobs you left behind in Rome—and they, you know,
Wish they had a garden like yours, and sheep, and all the wood
They could burn. The best thing, O bailiff, is to be happy where each of us is,
Doing the best we can with what we understand!

I, 15

Vala, my friend, what the winter's like at Velia, and the weather
At Salernum, who lives in the place, what sort of road they have
(For Musa tells me Baiae won't work for me, its springs
Are hot and here in the middle of winter I'm ordered to soak
My bones in frozen water. Of course Baiae protests, mumbles
I've deserted its myrtle groves, turned my back on its sulphur
Baths, famous for driving out lingering diseases—
And they're angry, there, at invalids—like me—who have the gall
To drench their heads and their stomachs too in Clusium's showers or at frigid
Gabii. But I've got to go elsewhere, ride my horse past
Those stables he knows so well. "Where are you *going*? Not to Cumae
And not to Baiae, damn it!" The rider can curse and haul
At the reins, but a horse's ear is in its mouth)
—And where the food is better, and more plentiful, and whether they drink
Rainwater or rely on never-failing wells (Their wines
Are irrelevant, there on that coast: I can put up with anything,
Down in the country, but once I'm at the shore
I demand a mellow wine, and lots of it, so my veins
Can run rich with hope, and trouble is washed away,
And my soul smiles, and words sprout on my tongue
The way a young man jabbers, and my mistress likes that)
—And where the rabbits are better, and where the boars,
And where the water's full of fish, and oysters too,
So I can come home fat like some luxury-loving Phacian
—Write me all of this, and my thanks in advance.
          Maenius, gallant consumer of everything he inherited,
Came to town as a kind of wandering buffoon,
Living (and eating) wherever he could: leave him dinnerless
And he'd rip you to shreds, friend or enemy alike!
He'd cook up spiteful tales, malicious, cunning,
Untrue, to get a chance at food—and how he ate! Like a cyclone,
An abyss: he shovelled anything and everything down to his gut.
If no one favored him enough, or feared him enough,
He'd eat plate after plate of tripe and the cheapest
Lamb in the market—he'd eat as much as three bears,
And then he'd brag, like Bestius, that people who threw away
Fortunes should have their bellies branded—him!
Give him something worthwhile, it was gone in a minute,
Smoke and ashes: "Well, by Hercules, no wonder

Estates get eaten up: is there anything better anywhere
On earth than a good fat thrush, a nice pig's stomach?"
    And I'm another! I praise what's modest and safe
—As long as I'm poor. Oh, I'm brave and prudent, poor!
But give me something richer, better, and Horace
The Stoic tells you, just as feelingly, that wise men
Are rich men, and live, like Vala my good friend, in shining mansions.

I, 16

Quinctius, my friend: no need
To ask how well my farm grows,
Counting out olive and apple trees, pastureland, rows
Of wheat, and elms covered with grapevines.
I'll ramble around and describe it all.

A solid ring of hills, cracked
By a shady valley, letting the sun fall
On the right as he rises, warm
To the left when he goes,
Flying high in his chariot: you'd like
The climate, Quinctius. And if you knew
How my trees droop
With plums, flower with dogwood? If you'd heard
How acorns and holly feed my cattle, and I
Lie cool in their shade, Quinctius, you'd say the South
Had come to Rome and blossomed.
And a spring, almost a river, as cool, as pure
As Hebrus winding down through Thrace,
Soothes aching heads, soothes
Aching bowels. This quiet place
Charms me, my friend, and keeps me sane
And sound even in the heat of September.

Life is lived, truly lived, when we are
What others think we are. Everyone in Rome
Calls you happy, has known
You happy—but you, you think
Too little of what you think
Of yourself, Quinctius, maybe you even wonder
If wise men, if good men, are even happy. Maybe
You hear too many voices telling you
You're strong, and you hide your fever—until
Your hands shake as you sit to eat.
Ulcers can grow on anyone: fools
Powder them over, filled with fake shame.

Let someone pour words in your ears,
Retelling the battles you've fought,

Saying: "O Jupiter, who knows if he
Loves Rome
Better, or Rome
Loves him"—you'd *know*
Augustus was praised, all right, not you.
But talk of your perfect
Wisdom, your perfect
Virtue: you let them say such things, right?
"Well, anyone likes to hear himself praised
For good sense and goodness. You too."
And those who label you
Today
Will unlabel you
Tomorrow,
Exactly as they please—exactly
As statesmen are made and unmade every day
Of the week. "Off!" they push us away;
"It's ours, not yours." They're right,
And we go, miserable. But let the same
Crowd shout "Thief!" or claim
That I throttled my father, that I lie
In my teeth: shall I cry
And change my evil ways?
Only the unstable
And sick cherish labels
They've never deserved, or are frightened
By disgusting lies.

But who is really good?
"The law-abiding; he who
Helps his neighbors keep from quarreling; who keeps
Land and people from seizure; who's believed
In court." But *him*
The world and all his own family
Know for a hypocrite, lovely surface
Rotten within. Let a slave tell me,
"I've never stolen,
I've never run off," and I say, "See
What you've earned? No one beats you."
"I've never killed anyone."
"Ah: you'll never hang

On a cross, feeding
Crows." "I'm useful,
                    I'm honest,
                              I'm good."
My Sabine neighbors just shake their heads:
"No."
And again:
"No."
Wolves are careful, they watch for covered traps;
And hawks are afraid of snares;
And fish worry about hooks.
Good men hate sin
Because they're good—but you,
You're simply afraid of being caught. One chance
To steal safely, and your holiness
Turns quickly secular.
Steal a bushel of beans
From my thousand, I've lost little;
Your crime is exactly the same. O law-abiding Good man,
Applauded in the Senate,
Favored in court, you
Pray to Apollo at the top of your lungs,
You call "O Father Janus"—but
Then you whisper, cautious, afraid
Of being heard: "O Laverna, Goddess of Theft,
Let me be hidden! Let them think me
Brave
And
Honest;
Cover my crimes in darkness, cover
My lies with clouds!"

To me, Quinctius, a miser
Is a slave, squatting down, prying
At a penny glued to the road: whoever
Lusts after things
Will live in fear, and whoever
Lives in fear
Is a slave.
A man buried in buying and selling
Is a man without arms, a man

Who's deserted from the army of the good. Sell him,
Save him, and let him be useful,
Somewhere, as a slave. Let him
Feed sheep, and dig up the ground, and sail
On the sea, and shiver on frozen waves.
Let him
Bring our bread
And carry our wine
And keep us warm.

A good man, really good, will stand like Dionysos
At the court of Thebes
And ask the king his punishment.
"All your goods."
"My cows, my land, my beds, my gold?
Take them."
"I'll lock you in chains,
Set you a vicious jailer."
"But God will free me
Whenever I please."

What he means, I think, is:
"I can die
As I will." For death
Is the line at the end
                    of
                        every
                            road
For everyone.

I, 19

Maecenas, my learned friend: according to old Cratinus
Poems penned by water drinkers please for a moment,
Then fade away. As soon as Bacchus put brainsick
Poets with his Satyrs and Fauns, the sweet-tongued Muses
Have tended to smell of wine, in the morning. Homer
Himself was a toper, if we believe his poem, which praises wine
To the skies. Old Ennius could never tackle an epic
Until he was drunk. "Wall Street and the Stock Exchange
Belong to the sober; but no grim-faced puritans can sing
A song." I said that, once, and poets have been
On binges ever since, day and night.
Lord! If some idiot imitated Cato, stalked the Forum
Savage, grim, his feet bare, his clothes skimpy,
Would he embody Cato's virtue, Cato's golden life?
Black Arbita ruined himself, matching tongues
With Timagenes the eloquent, desperate to be thought a wit, to rank
With the masters of the word: how easy it seems (but it isn't) to copy
A flawed pattern! If I turned pale, tomorrow morning, poets
All over Rome would be pasting flour on their faces. O mimics, O jabbering apes!
How often you've made me furious, how often you've made me laugh!
        I walked where no one had ever walked before,
Never in anyone's footsteps. Trust yourself
And you'll always lead the crowd. I was the first
To use iambics in Latin—but I learned the rhythm,
The spirit, from Archílochus, but never his stories, never his words.
And anyone who thinks I deserve some lesser wreath
Because I borrowed music from the Greeks, consider
Sappho, great as any man, who modeled her verse
On Archílochus—and Alkaios, too, though his songs are as different
As night and day, full of no invective, scolding
No one, he borrows his meter too from brawling Archílochus.
No Roman poet knew him, dared to name him: I made
Alkaios famous. My pleasure is the new, the unknown,
And the joy that gentlemen, and noble ladies, have known through me.
        And why am I praised, quietly, at home, but condemned
In public? And unjustly. O ungrateful readers! I've never
Courted my public, hunting for votes at the cost
Of fancy suppers and coats pulled off my back.
Noble writers are like my family, I revenge their insults,

I've never flattered the tribes of lecturing academics.
"And so we weep." If I told some professor, "I'm ashamed
To trouble your busy students with silly trifles
Like my poems," he'd answer, "Oh ho! You save them for Caesar!
Your view of yourself, I take it, is that all poetic honey
Is kept in your jars?" How could I sneer, how would
I dare? He'd rip me to pieces: professors have nails
Like lions! "A truce!" I bellow. "Some other time,
Some different place!" A joke is mortal, to men like that,
They're easy to anger, and they fight to the death.

I, 20

Book, you're staring
Wistful
At the gods of buying
And selling, two-faced gods
Of the marketplace, you're waiting
To lie
Smooth and eager and young, open
For sale. You hate
Decent bookshelves, closed
And modest, you want the world
To see you,
You sing the public life,
Though I never taught you
That song. You're itching
To get there: so go! go!
Once you're out, you'll never
Come back.

"Oh what have I done? Oh misery!
Oh what did I think I wanted!"

You'll cry, when someone insults you,
When you're thrown into a corner, squeezed
Like a sardine, when your lover, bored,
Lies back and snores.

And still, if I see straight
And true, even hating
Your stupid behavior as I do, still
Rome will love you, as long as you're young;
After your hide grows dirty, thumbed
By vulgar hands, you'll lie
In the dark and moths will eat you, or
They'll ship you down to Africa,
Or off to Spain. You were deaf
When I told you, and I'll laugh, book,
Like the angry man
Who shoved his stubborn donkey
Over a cliff. Who wants to save a donkey

Against his will?
And this, this too, book:
You'll turn gray and old, and stutter,
While schoolboys in tiny schools
At the edge of the city
Fumble out your A
                    and B
                        and C.

And still, when some temperate sun
Brings you more readers, tell them
Who I was: son of a freeman, taught
To fly on wings too wide
For my nest. So add to my talent
What you take from my birth. Tell
How the great of Rome smiled at me, in peace
And in war. Tell that Quintus
Horatius Flaccus was a small man, gray
Far too soon, loving
The sun, easily angry and easily
Quieted down. And if anyone asks
How old I was, say that
Lollius was Consul, and Lepidus was Consul,
And I'd seen forty-four Decembers
When they sat in state
In Rome.

II, 2

Florus, faithful friend to our great Tiberius,
If someone came to you with a slave, born at Tibur
Or Gabii, and bargained like this: "Now here's a blond
And handsome boy, lovely from head to foot!
He's yours for a mere eight thousand, a homegrown slave
Fit for service, ready to jump when you call—
Knows a little Greek—he's good at picking up
Crafts—mold him however you like, he'll be putty in your hands.
He sings, too—untrained, but sweet, if you've drunk enough wine.
Some men try to push up their wares, talk them up
Big—you know what I mean—it kills your confidence—not right
At all. Me, I'd just as soon keep him: I've got no debts.
No dealer would give you a bargain like this, believe me—and I
Wouldn't do as much for just anyone. Oh, he was lazy, once,
Ran off—you know how it is—afraid of the whip on the wall.
Just eight thousand, if his running away won't bother you?"
If he got his price, the contract would bind you, I think:
You'd buy knowing the problem, he told you about it—
And would you sue him, unfairly, knowing you were wrong?
Well. I warned you when I left: I'm lazy, I assured you,
Almost incompetent at writing letters. I wanted
To keep you from anger—and from scolding—when no letters came.
What good did it do, you're still angry, though I'm right
And you know it. And more: you're still complaining about
The poem I promised to send: I've broken my word!
          There was a soldier, once, who skimped and saved
And got a little pile—but one dark night, exhausted, he slept
Too sound and lost it all. And then, like an angry wolf,
Furious with himself and with the enemy, snarling, hungry,
He conquered a royal palace almost single-handed,
A fort strongly defended, and rich as Croesus.
He was famous, and honored, and showered with gifts—and he got twice
Ten thousand, too, all in plain hard coin.
Well, his general wanted to take some fort or other
And started to talk to this man, get him excited
With words that would stir up even a coward: "My hero,
Go! Let your courage call you to battle!
The rewards will be tremendous. There they are. You hesitate?"
The soldier came from the country, but was nobody's fool:

"Anyone'll do it, sir, provided he's lost his cash."
        I was lucky, brought up in Rome, taught
How Achilleus' anger hurt the Greeks. Athens
Added a bit, helped me to separate right
And wrong, let me hunt for truth in those groves
Where Plato and Aristotle walked and taught.
But the times went wrong, and I had to leave that lovely
Place, and civil war came and took me—though I'm no soldier—
And I fought for the losing side: who could defeat Augustus?
Brutus went down at Philippi, and I left the war,
Came home, my wings clipped, my father's estate lost,
Of course, even his house, and poverty—rash, arrogant—
Drove me to poetry-making. But now I've written enough:
What laxative could purge me clean, if I went on
Scribbling instead of resting, composing instead of composed?
        One by one the years go by, and one by one they steal
Our pleasures: laughter, love, friendship, fun.
They're taking poetry too—and what in God's name should I do?
Different men love different things: it's true.
Your pleasure is lyric, this man adores iambics, that other
Loves Bion's biting satires, sometimes coarse, always raw.
To me they seem like a trio of guests, each with a taste
Totally unlike the other's, all of them requiring different
Dishes. What should I serve? This? That? You take it, he sends it
Back. You refuse it—sour, disgusting!—he laps it up.
        And even more: do you think me capable of *poetry*,
Here in Rome, surrounded by worries, afflicted with work?
I'm needed to go bail, I'm demanded as a critic (the devil with poems
Of my own! Push them aside!), there's a friend sick at the top
Of a mountain up North, another's dying to the South, I need to visit
Both. But I'm centrally located? And the streets are straight
And clear, I can easily compose as I go? A contractor
Hurries along, pulling mules and porters behind him;
A derrick hoists up a boulder, a staggering beam;
Sobbing mourners in procession fight with heavy carts;
Here's a mad dog, howling, there's a mud-spattered hog.
Oh yes, a perfect setting for poetry: try it yourself!
Poets run to the country, to trees and streams, they flee
From towns, eternally loyal to Bacchus sleeping in the shade.
Do you want me singing in the middle of a riot, by night and by day,
A minstrel walking the narrow path sacred to Apollo—

Me? When an undoubted genius, choosing peaceful Athens
For his home, studies for seven years, grows gray turning
Pages in books, takes walks silent as a statue, all absorbed—
And everyone laughs! Me? Here in Rome, not Athens,
With Roman tempests, with business billowing down every street,
You think I can weave my words and wake my lyre?

      Two Roman brothers, one a lawyer, one an orator,
Praised each other endlessly: "You plead like Gracchus
Himself!" "And you're as eloquent as mighty Mucius!"
And this fever attacks our poets just as severely.
I write lyrics, my friend writes elegies: "The eighth wonder
Of the world, molded by the Muses themselves!" And note
What pride, what self-importance, smothers our thoughtful
Faces, studying the library shelves where our works will stand
(And our portraits hang)! And then come closer, listen to our talk,
Watch us weaving our laurel crowns. We beat each other
With compliments, heavy-handed like gladiators armored to the teeth,
Trading praise till the sun goes down and the candles are lit.
He calls me a veritable Alkaios. My view of him?
Callímachus, of course. But he may need more, in which case I make him
Mimnermus too—whatever he needs, titles and honors galore!
Oh, I suffer, I do, to keep these irritable poets
Soothed—as long as I write. I submit to my public.
But let me stop, recover my reason, and they can recite
And roar like drunken nightingales, I don't need to listen.

      Bad poets, believe me, are a very bad joke—but they love
To compose, and oh, they love themselves! Say nothing,
They smile and cheerfully provide the praise they adore.
The true poet, obedient to Art and its rules,
Becomes a critic the moment he picks up his pen.
Callow lines, words without sparkle, words out of place,
Ancient words too moldy to work: he bravely
Plucks them forth, though they fight to stay, and throws them
Away, out of the poem; they weep, but he's ruthless. Forgotten
Words, still able to shine, he pulls from the darkness
And polishes like brass, like gold—glowing phrases
Coined in Cato's mouth, spoken by old Cethégis,
Neglected now but unworthy to lie all moldy and gray.
And new words, too, as the language creates them. Clear and strong,
Like some crystal river, he pours out his treasures, and Latin
Gleams, lovely and rich. Like some Olympian gardener

He prunes out weeds, rubs the rough places smooth,
Cuts down sprouts that could never grow—running
Like a child at play but working, working hard,
Like a dancer doing a Satyr first, and then a clownish Cyclops.
      Myself, I'd rather be silly, and dull, as long
As my faults were pleasant (or at least invisible—to me): I hate
A snarling writer. At Argos, once, a distinguished citizen
Would sit in the empty theater and applaud actors who weren't
There, speeches that no one gave—but he was happy.
Everything else in his life was notably proper,
An excellent neighbor, an amiable host, kind
To his wife, gentle and forgiving to his slaves, never hysterical
If a wine cask came up from his cellar with its seal broken,
A man who walked around wells and never fell off a cliff.
His family cured him, finally, with hellebore and other such medicine,
And when his madness had been driven off, and he was himself
Again, he cried: "O friends! You've killed me, not cured me!
You've stolen the deepest pleasure I knew—an illusion,
Perhaps, but oh, how agreeable it seemed, how happy it made me!"
      Toys and trifles should be put aside, and wisdom should be acquired:
Boys should be left to play like boys, not struggle
With Latin and a lyre they can neither pluck nor understand:
Let children learn the rhythms, the tunes of life.
And so I repeat to myself, silent, remembering:
      If water never ended your thirst, and you drank and drank,
You'd go to a doctor: but now, the more you have the more
You want—and why not be brave and admit it?
An herb that could not cure you, a root that did you
No good, you'd give it up, you'd try something
Else. Perhaps you'd heard that the gods gave wealth
And took away folly—but rich as you are, and yet
No wiser, still the same as you were when you started,
Why listen to the same old lies, the same lying advice?
      And surely, if gold brought wisdom, if riches made you
Braver, immune to desire, you'd blush if anywhere
On earth a miser existed, more miserly than you!
If you own what you buy, measuring out your money,
And use entitles you to ownership (according to lawyers),
Then the land you eat off is yours, and that Orbian bailiff
Ploughing up fields of corn, and giving you grain,
Calls you his master. You pay for your grapes, the grapes

Are yours—and chickens, and eggs, and wine—you see? You pay
For the land a little at a time, a farm that sold,
Perhaps, for a quarter of a million—maybe more.
What difference does it make? Live on money inherited, money just made,
It's all the same. Buy a farm at Aricia or Veii
And you buy the vegetables you eat for dinner (you think you don't, but you do),
You buy the firewood that boils your kettle when nights turn cold.
Call it your own, all of it, up to the poplars
Planted for boundary markers (they stop quarrels with your neighbors)—
As if anything were ever owned, when an hour later,
By force, by purchase, by prayer, sometimes by death,
It changes hands and comes, suddenly, to some different owner.
No one earns eternal use, heir follows heir
As wave follows wave: what good are granaries
And profits, what good are Lucanian woods joined
To Calabria, when Death mows everything and everyone, great
And small, and gold never tempts him?
        Diamonds, marble, ivory, Tuscan vases, paintings,
Silver dishes, purple robes: some people have them,
Some don't—and I know one who doesn't want them.
Take two brothers: one's lazy, perfumed, a gambler,
He lives like Herod, surrounded by waving palm groves—
And the other, endlessly busy, piles up money, ploughs
His land, tames his trees, from morning to night.
Our guiding star controls us, high in the sky as we're born,
The god of human nature, one to each man, mortal,
Lasting a single life, some black, some white, changing
And changeable. I'll use what I need, and enjoy it; I haven't much,
But damned if I'll worry for my heir, and how he'll love me,
Or hate me because I've used too much. And yet I want
To remember the difference between a man with open
Hands and a tightfisted miser. For the way you spend
Your money matters, whether you scatter it all around you
Or—neither trying to hatch it like eggs nor working
For more—you take your pleasure as it comes, brief
And passing, as schoolboys delight in spring vacation.
Poverty's debasing: keep it away from my door! But a boat
That carries me, carries me, a rowboat or a yacht, and I stay the same.
Life's no steady North wind, blowing us on,
But it's not a dirty southern gale, driving us back:
We may not lead, but we needn't bring up the rear—

In fortune, in strength, in standing, in beauty and intelligence and virtue.
         You're not a miser: fine! And then? No other vices
Afflict you? What about empty ambition: is there any, deep
In your heart? You're not afraid of death, not worried at all?
And you laugh at dreams, and magic, and miracles, and witches,
And ghosts walking the dark, and Thessalian omens?
You're grateful for every birthday? You forgive your friends?
Are you calmer and gentler as you're growing old? Are you better?
Pull out a single thorn, and leave the rest: does that help?
Know how to live—or get out of the way for those who do!
You've played enough, you've eaten enough, you've drunk enough:
It's time to give it up, retire gracefully while you still can:
The young will find you ridiculous in your cups, and tell you so to your face!

II, 3 *The Art of Poetry*

A painter who puts a horse's mane
On a man's neck—who pulls feathers
From canaries
                    and doves
                           and parrots
                                  and owls
And grows them on a sheep's back—who lets
The upper half of a beautiful woman come
To a bad end, wriggling like a black
Fish: if he let you see her, friends,
Could you keep your laughter down?
And books are like pictures, and any book
Written as that canvas was slopped, empty brained,
Like a sick man's nocturnal
Editions, will read
Like a portrait of a one-footed hero,
Maybe blessed with a head at the top,
Even resembling *Homo sapiens*
Perhaps.

"Poets, like painters, can do as they like,
Have always done what they pleased."

True. And as poet I need,
And as critic I permit
Freedom—but not to let Africa lie down with Europe,
Not to have snakes
                    sleeping
                           with
                                  birds,
Lambs making love to tigers.
Give an inflated ass a windy plan,
And an Olympian
Hope, and he sews on purple patches of
        BRILLIANT SCENIC DESCRIPTIONS
                a shady grove
                Diana's peaceful altar
                and a lazy stream
                in a pleasant meadow

          tinkling clear
          or the mighty Rhine
          or the glorious arch
          of a rainbow
—Though
          no one was visiting Diana
          there were no streams
          no rivers
          no rain for the poet's bow.
No.
But maybe you can design
A cypress in the wind?
For a portrait (paid in cash) of
A sailor swimming to shore?
His ship ground in the rocks?
The potter's wheel
Starts on a wine jar:
               whoops,
                    a pitcher!
What?
Oh let it be what it wants to,
But let it be what it is,
Just what it is. Please.

Most poets, leaders and led,
Chase a will-o'-the-wisp of abstract Right.
Thus:
     I aim
         at concision,
     I hit
         on darkness.
I aim to be smooth, my lines go slack.
The eloquent idealist rants and raves,
The timid, the gutless, crawl like beetles,
Seekers after novelty hang dolphins in trees,
Float a boar in the sea:
               O rare effects!
               O marvelous.
Ugh.

Even if critics can't bite you

You can be hangdog dull. Witness
Painters who draw simply *exquisite* nails,
Sculptors who can curl bronze like a Roman barber
(But can't paint pictures,
Can't turn out statues
That
    stand and
           stare
              back).
Not for me:
Who wants to walk around with split and dripping nostrils
And have people praise
                your fine black hair,
                your deep dark eyes?
Writers!
Write what you can, and
Think: can you really? really?
Words will flow,
Order and ideas
Will feed at your hand,
If you pick what is yours.

Order: is: I think:
Just this:
      Saying, now,
What now needs said;
Not saying, now, everything that can be left unsaid for some other more
                                  [appropriate time.

Take one part, hold back on another,
And blend words like pigment, slowly,
Cautiously. Be proud
If some clean metal comes up out of the slag heap,
Some tired phrase
Shines. Invent words,
If new ideas need them.
Don't look over your shoulder: the graybeards
Won't like you whatever you do.
Freemen are right to relish freedom
But not to roll in it,
Arrogant.
New words are good words, no matter who makes them,

If Greek gets poured into Latin—
But
    drop
        by
           drop.
Who the hell is Plautus,
To have what Virgil and Varius cannot?
And who needs to envy *me*, if I coin
Some new ones,
When Cato made bushels, and Ennius,
And left our Latin richer?
Words from living mouths slide easily into poetry.
Forests turn and change, grow leaves,
Drop leaves. So old words die,
While new ones run like boys.
Death will take us all, in the end: no matter
If Neptune
         shelters or
              sinks
Our ships, or else some enemy fleet, or if
The soggy marsh, where boats ran, spills out, is tilled and then
Feeds cities, or if
The once-wild river is tamed,
Cherishing trees instead of drowning them—
Everything mortal dies; beautiful
Language is easily broken.
Dead words
        shall live
And live words
        shall die,
And only the mouths of men can decide.
Only what's said
        is said
           and therefore
              alive.
                And therefore
Correct.

Homer made meters for
        war
          and kings
            and the deeds of great men.

(Who sang the first songs of sorrow,
The first songs of love,
Who sang the two together,
Is a scholar's argument and so
Unsettled.)
And angry Archílochus shoved his rage into iambs.
And comedy,
And tragedy,
Walked in his shoes, shaping talk for the stage.
(And an actor must be heard.)
And the songs
          we sing
               are sung
                    for the Gods,
And the sons of the Gods,
And for Olympic winners,
And for fast horses,
And the painful love of young men,
And the freedom of wine. And why
Am I a poet,
          and praised,
If not because I see differences,
And know them,
And mark them
Just as they are?
To blush at wisdom is to lie;
I'd rather learn.
Thus: and Wherefore:
               Comic themes
               Need
               Comic verse.
Thyestes' gory supper
Can't take a vulgar tone, a comic tint.
Everything
        in
          its
            place,
I say.
And still:
Comedy of course can rail, can swell, can puff in anger,
And tragic heroes,

       poor exiles,
Must always forget their yard-long language
To have a prayer of melting indifferent audiences.
Poems (oh)
       can be (oh)
          so beautiful
And (oh) so dull.
Poets need charm, too, to seduce our minds.
We smile when we see smiling, weep at tears:
Ask me to sob
       when you can sob
          yourself—
Then (ah) tragic heroes are tragic
(To me). Not:
       when words are mouthed,
       never digested,
       square
       in round red lips.
I sleep, I laugh (oh) then.
Let sad eyes weep,
       angry ones burn,
          sly ones wink,
             harsh ones frown.
And in fact we are born ready-makable,
Flexible in every emotion to the touch of Nature's hands
—And once formed (ah) we show our lessons, our new-shaped minds,
With
   our
      tongues.
Let words jar
      with face
         or fortune
And Romans rich and poor will howl with laughter.
A God speaks
      so,
A hero
   differently,
Or a ripe old man,
Or a young man
      hot with passion;
So a patrician lady,

So a pushy nurse,
So a footloose merchant, or a farmer in his green furrows,
Or a man of Colchus or of Assyria, of Thebes or of Argos.
Different.
Describe
      either
           what is
                and has been
Or
   what might well be.
Writers: *Writers*:
           If Achilleus
Lives in your words, let him be brave,
Angry,
Unbending,
Fierce,
Scoffing at laws which were made for ordinary men:
Arms are the thing,
           and himself.
Let Medea be a fearless witch, give Ino her tears,
Make Ixion a dirty thief, Io a wanderer, Orestes sorrowful.
Or when you take your name in your hands
And invent unknown people,
Let them come from your brain in one piece, seamless,
The same from start to finish.
But literary property that belongs to everybody
Is the hardest to invent
          well:
Poets who carve up songs of ancient Troy,
Constructing well-shaped plays, work harder than
Poets who make it all up as it falls on the page.
Old stories are yours for the working
—*If* you walk somewhere off the beaten path
And never forget the exact words of tradition and
Never
Never
Use the names without the substance, without the spirit.
But (oh) if you begin:
          "O Muse,
I sing Priam's fate and glorious war!"
Oh Lord, where can you go, after such vigorous boasting?

The mountains will labor and
                         out
                   will come
                   a
                         shivering
                                 mouse.
But Homer (ah), Homer,
Dares nothing he cannot be sure of doing:
    "Sing, Muse, the man who, once Troy was down,
        Saw the ways of many men, and knew their cities."
His plan is not to use fire
To make smoke, but to turn smoke into light
And dazzle us with the dazzling sight of
            Antiphates
            and Scylla
            and Charybdis
            and the Cyclops.
And Homer hurries to the core, to the reality:
He neither pegs Diómedes' return to the death of Meleáger,
Nor the Trojan War to Leda's double egg and Helen's birth.
No.
Homer's reader can soar *in medias res*,
Right where things happen, and in the way they happened
And we know they happened,
And nothing impossible to mention is mentioned, but
Only what the poet can polish and present
                                alive.
Fictions are so carefully crafted,
Invention and history so blended,
That it does not matter whether
                         beginning
                            or middle
                                    or end:
Everything is part of a single whole.

Listen:
Do you understand what we want of you, poets?
Are you listening?
If you want audiences to clap their hands
Instead of sitting on them,
To beat their hands, to bang their hands,

Then
    watch men,
    learn men
    and manners,
How a man ripens,
          and changes,
       and grows.
Boys barely able to answer questions
Walk like bipeds, they love other boys
To play with,
They scream, they smile, they change
Hour by hour. Boys
Grown almost men, but beardless, play
With horses and dogs (no longer with tutors), love
Grass and meadows, and melt to vice
Like slender candles, glower at guardians,
Produce nothing, spend everything, want anything,
Enjoy desperately, hate—soon—what they once loved.
Men full-grown chase after friends
And friends' friends, cautious
In risking anything. And men grown old suffer,
Rich but afraid to spend, not daring to eat,
Sick of living but sicker at death's first breath,
Cold and slow, endlessly timid, greedy
For time but trembling, short-tempered, intolerant,
Able to see only what once they saw, bitter
To boys and men still growing old.
Flowers bring fruit as they come,
Take sweetness with them as they go.
Writers:
      Keep senility for the senile,
Adolescence for boys, and let your audience
Trust you to show that
           apples
               are
                 apples,
Pears, pears.

What's on the stage is either what is
Or what is said to be
(Though performed elsewhere).

What is heard, not seen, is weaker in the mind
Than what the eyes record faithfully as it happens.
Yet judge for yourself what the eyes must not see,
Leave to the ears what belongs out of sight.
Actors' tongues can stir an audience
Almost as well as actors' bodies: keep Medea in the darkness
As she butchers her sons, and Atreus brewing human guts,
And Procne running for her raped life, becoming a bird,
And Cadmus turning into a snake.
What I cannot believe I will loathe:
Let me believe and I love.

Let a play end
            not sooner
            not later
But at the end
And be played
            so
                  again.
Let gods be gods, not Gordian
Knot untiers: unless the knot
Is truly Gordian hard.
Only three characters may speak, not four.
Let the chorus seem like a living man,
Not standing trilling irrelevant tunes while the actors rest.
Let the chorus work for good and for the good,
And against the angry, and let it help the law-abiding
And preach abstinence,
                  simplicity,
                        justice
                              and right
And the open gates of peace. Let the chorus keep
Its peace and pray for the unlucky and against the proud.

And as for music, well: not the brass flute
Invented (this morning) to blare like a trumpet,
But the simple reed with simple stops.
This slender flute sounded the key
And kept the chorus in tune
And blew gently across a few rows of patient listeners—
Few because too many cannot be

                 modest,
                     decent,
Cannot sit quietly together.
Rome
First staggered the world, then swelled to fill it up:
Spilling wine in their Own Great Name,
Romans now feast like wild pigs, swilling loud.
And how could clods and bankers be quietly mixed,
Crooks and Senators?
So musicians gave up being quiet, grave,
Turning into strolling players,
                 sneered,
                 leered,
Pulled their sacred gowns like balloons across the stage;
The sober lyre was strung like a banjo;
Actors learned a bright melodramatic bray;
And our once-wise chorus began to read tea leaves
Like other gypsies.

Playwrights (fighting for nothing more than a goat)
Pushed a pack of naked satyrs into the public eye,
But tried to stay sober and in all things
Ennoble the stage, and audiences sat seduced,
                    coaxed,
                    titillated
Even in their drunken satisfaction,
Ready to piss on Zeus.
Naked satyrs are good for a laugh: (oh) yes:
But keep them, in the name of all that's holy,
Away from gods, and keep gods (and heroes) out of whorehouses,
Let them sound a little less like dirty deities
Floating up into empty space
With empty spaces in their faces.
Tragedy and barroom ballads don't mix:
Senators' wives, dancing in festival streets,
Are careful to hold their hems high.
My friends:
If I wrote parts for satyrs
I'd let them speak some noble Latin, too,
And I'd have nobles speaking nobly,
Slobs like slobs, professors like professors, apes like apes.
I'd weave my verse out of everyday stuff

But I'd weave it—and it would seem so easy
That anyone might try, and would, and would
Sweat like a constipated horse, trying.
It's all in the knowing how,
                and when,
                      and where.
A rock is only a rock
If you can't cut diamonds out of it.
Wood fauns running lightly on a stage
Should never carry switchblades or whistle at girls.
There *are* people (after all) who still have land,
And horses, and who know their father's name,
And care about these things,
And can be offended,
And have (oh Lord) no interest in whatever may please the bubblegum buyers,
The soda-pop crowd.

So: fine: now what about the rules
For writing poetry? Oh, we've got them, still:
     iambics,
     trochaics,
     spondees (a nice invention, that, and nicely brand new),
And we've got good Latin poets who like one
Better than another, or who like one
Too much, and hang it like wet blankets
Across sagging lines. (Are you listening, O Ennius?)
Not everyone knows the rules:
Too many of our poets get away with too much.
Writers: so what? When another Roman
Slops on a page, should I slop too, and hope for the best?
Or never slop, and never venture, and never gain?
No one wins races by being afraid to run.
Read the Greeks.
Read them again.
And so what if Plautus was praised?
Did he deserve it? Shouldn't you know the good
From the stupid for yourself? Train your ears to tell you?

Thespis (the old tale says) was the first to write tragedies,
He loaded his poems onto carts and carried them
Here and there to be acted, to be sung,

By worshipers with wine-smeared faces.
And then Aeschylus invented actors' masks, and noble costumes,
And covered the stage with boards, and taught players
To talk like gods, to stalk like kings. And comedy
Was born, and came to be famous, and fell,
From too much freedom, into disgrace, and needed law
To correct it, and a law was framed, and the chorus
Withered away, too accustomed to smut and slander.

In time, our poets tried everything, dared
To be different from Homer,
Sang Latin, sang Roman,
Some of them sang cheerful, some sang sad,
Many, many sang well. And Rome would rule
The world of letters, too, if our poets—
All our poets, friends: all—could stop
To blot and erase. My friends:
                                        Lock your desk
On uncorrected lines; poems written nine times over
Are nothing, ten is only the beginning.
Democritus can prefer inspiration to perspiration,
He can keep sane poetry out of *his* poets' heaven,
But why (oh why) let your nails curl black, your beard hang dirty,
Why hide in foul corners and stink like an uncombed goat?
(Democritus? Democritus? Who's Democritus?)
Can you get to be a poet by hurting the barbers' business
Or forgetting to purge poetry
                                        and madness
                                                        away?

Ass (oh), I'm an
Ass, letting spring purge me sweet:
Bile is pure essence of verse distilled. But
Is it worth distilling?
No. So
Let me play grindstone instead of cutting edge:
At least a grindstone sharpens steel.
I will professor poetry, myself professing
Nothing (but professors are well paid, these days):
Dig here, poets; drink this; stand
Just so; push the discipline button (whoosh!) and then try

If
   vice
       is
           nicer.
I'm serious: good sense is everything, in art.
Plato is the best guide to the best poems of all:
Words wag on the stick of substance.
Understand what your country asks of you
And your friends, and how to love
Your father, your brother, your new neighbor,
And what a Senator owes his country, and a judge,
And how a general issues orders—
And you can create them living,
                       breathing,
                               on the page.
Draw them as they are, see them as they are,
Let them talk as they talk.
A touch of reality goes down better
Than the sound of sweet music, even when the story
Is stale, and the point pointless.
Pretty Polly can sing all day for no pennies:
Be in tune with the turning world.

The Greeks (ah) sang for applause, and for honor,
Only applause, only honor,
And the gods gave them music.
But Romans grow up like accountants:
     "Tell me, son of Atticus,
       if we have five ounces
       and one is taken away
       how much is left?
       Tell me, quickly:
       long division need not be
       quite so long."

     "A third of a pound."

     "Marvelous! You'll audit
       your own accounts,
       you will. Fine, fine.
       —But then, what if we add
       An ounce, eh? How much then?"

"Half a pound."

Does anyone think that poems worth rubbing with oil of cedar,
Poems worth cherishing in cypress chests, can come
From minds rusted with this money-grubbing shit?
Poets should write for *our* profit, delight us,
Neatly frame us a thought, pass on good counsel. Or both,
Or all at once. Whichever,
Say it quickly, so he who runs can listen, and hear, and learn,
And be better for learning. A bursting head
Opens like a bladder, and leaks away.
Imagine, to delight us, only what is almost true.
Do not demand that we believe whatever your own cracked brain
Conceives for the stage: don't feed an infant to Lamia
And let her swallow and chew, then show him, squalling, whole,
Pulled alive from her belly.
Ripe old wisdom balks at empty display,
Dandies won't dance when the music's too slow.
Tame sense with a dash of sugar,
Stroke your reader's cheeks while you box his ears.
Then everyone reads you, your royalties mount
Like gushing oil, foreigners run for your latest title
And read you long after you've turned to dust.
So: make your own memorial!

You'll make mistakes: we all do: sometimes
Sin is forgivable, sometimes
A plucked string goes
                    yaw-yaw-yack
Instead of singing what you thought you'd sung,
Sometimes
     A♯
        emerges
        when you planned
     A♭
—And even archers
                    miss
                       sometimes.
But the forest excuses a few misshapen trees.
Give me more good lines than bad
And I'll read you cheerfully, in spite of bad luck,
Or a bit of bad judgment

Or carelessness. So? Writers:
A drunken clerk copying over and over the same mistake
Can be forgiven once,
                          twice,
                                    three times,
Maybe, but not forever. A harper makes us wince
When he mucks up a passage
                          once—
But we laugh if he stumbles in the same place, over and over.
So a hardened poetic sinner, forever irresponsible,
Sings to my ears like famous Choerilus, to whom
I offer only laughter, even when (by accident?)
He turns out a gorgeous phrase. I scowl, too,
When even Homer nods, though Morpheus (yawn)
Can't be kept out of a really long poem.
Poems are like pictures: stand and stare
And some look better close up, some better
At a distance. There are things that shine better
In the dark; things that shine only in bright light
(Where even critics can screw up their eyes and —with awful sight—
See); things pleasant the first time, others
Pleasant again and again. My friend,
Older of my young friends:
You've been shaped by your father's knowing voice
And you know, and you think, and you understand,
But listen: remember this:
        In some things, you've got to be good:
        flawed poets, medium-rare of talent,
        only halfway up the flagpole,
        just aren't all right.
Some lawyers know their stuff
And can't turn it all on like Messala (whose voice rolls like honey),
Can't ever get to know what Cascellus knows (which is everything),
And yet they're all right.
Not poets. No one,
No god, no publisher even,
cares about mediocre poets.
                Oh jangling drummers
                banging out Beethoven's Fifth
                when the party's getting hot
                and everyone wants to sing—

or that tablecloth soaked in perfume
and strawberries laced with poppy seeds:
who wants to eat such extravagant crap?
Food like that is better ignored—
And parties like that—and the poems (alas)
Of mediocre poets: slip anywhere—anywhere—
And you're down on your face, in the mud.
Stay out of duels, if you can't handle a sword.
Stay off the ball field if you can't throw, and you can't catch.
Sit still, just watch, unless you want rows and rows
Of spectators laughing at how dumb you are.
But EVERYONE writes poems (oh yes),
Just *e-v-e-r-y-o-n-e*.

Why not? Free and white (or black: it doesn't matter)
And twenty-one (or eighteen) (or less):
Sure, and his father's famous (for something),
And his mother's virtuous (really),
And his grandfather left him an income (ah),
And he's never been in jail (yet).
Oh Lord.

But my friends, my wise young friends, not you:
You'll speak when wisdom speaks to you, you'll act
When Jove tells you to. You know, I know you know.
But if you do write—anything,
                              ever—
Read it to Mecius first (a first-rate critic),
And to your father,
And to me,
And then lock it up for nine full years, lock it up tight.
Anything that's safe in your desk can be repaired, or canceled, but
Once it's out it's out for good and never comes back. Oh never.

Orpheus, with gods speaking through his voice, kept cannibals
From their feasts, held back tigers and raving lions;
Amphion, builder of Thebes, could move stones with his lyre,
Could pray them into place.
Ancient wisdom, which knew public from private, knew
What was holy and what was not, and told men
That every woman they wanted was not to be had, made rules

For marriage, created great cities, carved law onto wood and onto stone.
Fame and honor descended on holy poets, on holy poems.
Homer, and then Tyrtaeus, inspired heroes.
Oracle spoke in rhyme, and ordered our lives,
And kings were courted with music, with song,
And sacred festivals sung into being
—And I tell you this, friends, to remind you what Song
And Apollo
Can do.

Art or Nature: which egg opens into poetry?
I could argue it too, but in fact
How much can you do if all you exert is your effort?
What good is genius if it can't
                              scan
                                   or spell
                                          or parse?
It takes two to tango well. Runners
With everyone at their heels have worked like horses
Before they race, have sweated and shivered, refrained
When wine was offered, refrained
When women were offered. The harper who sings for thousands
At the Pythian Games started nowhere, sat awestruck
At his teacher's flying hands.—Today? *Today*!
"Poems? I write, you know, eks*TROAR*dinary poems,
You know"—and that does it,
Today.
        "Well, why should *I* get left out?
         Why should I be disgraced, I ask you,
         Admit what I don't know,
         Admit what I couldn't ever learn
         And didn't ever try?"
Like sideshow barkers or peddlers at a fair,
A poet who owns half a province
And has hundreds of interest-paying debtors
Lets flatterers praise him for profit. Suppose
A Roman who knows
                        peas from onions
                        steak from chops
And owns enough land to bail out a friend with zero credit at the bank,
And can hire lawyers for friends in trouble,

Can a man so rich, so blessed, tell—today!—
An honest friend from a fake? If you like
To give presents, if you ever gave presents, if you intend to give presents, if you
                                  might ever want to give presents,
Keep all your friends away when you read poems in public,
Or they'll gush:
                        "How charming!
                          How fine!
                          How true!
                          How very, very true!"
They'll faint with excitement, turn pale with fear,
Weep like a rainstorm (or ooze it out, drop by drop),
Leap for joy, beat time with their feet.
Like hired mourners, who grieve
More than widows, more than orphans, flatterers
Praise beyond words: no honest man
Could ever meet them on equal ground.
So emperors and kings fill cup after cup, torture with wine,
To find a friend really a friend.
Writers: poets:
Foxes in clever fur should never cheat you with praise.
Try Quintilus, instead, and he'll tell you
Which lines are bad, and why, and how
To repair them, if repair is possible.
Try to tell him you've done your best
Already, try to tell him how many times
You've tried, he'll still tell you
Which lines are bad, and why, and how
To repair them, if repair is possible.
Try to argue, try to show how right you are,
How wrong Quintilus, and Quintilus smiles and bows
And lets you strut unmatchable
On your imaginary pedestal.
Every honest man with an ear will tell you
The same: a clinker
                        is a clinker
                                  is a clinker.
And he'll tell you when you've raised
Your voice too high, when you've stumbled,
Wanting to dance the most elegant dance
Ever danced. If you've written darkness,

He'll call for light; if you've used six meanings
And only one will really work, he'll ask for clarity;
He'll wince where you've wandered
                                    and tumbled
                                            and coughed
—In a word, an honest man will seem like Aristarchus,
Never worrying about your precious poetic ego
Or the size of your mistakes (refuse to boggle at a minnow
And you might have to swallow a whale).

Mad poets are different. Admitted. Wise men
Close their ears, and their doors, when a madman comes to read—
As welcome everywhere as a malignant itch
Or a plague of yellow jaundice
Or a moonstruck gorilla with sonnets in his arms.
Boys throw stones when he walks, declaiming
(But the foolish run after him). Head in the clouds,
Belching poems like a sooty chimney, he staggers
Up one aimless street, down another,
Tumbling into ditches, into wells (like a hunter
Watching birds instead of his feet),
Yelling: "Help! Help!
        Oh your arms, citizens"
—For hours,
But left where he lies, no one willing to lend him
A hand. Suppose some fool went to him,
Lowered a rope, told him politely to climb,
I'd ask just one question: listen:
        "Did he fall, or
          did he jump?
        Does he *want* to be saved?"
And I'd tell of Empedocles, a Sicilian, a poet, and mad,
Who wanted to become a god, and leaped into burning Aetna,
Eyes open. Let poets die, when they want to:
It's as bad to save a poet against his will
As to kill one, unwilling to die (just yet).
Who knows how often he's fallen into wells before,
Or when he's pulled out, if he'll stay out forever,
Or leap to a hero's grave (oh yes) all over again?
And who knows, indeed, when a bad poet
Makes bad poems, and more bad poems,

Why he goes on and on and on and on and on and on?
Maybe he's punishing himself (and the world: don't forget
The world) for pissing on his father's ashes,
Or for wrecking a temple wall—but everyone knows (oh yes)
He's M-A-D, pure mad. Like a bear in a cage,
If he could break his bars he'd roar poems
Without mercy, he'd drive off anyone who heard him—
Knowing, unknowing—anyone. And like a bear,
Just let him fold you in his rapturous arms
And his poems will choke you to death—Oh
Worse than a bear—a bloodsucking leech
Who bites and sucks until your skin
Is an empty bag, until your blood is all
Drained
Dry. (Do I hear one now?
Run for your life!)

Afterword: Making It New Again

In the past few decades we have gotten used to hearing and seeing Greek and Latin poets look and sound like contemporary poets; perhaps we have even begun to realize that all, or almost all, translations of the ancient classics inevitably dwindle into mere curiosities as the aesthetic prejudices and the idioms that brought them into being are supplanted by new prejudices and new idioms. (Gilbert Murray's Victorian pastiche versions of Euripides bothered T. S. Eliot; now the verse plays of Eliot have begun to bother some of us.) Yet most readers, I think, will have seen the necessity for Pound's Propertius and Logue's Homer. For all that, I wonder if some readers will not be puzzled by the sights and sounds of Burton Raffel's version of the *Ars Poetica*; and I imagine that, though Mr. Raffel's version requires no defense whatever, it might be well to try to examine the varieties of problems that Mr. Raffel confronted in making this poem new.

For one thing, is the original poem not mediocre prose well versified? Or, to put it in another way, Mr. Raffel's poem not only has sparkle and tempo, but it also says interesting things about the nature of poems and about what it means to be a poet; finally, the man who is saying these things is witty, mercurial, undogmatic, not ungiven to minor malice, not much interested in the Laws of the Rules, very much interested in the anomalies about the problems of writing poetry. We miss here not only the handbook's stern lawgiver, continuator of the peripatetic (i.e., Aristotle's) tradition, but also the genial and opinionated don, feet on the fender, sherry in hand, wistfully pontificating; yet in most centuries one of these gentlemen (or, somehow or other, both) has been thought to have written this poem. Has Mr. Raffel tried to trick us? The persona that glitters everywhere throughout Mr. Raffel's version is very much like the personae of the satirist who wrote the *Satires* and very many of the *Odes* and the *Epistles*. He is, in short, the complex, sophisticated, dialectical iconoclast, the student of *rerum concordia discors*,[1] who fascinated Montaigne.

I am not arguing that everyone who read the *Ars Poetica* before 1974 misread it; but I am insisting that a number of readers from the Renaissance to the present have tended to emphasize certain aspects of the poet and his poem at the expense of others, and that this tendency has slowly but surely fostered a quite inadequate impression about the poet and his poem. But before we try to specify in what ways this impression is inaccurate, it would probably be useful to look at some of the problems that cluster around the central dogmas of neoclassicism,

---

[1] *Epistles* 1.12.19 "The disharmonious harmony of reality": the oxymoron perfectly mirrors the temper of Horace's times. Note that the emphasis appears to be put on the adjective—i.e., it ends the verse.

or, if you like, of classicism. Decorum, unity, structure, clarity, simplicity, what have you.[2]

It is a commonplace that just as Aristotle was losing his preeminence as scientist and philosopher he was, as author of the *Poetics* and as literary theoretician, soaring to a new preeminence, which was not undisputed, nor was it naively promoted. We glimpse the struggle for and against the new Peripatetic tyranny in those fascinating *disiecti membra poetae* (the limbs of the scattered poet), Ben Jonson's *Timber* or *Discoveries* (published in 1640) where the rules, standards, laws, and models that Renaissance writers delighted in having recovered jostle with Baconian and Senecan warnings against slavish imitation and exhortations to progress and new discoveries. Yet Aristotle's doctrines of *hen kai holon* (one and complete), of the supremacy of drama over epic, and his general predisposition to clarity of structure and clarity of style secure the foundation of the classical spirit, as it has been viewed from the Renaissance to the present day. In Jonson's case (whether he was dogmatizing about rules or copying down Seneca's remarks on originality), the major concern seems to have been the need for giving warrant to stylistic simplicity: i.e., the writer of epigram and comedy was interested in good *sermo humilis* (plain style), so that Martial and Seneca and other Silver Latin authors are, paradoxically enough, taken as best representing the classical ideal. However complicated and subtle the debate over classical issues from which the ideal of neoclassicism finally emerged, it is not a long step from the apotheosis of Aristotle and the Silverizing of the classics by Jonson and his academic sources to the wonderful absurdity of Addison: "The remarkable Simplicity that we find in the Composition of the Ancients."

I have not the expertise to undertake a precise explanation of the place of Horace's poem in the development of the neoclassicism of the seventeenth and eighteenth centuries. But two points are worth considering. First, some critics saw pretty clearly that the *Ars Poetica* was obviously preaching one thing (classical simplicity and structure) and practicing another. If this ramshackle poem was an example of unity, clarity, and simplicity, where did that leave unity, clarity, and simplicity? But, second, if one could not use Horace's poem as warrant for neoclassical doctrine, then the argument from ancient sources was not as strong as one might wish. The *Poetics* might be, in a sense, all one needed by way of warrant, but it was incomplete, and, wherever you went in the text, it was (and

---

[2]So the notorious unities of time, place, and action; consistency of character; *katharsis* (psychological purgation?); *hamartia* (sin or error or missing the mark or just taking the wrong turn at the intersection). You name it and Aristotle will have, in either the *Poetics* or the *Rhetoric*, the seeds for almost any desiccation of creativity that the human mind is capable of inventing. This doesn't mean that Aristotle is responsible for most of the idiocies that have been perpetrated in his name, nor does it mean that we are not tremendously in his debt for having put down foundations so deep and so sturdy (here as elsewhere): but it does mean that he must be used with massive caution.

remains) damnably difficult to understand much of anything that is being said. But who else was there? Quintilian? Indeed, and all the better for being Silver, despite his infuriating adoration of Cicero. Longinus? Yes, but he often said embarrassing things about passion and that sort of thing. Dionysius?[3] Good, a true Atticist who was pointing the way to good Silverism, but he didn't write enough on poetry. The most sensible thing to do was to ignore the problem of the apparent discrepancy between the canons of Horace and of Addison and to thereby insure a united Graeco-Roman front: Aristotle, Horace, Dionysius (Petronius), Quintilian, and Longinus, all of them bunched together:

> Thus long succeeding Criticks justly reign'd,
> *Licence* repress'd, and *useful Laws* ordain'd.
>> (A. Pope, *An Essay on Criticism*, 681–82)

As for Horace's peculiarities, they are not faults, but virtues:

> *Horace* still charms with graceful Negligence,
> And without Method *talks* us into Sense.
>> (*ibid.*, 653–54)

"Graceful Negligence" is a very handsome and very ingenious euphemism for the problem that had been worrying the neoclassicists from Scaliger down to Pope's own time: the *Ars Poetica* seems as indifferent to Peripatetic notions of beginnings, middles, and ends and their proper articulations as do most of the *Satires* and most of the *Epistles* and most of the *Odes*, but in these poems (whatever the metre) the problem is not really important (though still a bother) because these poems do not pretend to be giving a coherent exposition of literary first principles. But the *Ars Poetica* does pretend (or seems to be pretending) to do just this and if it doesn't do this, why doesn't it? And if it doesn't try to do it or succeed

---

[3] *Dionysius of Halicarnassus*, a Greek rhetorician and literary critic, taught in Rome ca. 30 to 8 B.C. He wrote on style in general and on style in the classical Greek orators in particular. He is a subtle and imaginative critic whose main weakness is his inability to grasp the fact that Plato was, whatever one thinks of *what* he said, the greatest of Greek prose stylists (Plato scrambles levels and modulations of styles with dexterity and a shining arrogance that boggle the mind; Dionysius, a schoolmaster as well as a critic, wanted something more in the way of uniformity—hence his enthusiasm for the mindless, monotonous platitudinizing of Lysias). Longinus, the name traditionally given to the genius who wrote *On the Sublime*, seems to have flourished in the early part of the last century B.C. He has wonderfully catholic taste, a superb eye and a superb ear, and, not surprisingly, the rules of the game seem to bore him. He cannot be institutionalized. Quintilian, after Cicero the greatest of Latin rhetoricians, flourished in the second half of the first century A.D. Like his master and hero, Cicero, he frequently echoes outworn dogmas about abstract Right, but, again like Cicero, he usually qualifies the dogma with such common sense and such humanity that the dogma withers away and something new blooms, fresh and bright, in its place. He was a professor, to be sure, but he was not a hack classicizer. None of these gentlemen was. That they came to be regarded as rigid neoclassicists is just another facet of the dreary neoclassical myth. (An important, authentic neoclassicist in antiquity appears to have been Apollodorus of Pergamum; q.v., *Oxford Classical Dictionary*.)

in doing it, then the canonical list of classical critics shrinks appallingly. "Graceful Negligence" (which is, neoclassically speaking, an oxymoron as well as a euphemism) solves the problem beautifully. Aristotle and Horace can still be saying the same sorts of things and legislating the same kinds of laws; they merely do the same thing in rather different ways:

> Poets, a *Race* long unconfin'd and free,
> Still fond and proud of *Savage Liberty*,
> Receiv'd his Laws, and stood convinc'd 'twas fit
> Who conquer'd *Nature*, shou'd preside o'er *Wit*.

> *(ibid.,* 649–52)

Horace, then, is safely restored to the classical Aristotelian fold, and poets as varied in temperament and in degree of talent as Jonson, Boileau, Herrick, Dryden, Addison, and Pope can all consider themselves the heirs of Horace in urbanity, in correctness, in inspiration, and above all, in concern for "meticulous application of rules," for "polish and propriety."[4]

I must here insist again that we are talking about emphasis, when we try to rethink what critics of the late sixteenth, the seventeenth, and the eighteenth centuries thought about the relationship between the *Ars Poetica* and the neoclassical ideal they were busy constructing. There were, doubtless, some mindless pedants who insisted utterly on the primacy of *ars* and *disciplina* (crafts, technique, art, rules), giving *natura* and *ingenium* (natural endowment, genius) a little lip service or none. But the major critics who forged the neoclassical ideal and refined it to its perfection were quite well aware that what one needs is an accurate balance between *ars* and *disciplina* on the one hand and *ingenium* and *natura* on the other. In phrases like "*Licence* repress'd" and "Savage Liberty" we may see a constant temptation to overemphasize *ars*, but in each of the great critics there is, at the last, a sensible willingness to try to give *ingenium* its due. Yet however scrupulous the attempts to be impartial in adjudicating the rival claims, and however subtle and exact the conduct of the debate, decorum comes finally to mean a need for the individual talent to subject itself to a fixed tradition that is sanctioned by both authority and collective experience and is susceptible of precise analysis and rigorous performance. The question now before us is to what extent Horace truly joined other classicists in viewing decorum in this way; or, to put it another way, in what relationship does he stand to Aristotle on the question of laws and rules? Where does Horace put the emphasis when he tries to rethink, in a vividly wavering poem, the problem of poetic decorum?

[4]Quoted from R. R. Bolgar by Robert Maxwell Ogilivie in *Latin and Greek: A History of the Influence of the Classics on English Life from 1680 to 1918* (Hamden, Conn.: Archon Books, 1964), p. 61.

I am afraid that the answer is all too simple; therefore quite suspect. Horace was sensible, as always, and quirky, as always. His central message is, quite properly, delivered very early in the poem.

denique sit quodvis, simplex dumtaxat et unum.

(line 23)

Mr. Raffel has rendered this with dazzling elegance:

What?
Oh let it be what it wants to,
but let it be what it is,
just what it is. Please.

A plain prose paraphrase would run: "Finally, do what you damn please, provided that you get it all together." The loveliness of this particular line is grounded in what C. O. Brink has called "Horatian dialectic."[5] You give freedom, then you take it away. But if, in the same line, you give freedom and then take it away, you have raised a very interesting argument about the nature of poetic license. Horace is not going to answer this question for you; he is going to make you think about it for yourself. That does not mean that he leaves you holding the dialectical bag. He helps you to think about the question by continuing to write a wild poem about writing poems either wild or tame, and in this poem the question of when liberty becomes unwarranted license is raised again and again, and the question is finally gathered up into such a witty cluster of yes/no, yes/no, that you *are* finally left holding your own bag. And this means that Horace demands that you have inner resources, which is what he usually demands elsewhere. In this single line Horace is telling Aristotle and Yvor Winters where to go by reminding them that simplicity is all well and good, so long as it is not simple-minded, and that unity is okay as long as it is not boring.

Horace's poem is simple only in the sense that it makes sense; it has admirable unity, and that unity is supplied by incredible and audacious variations. What Horace is telling prospective poets is: learn the art of variation after you have learned how to play the scales. This is not a silly thing to say, and he does practice what he preaches. Freedom and discipline are more or less the same thing after you have learned to fly. But the emphasis, because Horace was an Alexandrian and because he lived under Augustus, is on the freedom. *Decipimur specie recti* (line 25): "Most poets, leaders and led, chase a will-o'-the-wisp / Of abstract Right." I very much doubt that either Pound or Whigham could have quite hit that off so deliciously. In Horace's three words the radical neoclassicists

---

[5]See the long and enchanting essay on Horatian poetic in his definitive edition of the *Ars Poetica* (Cambridge: Cambridge University Press, 1971), passim.

have been given their walking papers. Mr. Raffel's version juices all the savagery and all the charm out of the epigram. The epigram is a poetical manifesto (Alexandrian) and a political manifesto (Augustus has come to bore me). In respect of Alexandria, most of what Horace is saying is that Pindar and the great tragedians are dead, so we must do what we please; in respect of Rome, quite a bit of what Horace is saying, by this time, is that Augustus is probably going to be around for quite a while, so we cannot ever again do what we please.

This interesting tension between poetic and political difficulties accounts for the permanent and relevant magnificence of Augustan poetry. The late news from Alexandria had not freed Augustan poets from tradition, but it had made clearer to them what their roles in carrying on the tradition had to be. They had learned from Cicero and from Catullus and from various Greeks that the only way to pass on a tradition is to change it; so they changed it. Augustan poetry becomes as luxuriant in oxymoron and catachresis[6] as anything that early seventeenth-century English verse or late nineteenth-century French verse can show. The Augustan poets were, to a man, metaphysical wits. The reasons for this particular outbreak of mannerism can be debated from now till forever. I opt for artistical arrogance (get daddy) and for a profound understanding of metaphysical and political confusion (find a new daddy, or look at daddy in a new way; turn him upside down and see if that makes him look better). That covers most of the ground in the current debate about mannerism, but it does not sufficiently explain the anguish and the joy these particular Augustans were partaking of. They had a poetic that required muscular dandyism, but they also wanted their country saved. Except that they knew their country was no longer theirs. "Iam non agitur de libertate; olim pessumdata est." "Let's not haggle over freedom; it went down the drain a long time ago." So said Seneca, in writing from the extreme comfort that tyranny affords. But the Augustans were still worried about the loss of freedom, because, for quite a while, they were not quite sure that it had gone down the drain. Hence the bustle and winding up that one finds even in the splendid languor of Tibullus. In most of the *Epistles* (and the *Ars Poetica* is one of them) Horace is chatting about how he does not like getting used to regimentation (i.e., "rex erit qui recte faciet"; "he will be king who learns to impose abstract Right by convincing the sheep that he is the living embodiment of abstract Right"). In short, the Augustan poets were in trouble. Alexandria had granted them poetic license, but year by year and bit by bit Augustus was revoking most of the license. What to do? Ovid didn't know and decided to write the *Metamorphoses* and spend an uninterrupted vacation by the Black Sea. But that was

---

[6]I.e., a deliberate and elegant misuse of words, often a judiciously scrambled metaphor (see *disiecti membra poetae* above).

when Augustus was baffled by and angry at the fact that all his successes turned, as if by magic, to bitter failures; Christ was then eight years old. Back in the teens of the last century B.C., all Horace could do was issue a formal warrant for Alexandrianism in poetry and register a strong statement of disenchantment about the politics of his times.

In examining what is specifically entailed in Horace's warrant for Alexandrianism the following issues need looking into. The poem is not, as has been constantly and fanatically maintained, about how to write plays. It is not about classical decorum. It offers advice to the tyro about how to learn to be his own man after he has learned most of the fundamentals. It is about the nature of the uniqueness of a poethood ("sumite materiam vestris, qui scribitis, aequam / viribus" [lines 38–39]: "Pick what is yours"). It is also about the hazards of poethood; namely, if you don't learn to listen to criticism and learn to take criticism neither art nor genius can save you.

Verses 1 to 85 are about poetry in general. Verses 86 to 284 are about writing for the theater, tragic and comic. Verses 285 to 476 are about the drudgery and obsessiveness of craftsmanship. What these divisions mean in terms of cold fact is that of the poem's 476 verses only 200 verses are specifically about drama. Furthermore, if we remove from the section on drama the passage on Homer's taste and judgment (128–52) and the passage on metre (251–74), both of which bear on the writing of drama only tangentially, we find that only 153 verses (less than a third of the poem) are about dramaturgy.

What then is the poem about, if it is not essentially a versified handbook on dramaturgy and Aristotelian abstract Rights? It is about the true nature of poethood and the hazards and drudgery of writing good verse. The passages on Homer and on metre are of special interest. Aristotle had dogmatized that drama is superior to epic, chiefly becuase it is more susceptible of the precious unity than is epic. In a passage that seems in many ways a witty paraphrase of *Poetics* 1451a, Horace not only repeats the refrain about the primacy of unity, but he underscores the paradox over which Aristotle palters throughout the *Poetics*; namely, though tragedy is superior to epic, it so happens that the greatest of the Greek poets is Homer, the writer of epic.

> And Homer hurries to the core, the reality:
> He neither pegs Diómedes' return to the death of Meleáger,
> Nor the Trojan War to Leda's double egg and Helen's birth.
> No.
> Homer's reader soar *in medias res*,
> Right where things happen, and in the way they happened
> And we know they happened,

And nothing impossible to mention is mentioned, but
Only what the poet can polish and present
alive.

Fictions are so carefully crafted,
Inventions and history so blended
That it does not matter whether
beginning
or middle
or end:
Everything is part of one single whole.

Peripatetic abstract Right would have us believe that drama is superior to epic because it offers a greater possibility of unity. The Horatian passage before us chimes in again with the doctrine of unity, but it points up the primacy of Homer, and in so doing it intimates what decorum in fact must be: *alive*. Not an abstract poet struggling to measure up to a fixed abstract ideal, but a particular poet using conventions that change as each good poet makes personal choices about how to make his own poem shine.[7] Each poet doing the right thing—for him—in the right place at the right time: that is decorum. The rules can change and do change, the alteration of the genre is what keeps the genre alive. The emphasis on individual talents and on personal responsibility is very Alexandrian, and what Horace has done here is to give a poetic warrant in very lively and witty poetry to the Alexandrian insistence that each man make it new in his own way.

The passage on metre is equally Alexandrian, both by virtue of its wry academic information and its insistence on craftsmanship. In a sense, the conclusion of the poem (285 to the end) is about what craftsmanship means. It means patience, drudgery, and humility. Horace never tires of asserting that he is not a poet but rather a mere versifier; whenever we hear this assertion (particularly in *Odes* 3.30), we know that what we are hearing is in fact an ironic self-glorification: "Not only am I a very good poet, but I am also the best damn shaper of verses that this country has ever had or is ever likely to have." Craftsmanship means constant revising and careful publishing and seeking out and paying attention to good critics. There must be discipline of the most exacting sort. But if this is what he is finally saying, is he not, after all, a member of the neoclassical academy?

---

[7]The passage is appropriately framed with images of splendor and light: "non fumum ex fulgore, sed ex fumo dare lucem / cogitat"—he is not plotting how to get smoke screens from brightness, but how to strike light from the dense smoke of oral tradition (143–44); "et quae / desperat tractata nitescere posse relinquit"—and whenever he finds that he can't get his materials to start to glitter, he drops them fast (149–50).

Not really, because the dialectic of the poem, the fruitful battle of unity against variety and of genius against discipline is never resolved; because this particular war, this particular zigzag of yes and no, must never end. What the conclusion of the poem says is that each man must carry on the dialectic with himself and by himself; and there will be different answers at different times, and nobody is going to be right once and for all.

But to carry this dialectic around within oneself all the time means that one has not only a profession but an obsession. It has been often thought that the mad poet who closes the poem symbolizes some Romantic idiot or other (Propertius, for example) who will not submit himself to the discipline of the academy. I rather think that the mad poet is Horace himself and all good poets. People who constantly have "chunes in the head," whose brains and inner eyes are magnificently blurred with rich clusterings of shifting shapes and colors, who will sit from twilight to dawn anguishing over a synonym or an intractable spondee—such people are, in a sense, in the best sense, crazy. The dialectic works at the close as it has worked throughout the poem. Horace insists that being a poet requires unpersuadable commitment and fatal dedication; then he says that men and women who make such commitments and so dedicate themselves are not quite right in the head. Not the least of the many beauties of Mr. Raffel's version of the *Ars Poetica* is that he has spotted this typical piece of Horatian mockery and dialectic (lines 472–76) and has rendered it grandly:

> Worse than a bear—a bloodsucking leech
> Who bites and sucks till your skin
> Is an empty bag, all your blood is all
> Drained
> Dry. (Do I hear one now?
> Run for your life!)

There is no warrant in the Latin for Mr. Raffel's last parenthesis; but if one needed any evidence that we may trust his reading of Horace, this final intuition of Horatian dandyism and Horatian seriousness—that incomparable, incomprehensible marriage of frivolity and earnestness—would be, I think, more than sufficient reason for our letting Mr. Raffel guide us through this poem.

INDEX

Index of First Lines

Design by David Bullen
Typeset in Mergenthaler Sabon
by Wilsted & Taylor
Printed by Maple-Vail
on acid-free paper